AN ANNIE COLLINS MYSTERY

A COLD CASE OF CONSCIENCE

HELEN STARBUCK

Routt Street Press

2023

A Cold Case of Conscience: An Annie Collins Mystery
Published by Routt Street Press
Arvada, CO

Publisher's Cataloging-in-Publication
(Provided by Cassidy Cataloguing Services, Inc.).

Names: Starbuck, Helen, author.
Title: A cold case of conscience / Helen Starbuck.
Description: Arvada, CO : Routt Street Press, [2023] | Series: An Annie Collins mystery
Identifiers: ISBN: 978-0-9992461-7-7
Subjects: LCSH: Women detectives--Colorado--Denver--Fiction. | Cold cases (Criminal investigation)-- Colorado--Denver--Fiction. | Murder--Investigation--Colorado--Denver--Fiction. | Arson-- Colorado--Denver--Fiction. | Sex offenders--Colorado--Denver--Fiction. | Secrecy--Fiction. | Man-woman relationships--Fiction. | LCGFT: Detective and mystery fiction. | BISAC: FICTION / Mystery & Detective / Women Sleuths.
Classification: LCC: PS3619.T3727 C65 2023 | DDC: 813/.6--dc23

Cover and Interior Design by Victoria Wolf, wolfdesignandmarketing.com. Copyright owned by author.

For information, email info@routtstreetpress.com.

Routt Street Press

Arvada. CO
info@routtstreetpress.com

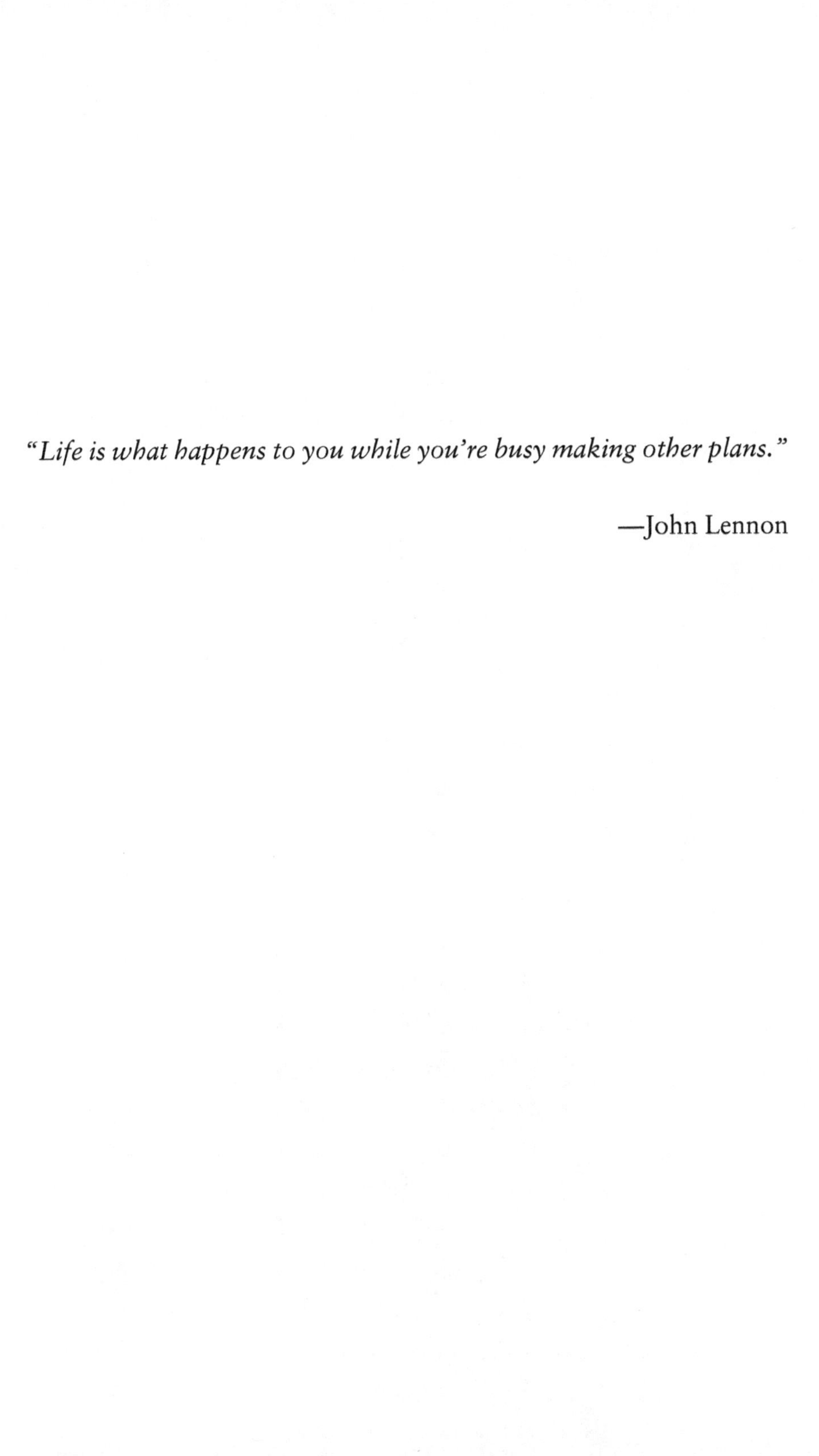

"Life is what happens to you while you're busy making other plans."

—John Lennon

OTHER BOOKS

THE ANNIE COLLINS MYSTERY SERIES
The Mad Hatter's Son
No Pity in Death
The Burden of Hate

STANDALONE ROMANTIC SUSPENSE
Legacy of Secrets

THE DENVER MAJOR CRIMES SERIES
Finding Alex
The Woman He Used to Know

PROLOGUE

*T*HERE IS NO RESISTANCE *when the back door, which should be locked, opens. Heat radiates from the nearby grill, but nothing is cooking. Not right, I think, not right.*

"I'm home." No answer. Not right, not right.

Furniture is knocked over in the living room and my husband, Angel, is tied to a chair, face battered, Ian stands next to him pressing a gun to his temple. I can hardly breathe, my heart pounds, panic starts to overwhelm me.

"Sit down now, or I'll blow his brains out."

I sit and take a deep breath trying to think. How can I de-escalate this? How can I get him away from Angel? How can I kill Ian before he can hurt Angel? I feel the hard bulge against my side under my jacket and it offers me some comfort. He doesn't know I carry a gun now. Time morphs as he taunts both of us waving his gun around, pointing it back and forth between me and Angel. I try, but I can't follow what he's saying. All I know is there will be no talking him down. I have to think of something, but my brain is paralyzed with fear.

"Please don't hurt her," I hear Angel say.

"It's me you want, let him go," I say to no avail.

"Do what you want with me, just don't hurt her," Angel begs.

"Okay," Ian says and turns the gun on Angel.

I hear the shot, and Angel slumps. My gun is in my hand somehow and I shoot. I watch Ian grasp his arm, stagger back, and drop his gun. I'm at Angel's side, my hands are covered in his blood, it saturates the ropes holding him to the chair and they refuse to let go. I hear a noise behind me and I turn to see Ian on his hands and knees grasping his gun and pointing it at us. I shoot to kill. And I do kill him, at last.

There is too much blood, and Angel is unresponsive. I pull and pull frantically until the ropes let go and Angel falls into my arms. No pulse, no breath, he's gone…NO, NO, NO, NO!

ONE

JOLT AWAKE SCREAMING and feel arms come around me. "Shhh, shhh, it's a dream, baby it's a dream. Wake up Annie."

Angel, warm, alive.

I run my hands frantically over his chest and abdomen searching and not finding any blood. I feel his heart beating under my hand and his breath on my neck as he gathers me to him in the dark of our bedroom.

"It's just a dream. He's dead, we're safe," Angel says and at last I relax into his arms. Ian Patterson may be dead, but he haunts both of us.

Normal is a funny word. Anything can become normal after a while, even killing someone. Maybe not normal—not many people kill—but when you do, it becomes your new normal. I've learned that people look at you differently when they know you've killed someone. They can't help but wonder what that's like, if it's changed you, and whether the act of killing another human being says something worrisome about you. It doesn't seem to matter that it was self-defense.

What I never tell anyone is that I wanted Ian Patterson dead more than I had ever wanted anything or that I have no remorse about killing him. There are limits to what you can expect people to handle.

The men I work with don't like it when I refuse to laugh at comments like the one a surgeon made recently, "Careful, don't piss her off—the last guy who did is dead." I thought about making a gun with my fingers and pretending to shoot them when they made a comment, but I figured that'd get me in serious trouble. Instead, I'd give them a dead-eyed stare and think to myself, *Head or chest shot?* It got the point across and eventually put an end to remarks made in front of me. God only knows what they said behind my back.

After a bad night filled with nightmares like last night, or worry about Angel, I spent the day imagining a bullet hole in the foreheads of people who pissed me off. It was why I no longer carried my gun with me; with escaped felon Ian Patterson dead there no longer seemed to be a need for it. He'd been the only reason for getting a gun in the first place. Its presence, in my mind, was riskier than not having it with me.

What worried me was that I saw Ian out of the corner of my eye at times, standing in the living room or by the bedroom door. I didn't tell anyone about it, not even Angel. He was dealing with his own issues, and I didn't want anyone thinking I needed hospitalization. *It would go away, it was a result of the trauma*, I kept telling myself. I hoped that was the truth.

What happened had bumped Angel and me off the paths we thought we would take and pointed us in new, unimagined directions. John Lennon was right when he said, "Life is what happens to you while you're busy making other plans."

TWO

HOMICIDE DETECTIVE ALEX FROST smiled when he saw me walk over to the booth he'd claimed at Cody's, the Denver restaurant where we often met. It was a small, quiet place where you could actually hear yourself talk while you ate. He stood up and gave me a hug when I got to the table.

"Hey kid, you look great—rested, relaxed. How are things?"

"Not bad," I said noncommittally. I smiled. He'd always called me kid and Angel was always 'your boy.'

I slid into the booth as the waitress walked over with menus and glasses of water. I noticed Frost's gently receding brown hair was now threaded with silver, his suit was rumpled, as always. I'd never seen him out of a suit and tie in public. He never seemed to be comfortable in one, though, taking every chance to loosen the tie, unbutton the shirt collar, and ditch the jacket on the back of a chair.

"I'm back working shifts in the OR, and Angel is back to full time at the DA's office. How've you been?" I asked after the waitress left.

"Been busy, always plenty of dead people," he said, his eyes crinkling as he grinned at me. He'd been a homicide detective for fifteen years and had seen a lot of dead people.

I rolled my eyes at him. "Lucky you."

We ordered and then settled in to wait for our food. "When Angel and I were in the hospital, you mentioned you had an idea you wanted to talk to me about but never said what it was."

"You two needed some time to recover. I didn't want to hit you up with it then. How's everything these days—really."

I reached out and put my hand over his. "We're good. Some shockwaves here and there."

He eyed me closely. "What kinda shockwaves?"

I shrugged. "Oh, you know—flashbacks that hit me from time to time, dreams. Angel doesn't really talk about it, but he dreams about it, too; there are nights when he can't sleep."

Frost waited, clearly not buying my casual act.

I sighed. "Before all this happened, if I had to describe Angel in one word it would have been optimistic. What's happened to us seems to have taken that away from him. I'm more realistic, I guess. In the OR, you figure out what's the worst that could happen and do everything you can to prevent it. I wasn't prepared for Ian's insanity, but I handled it; I put an end to it. The effect it's had on Angel breaks my heart, but I don't know how to fix it. And it's hard not to remember what happened every time I walk past my old living room."

"Have you thought about moving?"

"No, not really. I suppose we should, but it makes me angry. We both loved our original duplex, and Ian ruined that for us, and now he's cast a pall on our new place. I don't know, sometimes it feels like even dead, he'll never go away."

"He'll go away a lot faster if you aren't reminded of it every time you turn around."

The waitress brought our meals, and we were quiet for a bit while we ate. "You interested in hearing about my idea?" Frost said at last.

"Yeah, let's hear it."

"You've helped me before, so I wondered if you'd help me with some cold case work. With the caseload we have, none of us has the time to give the cold cases the attention they need. They're supposed to be reviewed periodically to see if any new lines of investigation could lead to a solve, but we can rarely do more than take a cursory look at the murder books. Lieutenant Walker wants to see if we can't move some along." He hesitated, and I knew that something about the proposal made him uncomfortable.

"But…?"

"Pretty sure Walker won't agree to you being an official assistant. They don't let civilians do that as a rule."

This time I watched him and waited, like Frost had done to me for ages; I knew there was more to come.

He finally huffed out a breath. "Okay, and before you reject it outright, hear me out." Frost took a bite of his sandwich and a swig of his coffee.

"You're stalling. Let's hear it."

"Um, I definitely could use your help on the cold cases. Pretty sure it'd have to be unofficial, 'cause you're not a cop." He moved his coffee mug around in circles on the table. God only knew what he had cooking. At last, he asked, "I wondered, though, if you'd ever thought about being one?"

I put my sandwich down and sat back against the booth. "*A cop?* Are you serious?" Frost nodded and looked a bit embarrassed. "Frost, you know that isn't me."

"Yeah, probably not. It was just an idea."

"I like the idea of the cold case stuff, though." I'd always been intrigued by what Frost did. I had been pulled into his investigation into the death of a friend of mine, and that seemed to have ignited a curiosity about what he did and a desire to get involved in his work. Now, after all that had happened, being around him made me feel normal. In his mind I wasn't a killer, I'd done what was needed to save Angel and myself.

"I figured you would. I don't want to upset Angel; I know he worries about you. I could talk to him, explain what you'd be doing. And with you working at the hospital, it'd only be part-time."

"I'll talk to him. He's having a hard time right now, but as long as I'm not working on active cases—or planning to go to the academy—I think he'll be okay with it."

Frost ate a couple of french fries, then nodded. "Working with you unofficially would get my ass fried if my lieutenant got wind of it, but I could bring copies of the murder books over for you to look at and give me some ideas to follow up on."

"Okay." I wasn't sure how much help I'd be, they were cold cases for a reason.

"Knew that'd hook you," he said, grinning. He took a huge bite of his sandwich, chewed briefly, and washed it down with coffee. "After you talk with Angel, let me know if you want to do it. I'll give you a couple of cases I have that you can review to see if you spot anything that might have been overlooked or seems weird or if there's anyone we might want to re-interview. You've got a good nose for stuff like that."

"If it's too soon for Angel, though, this might have to wait."

"I get it," Frost said. "If it has to wait a while, that's fine. These cases aren't going anywhere." He gave me the once-over again. "You really do look good, kid. The time off has been good for you."

"It has." I had regained some of the weight I'd lost, and the constant fear and anxiety over what Ian would do next was gone. Killing someone had a way of taking care of that.

"When you called, you also mentioned a 'sort of' retirement plan. What's that all about?" I asked.

"I was thinking about a private investigator gig when I retire. I've spent most of my professional life in homicide, and I don't know what I'd do if I wasn't poking my nose into somebody's business. I kinda thought, if I did that, maybe you'd partner up with me." He looked a little sheepish as he started to slide his coffee mug around in circles again. Frost had some definite "tells." He tapped pencils when frustrated and played with coffee cups or his tie when uncomfortable.

"I hope you aren't planning to retire anytime soon."

"Nah, probably not for a year or two at the earliest, but I wanted to see if you'd be up for it. It wouldn't have to be full time. I know you like working in the OR, but I thought if you were interested, you could maybe do what's needed to qualify for a PI license. It might come in handy, you know, investigating stuff for me. That might keep us both out of trouble if my lieutenant catches wind of your 'unofficial' help."

He took a sip of coffee and sat back in the booth. "I've been thinking about retiring though. Things are changing a lot at work, things that an old dog like me can't keep up with."

I waved him off. Frost was in his late fifties, and there was nothing that he couldn't keep up with; but he liked to fuss about it.

"Hell, half the time, I have to snag Roberts and have him help me figure out how I screwed up the damn computer. So, I figure another year or two and then retire while they still think I have something to offer, instead of waiting until they force me to leave."

"They're not going to force you to retire," I said. "I'm interested, but I'll have to think about the PI stuff."

"You can do most of it in online classes. A lot of it is just learning the legal statutes, which is kind of boring, but you'd get it pretty quickly. You could do that on your own time." He tugged at his already-loosened tie. "It'd give you and Angel some time to get back to normal. It's not like I'm retiring next week."

"I told him I was meeting with you today. He's worried you'll talk me into helping you with your current investigations or something risky. I don't think the cold case work will bother him, but he wouldn't be happy about me working as a PI. Not right now, anyway. I could do the courses though."

"Think about it, kid, and we can discuss it more. Tell your boy he doesn't need to worry; none of this cold case stuff is risky."

"I keep hoping things will settle down," I said. "I wish he wouldn't worry as much as he does."

He frowned for a moment and then said, "Both of you have been through hell the last few years. He needs a chance to relax and enjoy a normal life now that shithead is dead." He dragged a fry through the lake of ketchup on his plate and popped it into his mouth, chewed, and swallowed. "It wouldn't hurt you, either."

I gave him a resigned smiled. "No, it wouldn't. I'll have to give Angel some time before I spring the PI idea on him, but I do want to help with the cold cases. As long as they're not dangerous."

He raised his eyebrows and snorted. "My lieutenant and Angel would be fighting over who gets to kill me if I got you into anything dangerous."

"It was good to see Frost again," I said the next morning as Angel poured a cup of coffee.

A frown line appear between his eyes, under which dark circles resided, as he stood at the kitchen counter dressed only in his boxer briefs. His face was covered in dark stubble, making him look like one of those guys you see on romance novel covers. His uncombed hair tumbled in loose black curls over his forehead. His dark chocolate eyes were heavy-lidded from lack of sleep. He'd slept, but I knew at one point during the night he'd gotten up and spent an hour or two prowling the house, before he returned to bed.

"What'd he want?"

"He talked to me about helping him with cold cases."

Angel stopped stirring his coffee and the frown intensified. "Annie, I don't want you getting involved in some investigation he has cooking or in any scheme he may have come up with. We both need to have some peace and quiet."

"That's what he said, too, but it would just be reviewing case files for him on the side. I'm not a cop, so I can't work with him officially on the cold cases, and I certainly can't help with active ones. I could look through the cold cases in my spare time." I accepted the cup of coffee he handed me and started to walk past him. "D'you want something for breakfast, or will coffee do you?"

Angel caught my hand and stopped me. "Annie, please, whatever he has cooked up, please stay out of it."

I smiled and reached out to rest my hand on his stubbled cheek. "It's Frost; he won't get me into anything dangerous. I promise, if there's something risky on his agenda, I'll talk to you about it first."

He nodded, frown still in place. "Things will be changing for both of us," he said, leaning against the counter.

"They will?"

"Owen Cameron, a criminal defense attorney I know, offered me a job."

"As a defense attorney?"

"Yeah. Pretty nice offer, actually."

"What about the DA's office?"

Angel sighed, pushed away from the counter, and sat down at the kitchen table. "You know how you've been treated since going back to work?"

I nodded. I'd felt the stares and was well aware how conversations often stopped when I approached. People were either intrusive or avoidant. I wasn't sure which was harder to handle.

"What we went through has made work difficult for me, too. People can't stop asking or talking about what happened to both of us, and I'm tired of dealing with it."

"But you love prosecuting cases."

"Yeah, but because of all the insanity with Ian, plus all the medical leave, I'm a bit of a liability now. At least as far as my boss is concerned."

"Did he say that?"

Angel shrugged. "He hasn't come out and said anything to me, but it's pretty clear he doesn't want my notoriety taking center stage with cases. There's really no way to avoid it, at least for a while. The last few weeks all I've been doing is scut work, stuff that a brand-new ADA would be asked to do. It's made me wonder if he's trying to get me to resign."

It made my heart ache. Angel was a brilliant attorney and worked hard. He put in long hours that he considered part of the job—without complaint—and now he was being shunted aside because of me.

"They're lucky to have you," I said, angrily. "None of what happened was your fault."

"No, but it's a major distraction for the office and not likely to die down anytime soon. The press still goes nuts if I'm involved with a case. Half the time they show up and pester me for an interview about Ian. It's like they don't care about the actual case."

He took a deep breath. "Anyway," he said exhaling. "Owen made me the offer over lunch yesterday. He said he's been biding his time, waiting for an opportunity to present itself."

"That's kinda like going over to the dark side, isn't it?"

Angel laughed. "Yeah, I suppose so. Still, it's a good offer."

"What'd he propose?"

"Come in as a junior partner. I'd be helping the other partners with their cases until I learn the ropes; it's different than being a prosecutor. It'd double my salary right off the bat."

"Really?"

"Really. The private sector is where the money is, *chica*. I wanted to talk to you about it and make sure you were okay with the switch."

"It's such a different type of practice. Some of the people defense attorneys represent are pretty reprehensible—some probably guilty as hell."

"I'd say most of them are guilty of something."

"It probably won't go over well with the cops we know or the people you work with in the DA's office. Your family might even be upset about you switching to what they may see as helping criminals get away with whatever they've done."

We sat quietly drinking our coffee for a few moments, each lost in thought about the offer. At last Angel said, "I could hang in for a while and see how it goes at the DA's. The interest in what happened to us will die down eventually. I'm not sure, though, how long that'll take. Owen's offer would let me work behind the scenes for a while and get me out of the limelight."

I moved over to stand next to him. "As long as it's what you want to do and you'll be happy doing it, I'm fine with it."

I wasn't sure if that was entirely true. I wanted Angel to be happy, but I'd been around cops too long to have a very high opinion of defense lawyers. If he decided to do this, there would be repercussions personally and professionally. If that's what he chose to do, though, I would deal with it.

He smiled and pulled me onto his lap. "I told Owen I'd think about it and get back to him," he said, then kissed my forehead. "But honestly, if we can work out the details, I'll probably take him up on the offer."

"Be happy, that's all I care about," I said resting my head on his shoulder.

THREE

ALL YOU'D BE DOING is reviewing cold case files, right?" Angel asked when he got home that night. He'd clearly been going over the idea in his head all day, planning this discussion, identifying his concerns. It was one of the disadvantages of being married to a lawyer.

"Yeah, it'd be reviewing case files, looking for avenues worth re-examining, and letting Frost know if I find anything worth following up on."

"That's it?" The frown had returned to his brow.

I hesitated, then plowed on. In for a penny, in for a pound, as the saying goes. "For now. He's thinking about retiring in a couple years. He wants to do private investigation and wanted to see if I'd be interested in partnering with him."

Angel scowled and muttered something in Spanish as he walked into the bedroom, with me following in his wake. He took off his suit and hung it up.

"Meaning what?" he finally asked, pulling on jeans but neglecting to zip them up. They rested low on his hips. He watched me as he held a T-shirt in his hands.

My mind went a little off target for a moment. He was beautiful, an odd descriptor for a guy, but it was true. The surgical scars on his shoulder and abdomen hadn't changed that. They were his war wounds, testimony to what we'd survived. Angel lived up to his nickname; he looked like an angel, just one who had no aversion to fun.

Pulling my thoughts back to the current subject, I said, "Meaning I'd be his partner when he retires and help him with investigations." *Maybe this wasn't the time to broach the PI idea*, I thought.

He shot me an annoyed look as he jerked the T-shirt over his head, roughly tugged it down his torso, and zipped up.

The opportunity to divert him now gone, I plowed on. "He's not talking about doing that right now. I'd probably only do it part time, unless something changes my mind about working as a nurse."

Silence. When he spoke, his voice sounded tight and angry. "After everything we've been through the last couple of years, I'd think you'd enjoy some peace. I know I would."

"Frost said to tell you not to worry; he won't be asking me for any help other than reviewing case files. And you know Frost, he'll never retire."

"Thank God for small favors," he said under his breath, the frown still firmly in place. He could be stubborn as a mule, a trait he'd inherited from his grandmother, and I suspected this discussion wasn't over.

Frost had dropped off copies of two murder books the following morning, which was my day off, and told me to take a look. That was probably the way helping Frost with this was going to go—*Here are the files, kid, figure it out.*

"This first one isn't an old case, but it'd be great if we could solve it. The murder happened about eight months ago and there are no suspects, no witnesses, and no one who's sorry that the deceased is gone. I figured with it being relatively recent it might be easier to solve, so see what you can come up with." Frost said handing me two case files.

The books were digital now, but he'd printed off copies for me since I wasn't allowed access to the police files. *Well, Collins,* I said to myself, *think of it as a chart review. You've done those for countless patients. How different could it be?*

Murder books, I quickly learned on opening the first one, consisted of pages of documentation that began when detectives arrived on the scene and continued until the conclusion of the case or its classification as "open, unsolved." They included crime scene photos, forensic reports, documentation of interviews, transcripts of recorded ones, and notes from the investigators. Although it was similar to a hospital chart, I found it overwhelming, like reading something in a language I didn't quite understand. There was a report from the death investigator called to the scene, for example, and I had no idea what that meant.

"What?" Frost demanded when he answered my call.

"It's me. What's a death investigator?"

"It's a person from the Medical Examiner's office who goes to where the body is."

"I thought the ME did that."

He took a deep breath, annoyed that he wasn't going to get out of the conversation quickly. "He can't. We got too many homicides, accidents, and suspicious and unattended deaths in Denver. The death investigators work for the ME's office and go in his place."

"So, they show up and photograph the scene?"

"Yeah, but they also make a prelim determination of time of death using liver temp and degree of rigor, and they determine what most likely caused it, whether they consider it suspicious, and then turn the scene and the body over to the detectives and the forensic techs or, if it's clearly not a crime, they release the body for the EMTs to take to the morgue." I could hear conversations in the background as he talked. "I'm at a crime scene, gotta go."

"Okay, thanks," I said.

"No problem," he said.

You learn something new every day, I thought.

One major difference between hospital charts and homicide case files was in the autopsy report and photos of the crime scene. A hospital chart—also digital now—always had the surgeon's dictated report if the patient had undergone surgery, nursing and physician notes, dry pathology and radiology reports, and lab results. The charts rarely contained photos unless they were photos taken during surgery.

After glancing through the first file, I was grateful that I was an OR nurse. I had seen some frightful and stomach-turning injuries in my career, but these photos were far from medical. The deceased had died in a house fire. My stomach did a slow roll, and I seriously worried that I was going to lose my breakfast.

The large pediatric hospital where I'd once worked had a burn unit. Kids from a four-state area were sent to us if they had sustained a serious burn. That usually meant extensive second- and third-degree burns. In the OR, we performed the debridements that removed dead tissue and we harvested skin grafts that were used to cover areas that lacked viable skin.

I suspect that the only relief we offered the kids from the pain and torture of a serious burn was when we anesthetized them. At least then there was no pain, no awareness of what had happened. Otherwise, their lives were hell until they either healed or died. I used to imagine they were sorry when they woke up. I would have been.

I was grateful I had never had to care for one of those kids outside the OR. The strength and compassion of the nurses who worked in the burn unit always impressed me. It was not something I could have done.

I hoped that I never had to die like that. Or be drowned or strangled or—I had a long list of ways I didn't want to die. The scary part is that none of us get to choose how we die unless we kill ourselves.

I've always wondered if I didn't become a nurse so I'd have inside knowledge about illness that would keep me healthy or know what to do if I wasn't. I'd begun to wonder if my interest in Frost's work wasn't an attempt to learn how to avoid being a murder victim. I shook my head to get rid of those thoughts and brought them back to the task at hand, which was gruesome enough.

The person in the crime scene photos wouldn't have made it to any burn unit. The man—I had to double-check the autopsy report to confirm that—was a charred remnant of a human being. The muscles of his arms and legs were contracted by the fire, his skin blackened and split like barbeque gone badly wrong, and his body lay in the cindered remains of a living room couch. From other photos it looked like the fire had engulfed the couch and part of the living room around it before it had been put out.

The autopsy report identified no obvious physical injuries other than the smoke inhalation damage to his lungs. According to the ME, the presence of that indicated that the victim, Ken Stevens, had been alive when the fire started.

The on-scene investigators speculated that he'd fallen asleep smoking and his cigarette had started the house fire. He was known to be a heavy smoker, and the remains of an ashtray lay on the charred coffee table next to the couch. That theory lasted until the arson investigators found traces of accelerant around the couch on which he'd died. When the results of the toxicology report returned, it identified the presence of alcohol and Rohypnol, which struck me as odd.

Rohypnol is used as a date rape drug with street names like roofies, trip-and-fall, and mind eraser, and was used primarily on women, as far as I knew. I supposed it could be used on a guy. I didn't know many guys who required a drug to agree to participate in sex; Viagra maybe, if they had erectile dysfunction. I stopped; I wasn't thinking straight. The word *date* conjured up a social encounter until you added the word *rape*, which was never social.

Sadly, there were always situations where one person wanted sex and the other person didn't. In some cases that devolved into using drugs like GHB and Rohypnol to incapacitate the victim; in other cases the perpetrator forced the issue with no help from a date rape drug. But that didn't mean such rapes only occurred with heterosexual encounters. Sexual predators preyed on whatever gender appealed to them.

Predators also used date rape drugs because they erase or seriously cloud the victim's memory of the event. Rohypnol, in a large enough quantity, would work just as effectively to prevent someone from objecting to being left in a burning house. The question of course was who'd given it to this guy, and why did they want him dead?

Perhaps they'd set fire to the incapacitated victim in an attempt to get rid of the body. After a little Google research I discovered that house fires never actually got rid of a body. To cremate a body required a temperature of 1,800 to 2,000 degrees Fahrenheit and house fires averaged 1,100 degrees. That left a body, and during autopsy a surprising amount of information could be gleaned from a burned body, including toxicology results.

The ringing of my phone jolted me out of my thoughts. "Annie, Gabriela asked me to call you," Paul Roberts said when I answered. "I'm going to be at Gabriela's place tonight after work, and she asked me to invite you and Angel over for dinner." Angel's youngest sister Gabriela shared the next-door unit in our triplex with her sister, Marisol. Paul, a homicide detective who worked with Frost, had been dating Gabriela for about a year.

"Sounds good to me. Any time I don't have to cook is a relief."

He laughed. "She's still at school but said to tell you about seven."

"Okay, we'll be there."

"I hear Frost talked you into helping with cold case files. I hope he knows what he's doing."

"Everybody's a comedian. Who told you that?"

"Frost mentioned it. He figured with the family connection I'd hear about it anyway, and he wanted to warn me to keep it quiet."

"Keep it quiet, please. I don't want him getting in trouble. How are things with Gabriela?"

"Great, we're great. Things have gotten pretty serious for both of us."

"Any announcements due?"

"Uh, no. Maybe. We'll see. I kinda want to talk to you about that."

"Tonight?

"No. No. Sometime when we can talk in private."

"Everything okay?"

"Yeah, we're good."

"Okay, maybe we can get lunch and talk. Whatever it is, tread carefully. You know big brother—he gets a little protective."

Paul laughed. "I'm well aware."

I imagined he was absently rubbing the bridge of his nose, which Angel had broken during an argument the previous year over what Paul had said to me about Ian.

Angel came up behind me and wrapped his arms around me as I looked for my sleep shirt in the dresser drawer. "It was nice at Gabriela's tonight, but you look tired, *chica*. Long day?"

Angel had accepted the idea of my working on the cold case files, not graciously mind you, but he had let the subject drop.

"A bit. I can see it's going to be tiring, working full-time and then using my days off to go through those files. There's a lot to review. The one I'm working on is kinda gross."

"That's saying something, coming from you."

"Yeah, it is. But you can get used to anything." I turned and wrapped my arms around his neck. "Have you thought any further about Owen's offer?"

"Yeah, I've been thinking."

Smiling, he slipped my bra and panties off and traced his hands down my back as he spoke. True to form he'd managed to disrobe as soon as we walked into the bedroom. Pajamas were not a part of Angel's wardrobe.

"The hang up for me, and it's a big one, is if I can accept the fact that whether clients are innocent or guilty doesn't matter; it's always mattered to me. I'd have to defend them as if they were innocent, and according to Owen, it's better not to know whether they are or not.

"The first two things you learn as a trial lawyer is not to ask a question in court you don't know the answer to, and don't ask any you don't *want* the answer to. That's the only thing that gets to me. What if they aren't innocent?" He kissed his way down my neck.

"Yeah, that'd bother me too," I said, a little distracted. Angel always smelled so good. "Will you be happy if you take the job?"

"I'm still weighing the pros and cons. The money would be great, but if I find out or suspect that one of my clients is guilty, that would be a problem. I haven't figured how I'd deal with that yet. I'm going to talk to a couple defense attorneys I know and see what they say."

He walked us over to the bed, where we crawled in and snuggled up, the sleep shirt forgotten.

"Life has a funny way of changing doesn't it?" I asked, nestling my head on his shoulder and trailing my hand across his chest.

I loved the feel of his soft chest hair and the reassuring thump of his heart under my hand. I flashed for a moment on him lying limp in my arms, blood everywhere, terrified, knowing in my heart that Ian had killed him, and I shuddered involuntarily.

"What, *corazón?*" he asked, stroking my back.

I pulled closer to him. "Bad memories."

He kissed my forehead. "We're here, we're alive, and we're together. Nothing else matters."

He propped himself up on his elbow and gazed at me, his eyes dark and intense. Sliding a hand down my body, he murmured, "You've gained back a lot of the weight you lost..." His voice trailed off. "You're almost back to normal."

"Is that your tactful way of saying I'm fat?"

He laughed and dipped his mouth to mine. "Mmm, no—just delectable and beautiful." He softly kissed my lips as he caressed my breast, and I knew it was true—we were alive and together, and nothing else mattered.

"I love you so much," I said cupping his face, running my thumb over his cheek.

"*Tú eres mi corazón*," he whispered as his kisses deepened. *You are my heart.*

My desire for him, which never seemed to diminish, flared.

Making love had always been our refuge and our comfort. Tonight, my body was hypersensitive as Angel touched, and tasted, and stroked, then slipped into me at last. I sighed as we moved with each other, thinking how grateful I was for him.

FOUR

FROST SAT IN THE LIVING ROOM across from me. The murder book lay on the coffee table between us.

"I have some questions about that arson victim."

"Like what?"

"Like why arson? Why not kill him quickly? One reason would be to make it look like an accident, but every Tom, Dick, and Harry seems to watch CSI and would know that arson investigators can determine if a fire was deliberately set. I don't think making it look like an accident was the point."

I leaned forward, bracing my forearms on my knees, and continued. "The Rohypnol sedated him enough that he couldn't escape the fire, but I think it may also relate to the why of his murder. I think whoever did this wanted to erase him—not just kill him but make him disappear—and didn't realize that a house fire wouldn't completely destroy the body."

"Most lay people don't know a burned body can still be autopsied," Frost said.

"And it's a detached sort of killing," I said. "Sedate him, saturate him with an accelerant, toss a match, and leave. No blood, no actual contact with the victim, no watching him die, really, unless you wanted to, but because of the fire you wouldn't be able to stay to the end.

"Leaving him to burn," I continued. "that suggests to me someone who's never killed before, and based on what I've read, poisons are historically a woman's choice for murder. Rohypnol isn't a poison, but it certainly made it impossible for him to object."

"True. Where exactly are you going with this?"

"I think it was retribution, and the fact that a date rape drug was used makes me think he might have used it to rape someone who decided to punish him for it." I paused and thought for a moment. "According to the case file and people who knew him, there's no indication that before his death he was involved in any same-sex relations with anyone. No one ever saw him leave with a guy, and it seems unlikely that he was sedated because he'd changed his mind about having sex with some guy who picked him up."

"Right, we looked into that."

"But according to interviews with a couple of his friends, he was quite the ladies' man, or at least scored a lot of one-night stands. That would discredit the same-sex line of thought, although I suppose it's possible. Anyway," I said before I got too off track. "The sedative effects of Rohypnol would be quick. With a high enough dose, the sedation would be a perfect way to incapacitate someone enough to set a fire that would kill them. It wouldn't necessarily take away the victim's awareness of what was happening. That's a pretty serious payback when you think about it."

"Yeah, it's a nasty drug even if murder isn't your goal, but that was all noted and questioned at the time. The detectives assigned to the case couldn't figure out who had given it to him or why. They were convinced the dosing happened at his house. There were the remains of some glasses that had shattered in the fire on what was left of the coffee table. Forensics couldn't get prints off what was left. The amount of Rohypnol in his system would have made it impossible for him to walk." Scratching his face, Frost leaned back in the living room chair.

"He didn't have any steady women friends or boyfriends, no pissed off current wives or ex-wives," he continued. "According to the investigation, he hadn't been involved in anything dicey, like selling drugs or other criminal activities that might have resulted in his death, and most of those homicides are gun- or knife-related or worse. If he used a date rape drug he had to get the roofie from a dealer, so a drug deal gone bad was an option, but it didn't seem likely in this case."

"Right. Why would you kill your client?" I said.

"If he'd screwed his dealer over that would merit retaliation, but I doubt sedating him and setting fire to him would have been the method. No one he knew had any idea he was doing that so they had no clue who the dealer was. It's a homicide, no question about that, but who killed him or why at this point is unknown." He pointed a finger at me. "That's why the case stalled, and I'm hoping you'll come up with some ideas," he said with a grin.

"It's puzzling," I said, thinking about what I'd read. "He'd been out earlier in the evening with some buddies, cruising the bar scene, and according to them it was a slow night—apparently that means there weren't a lot of women to pick up. They say he left, alone, at about midnight.

"He'd been drinking a lot but managed to get back to his house without incident, at least according to the investigation reports. There's no record of him getting in a fight, being stopped for a traffic violation, arrested for a DUI, or being involved in an accident. No one saw him come home, and there's no way to know if he was alone or with someone he might have connected with after leaving his friends. A neighbor noticed the fire about one-thirty in the morning. He'd gotten up to pee, saw the flames through the bathroom window, and called 911."

"That's all in the file. Any ideas about who did it?" Frost asked.

"Just a thought. You know as well as I do, guys who run through women like he did often can make serious enemies. I'm wondering if he used Rohypnol on all the women he hit on. If he did, one of them could have done it, or someone close to them who found out."

Frost nodded. "The case was Ryan's and Keller's and they wondered about that too. It makes total sense. This guy was a sleazeball. According to his buddies, he never had more than a one-night stand with a woman. He didn't call them or email or text them afterwards. Hell, I doubt he even remembered their names. So, there was no way to find or contact any women he might have been with before the fire."

"I have some ideas about finding them, but I wanted to see what you thought first."

"I think he was a total dick, and somebody decided to put an end to his behavior. His death isn't a great loss to anyone. He had no parents, no siblings, no one who seems to care one way or the other. What we don't have is a suspect."

I watched as Frost rubbed at his chest, a frown on his face. He'd looked tired lately, but it had been my observation that most of the detectives in homicide looked tired.

"Everything okay?" I asked.

He stopped rubbing and smiled. "Of course, why wouldn't it be?"

Angel had been working late the last few nights on an upcoming trial, and we hadn't seen much of each other. He'd showered, saying it had been a long tiring day. He often showered after a day like that, as if he was washing away what had happened. Sitting in bed, I caught him up on the case I was working on. He'd been listening, with the frown that my working with Frost always generated firmly in place.

"I think you're probably right about him using the drug on the women he took home. He doesn't sound like a guy who'd be all that appealing otherwise."

"In his before pictures, he didn't look that bad. Not someone you'd reject right off," I said. "His behavior was another matter entirely. I think one of his victims killed him, but I don't know how to identify who did it. I don't have much sympathy for him."

"There were people I've had to deal with in the DA's office who were hard to feel much compassion for. And some guys are just creeps."

"True."

"So, what's your plan, Sherlock? Seems like they exhausted all the avenues for finding whoever did it."

I made a face at him. "I'm thinking about it, but cold cases are cold because the means to solve them didn't work or the team hit a dead end. I'm not sure I can help much and honestly, with this guy, I'm not sure whether finding his killer matters. If he drugged the women he took home, he deserved what he got."

"Remind me not to make you mad, *chica*," he said with a grin.

I smiled at him as I watched him run the towel through his hair. "You know, you really shouldn't stand there starkers; it gives me ideas."

He raised his eyebrows as Mr. Happy decided to stand up and join the party. "Yeah? What kinda ideas?"

"About having a little fun that doesn't need coercion?"

"You'll never need to coerce me for that, *chica*."

"You're telling me!" I laughed, pulling off my sleep shirt. "Come here, gorgeous."

FIVE

ANGEL'S GRANDMOTHER, Maria Sandoval, had been diagnosed and undergone surgery for pancreatic cancer a year and a half ago. The family had convinced her, at last, to undergo chemotherapy and she had done surprisingly well until recently, when her health had taken a downturn. She'd bounced back, but I worried that time was running out for her. I had always visited her regularly, but I hadn't seen her since Angel and I had been released from the hospital.

We were ensconced on the patio at Angel's parents' home, chatting. They owned a lovely two-story home in north Denver. Dubbed Denver Squares, the house was exactly what it sounded like, a two-story, square-shaped brick house with four bedrooms, in an area of Denver that had historically been Hispanic.

Gentrification had gradually taken over. Developers bought homes, scraped them, and built new, expensive homes, and many upscale restaurants and shops had popped up. Younger professional couples were taking over neighborhoods that once were filled with kids and extended families.

Maria shifted carefully in her lounge chair and watching her I worried that she was in pain. "Are you okay? Do you need anything?"

She smiled. "I'm fine, *querida*."

I took a deep breath, inhaling the scent of the roses and lavender that bordered the yard, and closed my eyes to listen to the birds chirping in the trees. "Good," I said.

She reached out and took my hand, and asked, "Are you troubled by killing him?"

I opened my eyes; her question took me by surprise. We had never discussed my killing Ian. I wasn't sure what to say. She was a devout Catholic and I worried that the truth would offend her.

"No," I said at last. "I'm sorry if that upsets you. He was evil and I don't regret what I did."

She squeezed my hand reassuringly. "I am glad to hear that. Even the church does not see killing in self-defense as a sin. Nor do I. He *was* evil and I am glad that you and *Angelito* are safe."

We sat quietly for a bit. I was relieved; Maria was someone I never wanted to upset. "My grandson tells me you are working with that policeman, the one you are friends with," she said.

According to Angel, Maria never called him *grandson* unless she was annoyed with him, and I wondered what they'd discussed. I nodded.

"He is worried and wishes you weren't working with the detective."

"I know," I said. "Going back to the OR has been…complicated. Working with Frost in my spare time is interesting."

I took her hand. "There's nothing to worry about, and I wish he hadn't said anything to you. It's not something he should have dumped on you."

"I am not worrying about it. You're a strong woman, *querida*, and an intelligent one. Neither my grandson nor I need to tell you what to do. I told him that, and he was not happy."

"I'm sure he wasn't."

She smiled. "I think he hoped I would persuade you to stop. It takes a while sometimes for a man to realize that his wife can think for herself."

"It does."

She laughed. "And sometimes we have to think for them, too. Do what you need to do, *querida*, just be aware that he loves you deeply. I have never seen *Angelito* feel the way he does about you. He needs you to be safe, we all do."

"The more I find out about this guy, the more I'm convinced that one of his one-night-stands is probably responsible for drugging him and setting the fire," I told Frost.

I had begun thinking of the cold case fire victim as "Crispy," which wasn't respectful of the dead. He was a creep, though, and my OR humor had taken over. I knew that Frost, or anyone else in homicide, wouldn't be offended; cop humor was often far darker than mine. It was a defense against allowing the dark and difficult things each profession faced to overwhelm us. Some days it was either laugh or sob until you couldn't function.

I had met Frost in a coffee shop near the precinct. "Would it be possible to contact the guy's friends again and see if you can jog their memories about the last few times he left a bar with a woman? Maybe get some descriptions of the women, if there was a specific type he favored? Talking with them again might trigger something. It's been a while; it may be hard for them to remember much. Depends on how much drinking normally went on."

I paused, thinking. "If they don't remember specific women, then find out what bars they frequented. We could talk to employees at the bars and see if anyone knew women he hit on or could provide names."

"Not sure they'll remember much; they didn't when Ryan and Keller talked to them."

"Maybe not, but it's an avenue to explore. I'd also show the photo of him pre-barbeque to women who come to whatever bars he and his friends frequented, see if anyone remembers him."

"*Pre-barbeque?*" Frost laughed and shook his head. "Jesus, every time I eat barbeque from now on, I'll think of this guy. Thanks."

I shrugged. "I don't feel much sympathy for him. Even his 'friends,' and I use that term loosely, thought he was kinda sleezy, according to the statements I read. Not sure why you'd want to be friends with someone like that."

Frost shrugged. "If he was good at getting women to leave with him, his friends probably hoped that his luck would rub off if they hung out with him. 'Sides, guys like this, they're not so much friends as hunting buddies."

Hunting buddies, that sent a chill down my spine. Hell, his "friends" probably drugged the women they took home, too. Maybe we're all a little naïve, but I never worried about things like that when I was single. Women probably should, I should have, but most of us don't. You know something like that *could* happen but dismiss the possibility of it actually happening to you. I sighed and finished my coffee.

"If one of his victims decided to make him pay, then I hope you don't find her."

"We don't get to decide that, Annie. But the case hit a dead end, and it's entirely possible we won't find the person who did it. Can't say I disagree with you, though, if you're right." He pounded his fist lightly against his chest, pulled a roll of antacid tablets out of his jacket pocket, and popped two. I saw him flexing and releasing his left fist, and my concern for him spiked.

"Damn heartburn," he said, crunching the antacid tablets up and swallowing them with the last sip of his coffee.

"If it's heartburn, you need to ease up on the coffee. Maybe go see your doc?" I worried that it could be much more serious than heartburn. It looked like heart-related chest pain to me.

He waved me off. "I don't need to see anybody, stop worrying."

We stood up and as we walked toward the door of the restaurant, he said, "Just to be clear, *we* won't be investigating anything. Your job is to come up with ideas about where to go, and my job is to investigate. I'm not having Angel come after me for dragging you into anything."

Angel decided to take Owen Campbell's offer and had tendered his resignation. For now, while he finished his time at the DA's office, he was also putting in time at Owen's firm. I wasn't sure how he felt about the new job; he hadn't talked about it much. I wasn't sure if he was fully onboard with the change, but chose not to ask.

It surprised me to discover I was on the fence about it. It was my fault Angel had been put in a position to have to make the decision, and I wondered what the repercussions would be for him. I had always thought of criminal defense as game-playing. Prosecution seemed more straightforward, to me. Angel had joked about working for "truth, justice, and the American way," but as far as I could see, the legal system wasn't about truth or justice; it was more about which side could play the system better. Deep down, I wondered how either of us would deal with that.

I hadn't broached the news to Frost yet. In most cops' minds, defense attorneys were bottom feeders who prevented cops from bringing criminals to justice. They were the lawyers you love to hate, until you needed one. Like other sensitive topics between me and someone close, I tended to put discussing it off until forced to do so. Not a good idea as I had learned over and over, yet I continued to do it.

On top of all that, my helping Frost had triggered some serious hovering from Angel. He knew how involved I could get in an investigation. As a result, he was anxious and irritable about pretty much everything. I wasn't sure we'd ever get to a point where he would accept the PI idea. Unfortunately, it had become increasingly appealing to me.

I liked to solve mysteries about the human body, it was why I'd always loved working in the OR. You could find and solve the problem—most of the time. Medicine had its 'cold cases' too.

I had looked into taking the classes that were required to be licensed, and with Frost's help, had found one to sign up for. *What harm was there in that?* I asked myself. The classes might help me to decide if it was really something I wanted to do. I hoped it'd be a few years, though, before Frost retired. Maybe by then things would settle down for Angel and me.

Angel wanted peace—I did too—but apparently you don't always get what you want. And apologies to Mick Jagger and Keith Richards, but I wasn't sure you always got what you needed, either.

SIX

FROST CALLED ME as he was getting ready to leave work for the day. I happened to be on a break and walked out the main OR doors to talk. "How're the interviews with the Crispy's friends going?" I asked.

He snorted. "Only you would call him that."

"He's dead, he's not going to care, and I don't like him much. I promise to keep the name between us."

"I don't think anyone at the precinct would object if they heard it. I probably won't say it to the lieutenant, though. I've talked to several of the guy's friends, and they weren't all that helpful. They remembered a couple of women, but their descriptions are pretty worthless—pretty, great boobs, hot—that kinda bullshit."

"Guess his friends are creeps, too."

"They're guys who hang out in bars; it's not surprising. I did get a list of bars they frequent. It might be worthwhile to take his photo around to see what I can find out." I could hear Frost's footsteps echoing and figured he was in the garage on his way to his car. "Evie said to ask if you and Angel want to come over for dinner tonight."

"Angel's tied up with work." I didn't say he was working at Owen's office. I still couldn't think how to tell Frost. "But I'll come, if that works."

"She's been wanting to get together, but what with everything that's gone on, it never happened. I'll swing by and pick you up. We can have you both over another time."

"I should be home by four-thirty. See you then."

Frost and his wife lived in a nice home near University Hills, south of the University of Denver. It was a ranch that had become rather large for two people, but neither one of them wanted to downsize. Evie loved the yard and the house. I think they kept hoping their boys would marry and there'd be grandkids to come visit. It hadn't happened yet. I suspected their sons frustrated Evie as much as Angel frustrated his mother.

"It's good to see you at last. I'm sorry Angel couldn't make it," she said, giving me a hug as Frost and I walked in the front door. Something smelled wonderful, and I was starving.

I liked Evelyn Frost—Evie to friends and family. She was small, about five foot two, a handsome woman with salt-and-pepper dark hair in an appealing pixie cut, which made her seem even tinier. Her blue eyes sparkled, and her laughter came easily. She was a practical, no-nonsense woman who had put up with Frost for nearly forty years. That took some strength of character in my opinion.

Frost, in contrast, was a tall, weary-looking man who seemed to have a perpetually annoyed look on his face, unless he was looking at Evie. He was a testament, I supposed, to what being a cop for thirty years can do to a person.

Frost had told me once that they'd had a few "bumps" in their marriage, as he called them. One he'd admitted had nearly ended the relationship. He didn't give details and I hadn't asked for them—but they were still together. Theirs was a comfortable, lived-in relationship. They weren't together out of necessity or inertia; they really liked each other. Easy smiles, casual caresses, and their banter spoke volumes about their love. Seeing the glint in Frost's eye when he spoke about Evie always reassured me that, while love for some couples might not last, it could and did for others.

"Dinner's almost ready. How are you feeling? Have you and Angel recovered from everything?" She helped me out of my coat and added it to the jumble of coats in the front hall closet.

"Jeez, Evie," Frost said. "Give the kid a chance to get in the door before you start bombarding her with questions."

"Don't fuss at me," she admonished him, patting him on the cheek and planting a kiss on his lips. Taking my arm, she pulled me into the kitchen and motioned me to take a seat at the kitchen table. "How are you? Alex tells me you're helping him with cold cases. Are you still working at the hospital?"

"I'm good. I'm still working in the OR. You know, once a nurse always a nurse, but people can't let go of what happened, and I need something to distract me. Your husband's cold cases are filling the bill."

She brought me a glass of wine. "How's Angel?"

"Evie, stop with the interrogation. Annie doesn't need to rehash all of that." Frost retrieved a beer from the fridge and eased down into a chair across the table from me.

Evie glanced at him, clearly ready to let him have it. "We're family. For God's sake, you walked her down the aisle. I can ask a few questions."

"Frost, it's okay. You guys *are* family, you're allowed." I took a drink of wine. "Angel's having a hard time, but overall, I think we're doing okay," I replied with what I hoped was a reassuring smile.

"It scared all of us, sweetie. But you're my hero. You were incredibly brave in a horrific situation." Evie bustled around the kitchen, checking whatever was cooking in the oven.

"That one," she said, pointing a wooden spoon in Frost's direction, "was scared to death when he got the call about what'd happened."

"I'm sorry for all of that. I wish none of it had happened, but at least it's over." Suddenly my throat closed, and I could feel the sting of tears.

Evie looked horrified and rushed over and wrapped her arms around me. "Oh sweetheart, oh, I apologize for bringing all that back."

I hugged her back, and she let go. "It's hard to remember, but it's good, too. It reminds me of what I almost lost," I said.

She nodded and returned to her dinner preparations. "We can talk about something else." I saw a momentary glitter of tears in her eyes. Then she cleared her throat and gave Frost a smile. "Here," she said, handing him a stack of dishes. "Set the table, make yourself useful."

So, I thought watching her, *the fear that someone you love could be taken away never leaves, does it?*

I was in the darkened living room of a small house I didn't recognize and wasn't sure why I was there. I could see a couch where a man lay sleeping. A figure was standing in front of the couch.

I started toward the figure to ask if something was wrong, when I realized it was Ian, and froze. He held a small can in his hand and a lighter in the other.

He smiled at me, but the smile never reached those dead eyes. He turned back to the man on the couch, and poured the can's contents on the sleeping figure and the cushions he lay on. Grinning at me over his shoulder, he flicked the lighter on, leaned down, and held it to the man's shirt, which burst into flames.

Then he turned to me. "Gonna stay and watch Crispy burn?"

I awoke with a gasp, sat up, and looked around trying to orient myself. I could see Angel's sleeping form lying on his side in the bed next to me.

I'm home, I thought, letting out a breath I hadn't realized I was holding. *Home. Safe.*

"It's just a dream," I whispered, relieved to hear my voice, to know this was real, not the dream.

I took a deep breath and lay back down. Spooning up against Angel, I wrapped my arm around him. He pushed back against me, making a contented sound, pulled my arm tight against his chest, and mumbled "*Corazón*," before he drifted back to sleep.

It was a while before I slept.

SEVEN

HOW MANY BARS did they hang out in?" I asked Frost.

He gave me the names of the five he had discovered. "I plan to hand copies of his photo around and ask people to pass the photos to others, if they don't recognize him."

"Maybe we'll get lucky and someone will."

He shot me an annoyed look. "Again, it's not *we*, it's me. Got it?"

"I've got it," I said snottily. "It's a figure of speech."

"Right." He gave me one of his *You don't expect me to fall for that, do you?* looks. "I'll check it out, *you* stay out of it."

"I will, for crying out loud. You don't have to keep reminding me."

"So," he said, leaning back in his desk chair and pinning me with a look. "Rumor has it Angel quit the DA's office and has defected to the defense side of the courtroom. Is that true?"

"I was gonna tell you, I just hadn't figured out how."

He shook his head. "I can't believe he'd do that."

I frowned at him. "It hasn't been easy for him since he returned to work. He's been pushed to the side because of all the Ian crap. His boss wants him out of the public eye, no trials, nothing but scut work, and who knows how long that will last? Owen Campbell made him an offer he couldn't refuse." I watched Frost and waited for a reply. Getting none, I said, "If you're going to give him hell for this, then I'm done, and you'll be free of both of us." The idea that I would lose friends like Frost over this made me angry. I hoped it wouldn't come to that.

"I've never liked lawyers, it's all politics and games to them, but prosecutors are at least on our side. I don't see how he could be happy doing defense."

"I'm serious, Frost, don't hassle him, please. The DA's basically put him on a shelf. Angel feels shunted aside and this was a good offer. Who knows? When we get around to this PI work, you may be working with him from time to time. I wouldn't burn any bridges if I were you."

I walk when I have something on my mind. It's always helps me think, and I had a lot on my mind right now. I was worried about Angel and Frost. I couldn't tell if Angel was happy about taking Owen's offer—I wasn't sure if I was, to be honest—but it was a done deal. He'd given his notice and was coming to the end of his tenure at the DA's. He'd be full-time defense counsel at the start of the coming week. He was an adult, a logical, sensible adult, I kept telling myself, he wouldn't have taken the job if he hadn't wanted to.

But the worry was there, nonetheless. What if leaving the job at the DA's had been a mistake? I'd told Frost not to burn any bridges, but by leaving the DA's office, Angel had burned bridges. What if he didn't like defense work? What would he do then? It made my brain hurt.

Frost had said nothing to Angel. There hadn't really been an opportunity to, but I wasn't sure what, if anything, he'd say when they finally had a chance to talk. Frost and Angel had always gotten along well, and I worried Angel's professional move would damage that and in turn damage my relationship with Frost. They would sort it out, I reassured myself, they were adults after all. And yet I worried. I was good at that.

More worrisome was Frost's behavior. He ate antacids like they were candy, a frown seemed to be permanently in place, and he was more irritable than usual. He looked like someone who hadn't had a good night's sleep in months. I was sure he was experiencing heart-related issues and I didn't know what to do.

He needed to see someone, but I knew he wouldn't unless forced, and I had no idea how to do that. He'd become like a surrogate father to me and a mentor. I couldn't imagine life without him, and didn't want to, but I had yet to figure out a way to force him to see a doctor.

I didn't have to be at work until three p.m. so I bundled up and drove to City Park, to walk and think for a bit. There were walking paths along the Platte River that split Speer Boulevard into north and southbound sides, which were closer to where we lived, but you never knew who you'd meet, and some of the homeless people who often congregated along those walking paths were a little worrisome if you were a woman alone. I was distracted enough that I didn't want to worry about my surroundings.

A light snow blanketed the ground at the park, and my breath produced clouds of vapor, but the sun was out, and it was peaceful. There weren't many people in the park other than the occasional hardcore runner or dog walker and me. I breathed a sigh of relief in the fresh, cold air and began to walk on the path that ran around the outer perimeter of the park. Deciding to let my worries about Angel and Frost go, I thought about the cold case.

Frost was in the process of polling the bars again for people who might have seen the victim leave with women and handing out photocopies of Crispy's picture along with Frost's business card in the hopes that he could find someone who knew something. I hoped it would. This far out from the murder, I wasn't sure anything would come of it but Frost was willing to give it a try. If the effort didn't pan out, then this was one cold case that wasn't going to get any warmer.

As I walked, I thought about how frightening being drugged and sexually assaulted would be. The problem with Rohypnol was it made remembering what had happened difficult, if not impossible, and if you weren't tested for it within a certain timeframe there often was no trace of it left in your system.

Many victims were unsure what had happened and didn't decide to be tested soon enough. If they suspected rape, many were embarrassed to seek care and often didn't report the incident to the police. Because of their memory issues and the fact that they'd been drinking, they figured no one would believe them, and often no one did.

My guess was, if Crispy had drugged them, the women he'd assaulted would remember him and their initial conversation with him, but not be entirely sure what, or if, anything had happened afterward. I was hoping that any women who'd had contact with Crispy would at least contact Frost and tell them what, if anything, they remembered.

You might be physically aware that you'd had sex but would have no reliable memory of it. Most women would attribute that to drinking too much and blacking out, again something that many would be too embarrassed to report.

Sadly, in our society, some people still believe rape victims deserved or encouraged their assault. A recent candidate for office had actually said, "If it's inevitable, then you should lie back and enjoy it."

That callous attitude about rape—the blame the woman attitude—excuses men like Crispy and has always contributed to the reluctance of victims to come forward. And why would anyone, when the first reaction was to blame the woman not the rapist, as if a woman somehow deserved what she got?

What made me so angry was that sense of entitlement—boys will be boys—and the disregard for women who are assaulted. It made me hope that we never discovered or arrested whomever had been responsible for Crispy's death. If he'd drugged and raped women, then he deserved what had happened to him.

For a while, I just walked and let everything go. The Canada geese congregated on the frozen surface of the small lake in the middle of the park and several paddled around peacefully in the middle where the water hadn't frozen over. I laughed watching an older woman unsuccessfully trying to get her tiny white fluff of a dog to stop barking at a much larger dog who shot the small dog a look of disdain. Small dogs never seemed to be aware of their size and had no hesitation about aggression toward dogs far bigger than themselves. Men were a bit like that. The smaller they were, the more they seemed to have to prove.

It didn't take long, though, before the worry about what was going on with Frost popped up. The night I'd had dinner with Frost and Evie, she had taken me aside when Frost excused himself to use the bathroom and asked that I keep an eye on him.

"What's going on?"

She shrugged, watching the door Frost had gone through, evidently not wanting him to hear the conversation. "Probably nothing, but he's not himself. You're a nurse, please just keep an eye on him, okay?"

I had agreed, and her worry had added to my own concerns about him. Unlike Evie, I was pretty sure what was going on was more than probably nothing.

I felt weighed down with the worry and that there was no way to offload it. It was mine to carry.

I met my friend Chip Elliot, an ICU nurse I'd been friends with for six years, at a restaurant the next evening, leaving Angel to fend for himself. I hadn't seen much of Chip in the last few months, but he looked much the same as he always had. His blond hair was on the long side and made up of varying shades of gold. He had a quick smile and bright blue eyes. The quintessential surfer boy, a look that was popular with the ladies.

He'd surprised me, his dads, and his other friends by signing up for traveling nurse work. His reason being that he was getting a world of experience in different ICUs across the country, and it allowed him to see places he'd always wanted to visit. As he'd said when he'd told me what his plans were, "I'm single, no wife, no kids, no mortgage, better to do it now, rather than end up wishing I had."

He was back in town for six weeks, working in the ICU at Saint Anthony's Hospital out in Lakewood, a suburb on the western outskirts of Denver. "It's a great job, we get lots of trauma, and the people are a nice bunch, plus it's good to be home for a bit. The Dads miss me."

"And you miss them."

I had always been fond of Chip's dads, Phil, the tall cautious, serious one, and Allen the funny one who'd always reminded me of David Sedaris in looks and sense of humor. I knew they missed him, I had missed him, too.

He grinned. "Yeah, I do. They aren't happy with me being away as much as I am, but I'm living at home until this assignment ends, and they're happy for now." He shrugged his shoulders and resumed eating.

After we'd caught up on his life, he wanted to know how things were going for Angel and me. I filled him in and then cautiously told him about the cold case work I was doing and Frost's post-retirement plan.

"You're serious? Jesus, I'm not surprised Angel's worried about you."

"You'd think I was talking about working for the CIA or something."

"Annie, you're helping Frost with cold cases, and now you're talking about *working with him as a PI?* Christ, *I'm* worried about you."

I frowned. "Don't be. I haven't made my mind up about that yet." I didn't mention the PI classes I was taking. "I'm just helping Frost with the cold cases, and he isn't anywhere near retiring."

"Tell me what he's got you doing."

I did and Chip looked grim. "I don't know why you get caught up in this shit," he said.

I sighed. "I like helping Frost. What he deals with…I don't feel like such a freak when I'm helping him." I took a drink of my wine. "And…I knew a girl that happened to in college. She reported it and tried her best to get the guy prosecuted, but it went nowhere. She was a wreck and then found out he'd given her an STD."

"What happened?"

"She killed herself, and I found her. She'd hung herself; trust me, what they show on TV or write about in novels doesn't even compare to the reality. Every now and then, I still see her hanging there. "

"Oh God, Annie, I'm sorry." He reached out and held my hand.

"Thanks." I took a few deep breaths and sighed. "If that's what this guy did, I hope we never find the person responsible. I'd've set the bastard who did that to my friend on fire, if I'd had the chance."

We sat quietly and sipped at our drinks, each lost in thought. Again, I wondered if it wouldn't be justice to let the case die and figure karma had seen to it the guy paid for what he'd done. The problem was no one knew for sure why he'd been killed. Payback for date rape was possible—probable, in my opinion—but there was no proof, and I was trying hard not to jump to conclusions. As Frost said, we didn't have the right to be judge and jury. Our job—his job—was to solve the case.

"Tell me more about the traveling nurse job," I said at last, changing the subject.

I spent the rest of dinner listening to stories about his exploits. Before we parted ways, he hugged me and said, "Cut Angel and the rest of us a little slack, sweetie, and take care. I know you, be safe okay?"

It occurred to me as I headed home, that I probably didn't worry enough and thus gave people close to me too much to worry about.

EIGHT

THE DAY AFTER MY DINNER with Chip, I began my review of the second cold case Frost had given me. Crispy's case was as stalled as I had thought it would be. I hoped this one would be easier to figure out. It was a cold case, and an older one, so it was unlikely to be easy. Frost had stopped by on his way to work to see how things were coming. We talked about both cases, but like me he wasn't hopeful about either one. He looked exhausted, as he had looked for the last few weeks.

"Frost? You look worn out. Is everything okay?"

"I'm just tired, kid. Hazard of the job."

"Take some time off? Rest a little? I worry about you."

He grinned. "I worry about you, too, for all the good it does either of us."

"I'm serious, you need to see your…"

His phone rang and halted the conversation. "Frost. Okay, let Talbot know. Tell her to meet me there in fifteen minutes."

"What was that all about?" I asked when he hung up.

"Walkers in City Park stumbled on a young woman who'd been hit in the head and died, probably a while before the couple found her. I gotta get going." He grabbed his jacket and fished his keys out of its pocket.

"Who's Talbot?"

"She's a detective who was recently transferred to the unit, and my unofficial partner, at least for this case."

"Catch me up on it when you can?"

"Yeah, sure," he said distractedly as he left.

When he stopped by just before ten p.m., he plopped down on the couch and leaned back closing his eyes. I didn't like his color but he'd rebuffed my attempts to question him or suggest he might need to see his doctor and I doubted, as tired as he looked, he'd be open to hearing that now. He really needed to see his primary care. I didn't think that was likely to happen, though.

"Fill me in, can you?" Angel was out to dinner with Owen Cameron and the other two partners and had texted that he might be home late. I was relieved that Frost and I would have time to talk about his new case privately.

He rubbed a hand over his face, and I could hear the rasp of his beard. "Looks like she'd been hit on the back of the head. The DI thinks there might be a drug overdose involved, she had what looks like a needle mark on the inside of her left elbow. Won't know until the autopsy and tox reports come back. She could be an addict, you know, an overdose, but she doesn't really look like one to me and that doesn't explain the bash on the head. There was nothing around the scene that might have been used to hit her or that she might have fallen on to cause the head injury. It's pretty hard to fall on the back of your head, though, unless someone pushes you. I think she was whacked from behind."

"Who was she?"

"We're trying to ID her by fingerprints. She had no ID or personal effects on her. Only identifying marks are a tat that read *Per ardua ad astra* on the inside of her wrist." He paused and scratched his chin then frowned. "Not sure that's going to be any help if her fingerprints don't pop."

"I wonder why she'd have that? It's Latin for *Through adversity to the stars*. It's the Royal Air Force motto."

"How the hell do you know that?"

"I was in a college history class, and a student who was British had a grandfather who was an RAF pilot in the Second World War. She mentioned it when we were studying the London blitz. But it's not likely your victim was RAF."

"No, pretty sure she wasn't." Frost laughed, then knit his brows. "But who knows why people get tattoos? Maybe she has a boyfriend who's an RAF pilot or a grandfather like your classmate. People put tats in the weirdest places and for the weirdest reasons these days."

He grinned. "I saw a corpse once that had a fly tattooed on the end of his dick. Must have hurt like a son of a bitch to get it." Frost seemed to remember who he was talking to and blushed. "Anyway, my point is people are weird."

I raised my eyebrows at him. "Yes, they are, and just for the record, that's disgusting."

He snorted a laugh. "No shit."

I frowned. "I wonder if it means something else that's unrelated to the RAF. It's weird."

"Kid, when you've been around as long as I have, you realize people do a lot of things that are weird."

The following day I didn't have to be at work until three, and I decided to investigate the tattoo motto. I called a priest I had met the previous year regarding the death of another priest. Father Giraldi served a parish over by Rose Medical Center and had been helpful and pleasant to talk to, and priests knew Latin.

"It's the Latin motto for the Royal Air Force but that makes no sense. You know Latin better than I, perhaps you could think of something else it might mean."

He thought for a moment. "I suppose if you went from adversity to the stars, you'd be going toward happiness or success. From something difficult toward something beautiful or something to aspire to?

"Your translation is correct, there's really no other translation. The British seem fond of Latin slogans for buildings, colleges, and groups. It makes sense as an RAF motto, but there could be all sorts of interpretations or personal meanings for the phrase. Perhaps this woman knew someone who was in the RAF? If not, then it would likely depend on what the stars meant to her."

"That's a good point. I'm not sure the police will know until they can ID her. But that's helpful, Father, thanks."

"How are you and your husband doing? I read about what happened. You're lucky to be alive. I prayed for your recovery."

"Thank you, that's kind of you. We're doing okay. A few bumps, but definitely glad to be alive," I said with a self-deprecatory laugh.

I heard the concern in his voice and the kindness. "If…if you are experiencing any distress over what happened and I can be of any help to either of you, please don't hesitate to call."

"Thank you, I appreciate the offer." I liked him a lot.

Angel was struggling. Insomnia plagued him and when he slept, dreams took its place. Both of us should probably see someone about what had happened, but life had taken over and I had pushed the idea of therapy to the side. I wondered, hearing Father Giraldi's offer, if Angel might be more willing to talk to a priest than a therapist. I'd have to find a way to ask.

Now that I knew about the death of the young woman in City Park, I found I couldn't concentrate on the other cold case. A girl at my high school had disappeared one weekend toward the end of my senior year. I didn't know her well, but her disappearance and the eventual discovery of her body had left its mark on me. It turned out she'd tried to breakup with her boyfriend, and he hadn't been happy about it. She, too, had been bashed in the head and left to die not far from our high school. The current murder victim had brought all of that back.

After badgering Frost, he reported that fingerprints had finally ID'd the woman as Laura Hutchinson. It gave her a name, which was important to me. I had told him about my high school classmate and he had finally relented and agreed to talk to me about the case.

"Look kid, I shouldn't discuss this with you, but if I do, you need to keep quiet about it."

"I will, Frost. I just want to know what's going on."

He made a face. "Angel's not going to be happy about this…"

"I'm not involved, I'm just interested."

I shifted in the booth at Cody's where we'd met for lunch. "D'you know what happened yesterday at work? I was circulating on a general surgery case and I'd been on the phone with a tech in the sterile processing department for ten minutes trying to locate an instrument set.

"I kept getting this, 'I don't know where it is, it's not my job, not my responsibility' bullshit, and I lost it. I told the technician to find his supervisor and find the tray or I'd come down and find it for him, and he didn't want that to happen. I hung up only to hear the surgeon say, 'Guess the tech doesn't know she popped the last guy who pissed her off.' And he and his assistant laughed about it.

"Some days I hate my job. Listening to what's going on with your active cases and reviewing the cold cases makes me feel normal for some bizarre reason. Can you just talk to me about it?"

He reached out and patted my hand. "I'm sorry, kid." He sat back and took a sip of coffee. "I'll keep you informed if you'll promise not to kill the asshole surgeons you work with."

That drew an unexpected laugh from me.

Frost reported that the results from the autopsy wouldn't be available for at least forty-eight hours, assuming the ME's office wasn't backed up. The toxicology reports could take anywhere from three to eight weeks, but the ME could often make a preliminary determination if drugs had contributed to the cause of death, which then would have to be confirmed by the tox report.

He was in the process of searching to see if she had been treated at any of the Denver hospitals, ERs, or urgent care facilities. If so, he'd obtain the records. If nothing turned up in the Denver metro area, then he'd expand the search to the other suburbs near Denver. He hoped to find next of kin and some contact information.

Frost had found no record of her birth in the Colorado system. Her driver's license on record with the DMV had expired and did not list any emergency contact info, other than an address for a low-rent apartment house. The manager of that had no recollection of her at all.

I'd discovered that her tattoo was also the motto for the Royal Air Force in New Zealand and Australia, but as Frost had pointed out, it was interesting but of no help. It was also the state of Kansas's motto. Frost checked birth records there and came up empty handed. Neither of us had found an explanation for why she'd had it tattooed on herself. Perhaps her parents might know, if he could find them.

When the autopsy report finally arrived, Frost said the ME theorized that she had been incapacitated by the blow to the head and then killed by an overdose. Frost had dropped by on his way home. He'd kept his promise to keep me updated, and I hadn't killed any surgeons—yet.

"According to the ME, she weighed on the low side for her height, suggesting in his opinion some malnutrition or perhaps an eating disorder. He said it would be hard to tell if she was malnourished because of some diet she was on or some type of dietary restriction like being vegan or a vegetarian and not knowing how to ensure she was getting everything she needed nutritionally, or just not able to eat regularly.

Until family or friends are located there's no way to verify an eating disorder, although none of that contributed to her death."

Frost scratched his head, "Never understood why anybody would give up meat." He shrugged. "There were no signs of defensive injuries. She had scrapes on her palms and knees that were from hitting the ground. The ME surmised she hadn't seen the blow to her head coming."

"No signs of chronic drug use?" I asked.

"Nope, no nasal septum perforation, old needle track marks, or skin abscesses from popping." I knew that meant injecting drugs just under the skin. "There was no body packing, which, if one balloon of drugs had burst, could have caused an overdose."

"So that rules out chronic drug use or trafficking, doesn't it?"

"Probably. But he listed two findings that indicated an opioid overdose—froth in her mouth and the one needle mark. Based on that, she most likely was injected with an opioid after losing consciousness. He'll have to wait for the tox reports to confirm the overdose, but between the blow to the head and the suspicion of an overdose, in someone who showed no sign of chronic drug use, he declared her death a homicide."

When Frost received the postmortem toxicology reports two weeks later, it showed she had high levels of fentanyl, a synthetic opioid that has skyrocketed to popularity on the street, in her system. The part of the autopsy that made my heart ache was that she was twelve weeks pregnant.

With a name to go by, Frost had searched police records to see if Laura had any record that might help explain why she'd been killed. She had no arrest record as an adult, but he discovered that in 2006, as a seven-year-old, she had been sexually assaulted and left in a culvert, miles from the wealthy subdivision in Evergreen where her parents lived. A woman who lived in the isolated area and had been hiking and had stumbled onto her. She was injured, hypothermic, and dehydrated.

Police estimated she'd been lost for about twenty-four hours. The child refused to talk or give her name when found. At the time, no one knew if this was her normal state or caused by the trauma she'd experienced. Initially, no one knew who or where her parents were, they were eventually located and now Frost had their names.

Frost had asked me once before to review patient records for an investigation of a rash of patient deaths on the ICU step-down unit at my hospital. The medical consultants the department routinely used had been unavailable, so Frost's lieutenant had cleared me to review the records. I couldn't formally review Laura's patient chart, but Frost wanted me to take a look at it.

He wasn't sure that what had happened to her as a child had any bearing on her death, but Frost liked to be thorough. He didn't have the time to review the chart, and his lieutenant had dismissed his request for a medical consultant to review something that had, in her opinion, "Nothing to do with the current case and would be expensive." Frost thought the two incidents might be connected and, in his inimitable way of getting what he wanted, he quietly provided me a copy.

"Her original abduction and assault is a cold case, they never found the perpetrator, so I figured you could review the chart and see what pops for you."

"Lord, she was an unlucky person."

"Yeah, some people are. I think it's possible the two events are connected."

The photos documenting her injuries at the time showed a dirty child with pale blonde, tangled hair and blue eyes wide with fright. Her feet had been cut up badly because she hadn't been wearing shoes and there was a deep laceration to the side of her head. Her arms and legs were badly scratched from the terrain she'd wandered through; more than one required stitching. I thought of the trauma Laura had already experienced, which was bad enough, but what she'd faced in the hospital would have been nearly as traumatic for her.

Hospitals in general aren't welcoming places, and the OR is even less so. The ambient temperature is low, there are odd smells, and everyone is dressed in scrubs, hair coverings, and masks. As a patient, it can be hard to recognize people without the social cues of hair and normal clothing. Add to that faces covered by masks and eye protection or face shields, and the whole experience is anxiety provoking for any patient, but especially for a child.

With children, rules have to bend, you can't treat them as you would treat adults. You can introduce yourself and try to reassure them, but often they are too upset to pay much attention. Then, the goal is comforting them, helping them feel as safe as possible, and getting on with the procedure as quickly and in the least traumatic way possible.

According to the ER nurse's notes, Laura had been given a mild sedative pre-op. Despite that, she had refused to lie on the gurney for the trip to the OR, and the OR nurse carried her with the ER nurse bringing the IV. Laura had panicked in the OR and couldn't be convinced to lie down on the table, so the anesthesiologist had injected sedation into her IV while the nurse held her. When she had finally gone limp, the team began their jobs, and the nursing notes carefully documented the procedures performed.

Once anesthetized, the pediatric sexual assault nurse examiner began documenting and photographing the injuries and collecting evidence. I quickly and uncomfortably glanced at those photos. They were heartbreaking, and I wondered how a child could possibly recover from an experience like that. The physical damage would heal, but the emotional damage was permanent. No child should have to experience what the photos so graphically depicted.

I had no sympathy for Crispy, and I had even less for the perverts who preyed on children. When the nurse finished, the plastic surgeon and the pediatric gynecologist did their best to repair her physical injuries.

Frost had also provided me with the police records for the event. Her parents had finally turned up, and said she'd been playing in their back yard when she disappeared. Her mother had been in the house cleaning and doing laundry and had no idea that she'd wandered off or how long she'd been gone.

Laura's parents had moved to the area the middle of the previous school year and had no close friends who could have helped find her. They had looked for her for nearly twenty-four hours before reporting her missing to the Evergreen police. Initially, assuming the child hadn't wandered far from their home, they thought they would be able to find her. Laura had made friends with one classmate before school had ended and had visited her house regularly over the end of the school year and during the summer. Other than casual conversation at drop-off and pick-up, however, Laura's mother didn't know the friend's parents well.

Laura's parents had knocked on doors, but many close neighbors had left for the Labor Day holiday or had said they'd not seen Laura. The friend's parents said the same. When questioned, Laura's stepfather said he didn't think the police would consider the child a missing person until after she'd been gone forty-eight hours and had convinced his wife that they should just keep looking. Ignoring her husband, Laura's mother had finally called the police. The police weren't sure if it was a misconception on his part or an attempt to delay notifying them.

Their reluctance to call the police was puzzling to me; what parent isn't instantly frantic when a child is missing? But they'd waited to notify anyone. The lead detective had noted that Laura's mother had been distraught when they'd finally reported her missing. Doctors and nurses try their best to stay neutral, but some cases hit you like a ton of bricks, and this was one of them. My first instinct was to suspect the stepfather, as had the police.

She had been found before her parents had reported her missing. The police had broadcast a bulletin statewide and released it to the news channels the day she'd been found in an attempt to find her parents. Her stepfather claimed they'd been consumed trying to find her and they hadn't seen the broadcasts or left the subdivision where they might have seen newspapers or TV broadcasts.

It was early September, and Laura had disappeared at the beginning of the long Labor Day holiday weekend and, because of the holiday, no one from the school knew she was missing.

It was hard for me to believe either explanation in this day of media overload. I had to remind myself, though, that the incident had happened in 2006; no one was as connected then as we are now. Still, it *was* 2006, surely people weren't that out of touch. I Googled it and discovered only about 11% of the general population was online on a regular basis then. Perhaps it wasn't that odd that her parents hadn't seen or heard anything, The question for everyone at the time was, were the parents guilty or simply inept and panicked?

When questioned by the police, the parents adamantly denied knowing about the sexual abuse. Until the police had completed their investigation, they insisted the child be under the care of Child Welfare and that the parents not have contact with her. The cops had hoped that Laura would talk to them, but she remained mute. Each time they tried to interview her, she became hysterical. Despite several attempted interviews by a child psychologist and the help of a play therapist, they could get no information from the child who refused to talk.

The police put the stepfather under a microscope. He had adopted the child and the birth father was out of the picture. The police found no conclusive evidence to implicate either parent. They collected DNA, which eventually ruled out the stepfather as the abuser, but had ID'd no one else. Whoever had assaulted Laura was not in the DNA databases. He could have been anyone, all that was certain was that whoever it was hadn't been arrested or incarcerated, and that was of no help.

There were no custody issues between Laura's mother and her biological father, who lived in Fort Collins, seventy miles north of Denver, and there seemed to be no reason he'd abduct the child and certainly no reason to sexually assault her. He'd had little contact with his ex-wife and none with his daughter since their divorce and had no record of arrests or convictions for anything. He'd had an alibi, but police had collected DNA to be sure and it cleared him. There were no registered sex offenders anywhere near the neighborhood where the family lived.

Aside from Child Welfare, who would continue to visit the family, requiring that she be placed in therapy, and that periodic physical examinations and interviews be conducted, the police could do little more. Once the police investigation had hit a dead end and Laura was discharged, the nursing notes documented how the child had screamed and held onto the unit nurse who'd taken care of her when the parents tried to leave with her.

I remembered her tattoo, *Per ardua ad astra,* through adversity to the stars. She had certainly been through the adversity, but based on her murder, she hadn't made it to the stars, unless you believed that was where heaven could be found.

NINE

JESUS, FROST, TALK ABOUT UNLUCKY," I said after reading the autopsy report and the medical records. I had made a trip to the precinct after work to catch up with him on the cold cases and return the copy of the records about Laura. I was beginning to feel like Frost looked, exhausted. Working forty hours a week, then working on my days off on the cold cases was adding up.

He looked up from a pile of paperwork he'd been sorting through. "Yeah, it's pretty depressing."

"I can't believe they sent her home with her parents. I would've thought that maybe they'd put her in foster care until an in-depth evaluation of the family situation was done. Losing track of her and then not reporting it for twenty-four hours suggests questionable parenting to me."

Frost shrugged. "They were her parents, and the stepfather had been cleared. It sounds like the hospital and the cops did all they could. Child Welfare kept an eye on them for six months and she was fine. I do wonder, though, if the two incidents are related. They probably aren't, but you never know."

"I want to be involved. I want to know what's happening and help if I can. I don't know what it is about Laura—but I feel…like I know her. I want to help, if I can."

"As we've discussed, I can't let you officially help unless you're a cop."

He sat back in his desk chair and laced his fingers together across his abdomen. "I can keep you informed unofficially, but that's all I can do. Life would be easier for me if you were a cop."

"That's not going to happen."

"Then what you can do or be involved in is limited. My hands are tied. In the past, you've been a witness or an informant, or were cleared to assist in the investigation related to your hospital. I can't let you help with this investigation without you being official. There's no connection to you to justify that. Helping interpret the old hospital records and reviewing the cold case file on the sly is as much as I can let you do without getting my ass in a sling."

I looked at him for a moment. "I want to help even if it's unofficial. I'll figure out some way to placate Angel or reassure him about that or maybe not tell him at all."

Frost pursed his lips and frowned. "That's not a good idea and you know it. He's not a child, he's your husband. He'll be twice as pissed when he finds out you're involved in this case. And he will."

Okay, fine, I thought. *Frost is probably right.* Now I had to figure out how to tell Angel. "Fine, I'll talk to him."

I was reluctant to tell Angel about the case Frost was dealing with and that I wanted to be a peripheral part of it. I knew Frost was right, not telling Angel was a recipe for disaster, but I argued with myself all the way home about whether to tell him or keep it to myself. I decided to tell him. I thought, if I explained that I wouldn't be actively involved, he'd be okay with it. It turned out to be a huge miscalculation on my part, and I should have known it would be. My reluctance to tell him should have warned me it wouldn't go over well. It's funny how blind I can be.

"I'm reviewing the cold case file, like I would any other cold cases he gives me. As far as her murder, I would only be helping him sort through what he finds out. I won't be officially involved or doing anything dangerous."

He'd stared at me with a blank face all the while I had explained about the case, trying to reassure him—which wasn't a good sign—and that had made my heart rate speed up. When upset, he used his trial face to cover up any emotions he had.

Angel closed his eyes and took a deep breath, exhaling slowly, then shook his head, abruptly stood up, and walked away. I was taken aback. He'd never walked out on a conversation, or an argument, before. We were both pretty hot-tempered, but Angel didn't disappear on me when things were rough. If anything, he dug his heels in.

I waited for him to come back and was surprised when he didn't. I debated whether to follow him or leave him alone. Finally, I walked to the bedroom he used as his office. The door was closed. I tapped on it, then opened it. He looked up at me. His carefully schooled trial face was gone and a deep scowl had taken its place.

"Go away, Annie. I really don't want to talk to you right now."

"Would you at least hear me out?"

"No. You need to leave me alone."

"I know you worry…"

"You don't know *fuck all!*" he shouted, pounding the desk with his fist and making me jump.

"You do as you damn well please and don't give a rat's ass how it affects me. You never have. I don't suppose you ever will."

Leaning back in his desk chair, glaring at me, he said, "I hoped that you'd stop insinuating yourself into things like this, but now you want to get involved in this murder case? *Have you lost your fucking mind?*" he shouted. "Your insistence on doing things like this is what brought Ian down on our heads!"

"That's what it always comes back to, doesn't it? *I brought Ian down on us.* So that makes all my decisions wrong? Yes, I am responsible for him and all the insanity he caused. But I'm not dealing with a psychopath this time around."

"You don't know what you're dealing with, and neither does Frost." Angel pressed the heel of his hand against his forehead, then shook his head. "You're ignoring the risks, just like you always have."

"Angel, I'm not actively helping with his case, I can't. I'll just be helping with phone calls and—"

Stabbing his finger at me, he said, "This! This is *exactly* why I didn't want you working with Frost." He ran his hand over his face tiredly. "You need to leave me alone, or I'll say something I'll regret."

I stood in the doorway, not knowing what to do. I wished to hell I could take it back and start over, but I had opened this can of worms, now I had to deal with it. He stared at me with a look of anger and bitterness I had never seen before, and it terrified me. What if I'd finally pushed him too far?

"I...I want to continue to help Frost with the cold cases, but I'd like to help with this other case, too."

Angel stood up abruptly, walked around his desk, and gripped my shoulders—I had never seen him this angry.

"*I don't want you involved in this,*" he said, spitting out each word. "You pry into things you have no business getting involved in. It puts you at risk, which, if the past is any predictor of the future, is a pretty serious risk. Do you *ever* think about that?"

"Your job is risky, too!" I shouted, roughly pulling away from him. My heart was pounding. This conversation was getting out of control and heading in a dangerous direction, but I couldn't stop.

"You were prosecuting people involved with serious crimes as an ADA—psychopaths, criminals, gang bangers—now you're defending people charged with serious crimes, most of whom are guilty."

He turned away, which infuriated me. I stepped in front of him. "What if one of your clients doesn't like the job you did, or a relative of theirs doesn't like it, or the victim or their family thinks you got a guilty person off? You know as well as I do your job carries risk, a lot of risk. How many attorneys get blown away by angry clients or other people who don't like what's happened in court? I've *never* objected to you doing your job at the DA's or at Owen's firm. Do I not have the right to do a job I find interesting?"

He walked over to the window and stood with his back to me, bracing his hands against the window jamb, head lowered.

"Angel…"

He spun around. "No! *Just stop.* I don't want to hear it. You're *always* getting involved in shit that's none of your business, but I have no place in your world. My concerns are irrelevant."

"That's not true, I—"

He shook his head hard, cutting me off. "It doesn't matter how many times I ask you to stay out of shit like this, you ignore me."

"That's not fair! I haven't asked you to stop what you're doing."

"After all we've been through, why can't you give us both time to get back to normal, *give me time* to get over what happened? What I want—*what I need*—is peripheral to you wanting to save the rest of the fucking world and play cop."

He closed his eyes, clamping his hand over his mouth for a few seconds as if trying to prevent saying what he was thinking.

At last, he dropped his hand and said, "I can't do this anymore, Annie."

I couldn't breathe, stunned by what he'd said. What did he mean he couldn't do *this* anymore? *Did he mean us?*

"Angel…" I managed before my throat dried up. I had no idea what to say, and I was afraid to ask him what he meant. What if he meant us? What if he'd finally reached a tipping point and wanted out of our marriage?

His voice was choked. He held his hands out in a gesture of… confusion or supplication or surrender? I couldn't tell. "I don't get it.

I don't understand why you do this or why, in God's name, you're so attracted to this crap."

He crossed to his desk and sat down, lowering his head into his hands, refusing to look at me. "If you get hurt because Frost dragged you into his little scheme or you piss someone off, I don't know what I'll do. Why can't you be a fucking nurse? Nurses save people, too. Why can't you stop with this cop wannabe shit?"

Hearing the intensity and the note of despair in his voice, I was afraid to say anything. My heart pounded and my hands shook.

He looked up at me, and his face had closed down again. "I asked you to leave me alone. I need you to do that, or this is going to get out of hand. Words can't be taken back, and I may say something I'll regret. I probably already have," he said quietly.

I hesitated, trying to think what I could say to fix this. I wanted to touch him, wanted to anchor myself to him to prevent feeling as if I was standing on thin ice and could hear it cracking beneath my feet. But I was afraid to, as if trying to touch him would push him over the edge. Suddenly I felt like the ice had opened, and I'd fallen through, and it was closing over me. I had never felt as cold or scared.

"I'm sorry," I finally said. "I'll tell Frost I can't help him."

"I know you think you mean that, and I know you'll try, at least for a little while; but Annie, it never lasts. So do what you want. I have no way to stop you."

"Angel, I'll stop, I promise. I'll give you whatever time you need... I'll..." I trailed off, not knowing what else to say.

He stared at me, his eyes moving restlessly over my face, as if he was trying to memorize it. Abruptly he stood. "I need to get out of here."

He walked around the desk, forcing me to back away from him. He stepped around me as I grabbed for his arm and missed. I watched in disbelief as he walked out of the office. I heard him walk into the living room, set the alarm, and leave, pulling the door closed after him.

I used to think finding a man who knew me—really knew me, warts and all—who would still want me, was impossible until I met Angel. He knew me. In spite of that, he loved me. Now I wondered if I had finally managed to ruin everything.

↶

I woke when I heard the alarm beep and listened as he shut it off, closed the front door, and reset it. I heard him stumble against a piece of furniture. I sat up and groped for my phone. It was nearly two in the morning. I'd discovered, after he left, either someone he knew had picked him up or he'd called for a ride from a car service. Based on the state he was currently in, I was glad.

I waited and saw him come to the bedroom doorway. He leaned into the jamb to keep from swaying but made no move to enter our bedroom. At last he said, "Just wanted to let you know I was home."

"I'm glad, come to bed."

He shook his head no, then grimaced as if in pain. "I don' wanna go through what we've been through the last few years anymore, but I dunno how to put a stop to it."

He let his head fall down as he braced himself against the door jamb with both hands. "Fuck, I can hardly think straight. This whole conversation is pointless."

"Come to bed. We'll think of something."

He sighed loudly. "Not sure I believe that," he said, as he made his way unsteadily toward the guest bedroom.

↶

I stood in the doorway of the guest bedroom the next morning watching him sleep. He was lying on top of the covers still in his slacks and dress shirt. His jacket lay on the floor next to his shoes, and the tail of his wadded-up tie lay half out of the jacket's pocket. He was pale, eyes shadowed, his face covered with dark stubble; his long lashes lay against his cheeks. My guess was he would have a monstrous hangover when he finally woke up.

I stood over him, watching his chest rise and fall. I saw a pulse beat in his neck. The guest bedroom smelled like a distillery, and I wasn't sure if he was asleep or in an alcohol-induced coma. At least he was breathing.

His lips were parted, and it was all I could do not to lean over and kiss him, but I was worried and struggling with what to do. Part of me, the part that loved him at all costs, wanted to crawl into bed next to him and tell him I was sorry, that I wouldn't work with Frost if he didn't want me to. And the angry part of me kept thinking, *He needs to go see someone.* Then the damn nurse in my head would start lecturing me about how much he'd been through since our wedding, how I needed to take his needs into consideration and cut him some slack. All of it was true. I wanted to give him what he needed, and working with Frost was blinding me to what he was going through.

I was due at the hospital in half an hour, and he was due at work. I wrestled with calling his office and letting them know he wouldn't be in, or just letting him deal with it. In the end, I made a quick call and left a message that he was ill, wouldn't be in, and would touch base later. I scribbled out a note to that effect, then gathered my purse and car keys and left him to his hangover.

His comments had upset me deeply. At some point we were going to have to figure out how to get to a compromise that both of us could live with. The problem was, I wanted to help Frost, and the idea of eventually working with him as a PI had become more appealing. Because Angel was vehemently against that, I didn't know what would happen, and it scared me. I spent the day at work obsessing over fragments of the conversation from the previous night.

If I were single, I could have done as I pleased. My friends might think I was insane or try to talk me out of it, but ultimately, it was my decision. Being married complicated everything. I was pretty easygoing regarding what Angel did. I had to admit, though, he rarely did anything overtly dangerous or questionable. Over his career as a prosecutor, he'd worked with victims and prosecuted criminals with few repercussions.

Now, as a defense attorney, it would be anyone's guess whether he was representing an innocent client or a guilty one. The risk he was exposed to as an ADA or a defense lawyer was far higher than he would ever acknowledge. It was the pot calling the kettle black when it came to either of us realistically assessing the risks to what we did. His one saving grace was he thought things through and didn't leap off cliffs. I, on the other hand, tended to find myself hanging by my fingertips from those cliffs on a regular basis.

I was scared, too. I hadn't considered where Angel was in his recovery from the terror we had been through. I feared my blindness to his trauma might have pushed him too far. He was right; I didn't think about him enough when I made decisions. It was something that we needed to talk about and I needed to face. I feared there might not be any way to compromise on this, and that made my stomach burn.

When I came home from work that evening, Angel was nowhere to be found. I texted him to see where he was, but got no reply. Walking into our bedroom, I saw a note lying on my bedside table, and my heart began to race.

Annie

I don't want to fight with you or discuss this right now. I need a couple days to try to get my head straight. I love you; I'm just having a hard time dealing with everything right now.

Angel

I walked over to our closet and saw that several suits and their accessories were missing. A few pairs of jeans and sweaters were gone.

In the bathroom his toiletries and toothbrush were no longer there.

I sat on the closed lid of the toilet and rubbed my neck, fighting the tears that threatened to overwhelm me. I had made a lot of mistakes in my life, but this one had the potential to destroy my marriage. My headstrong, stubborn nature had blinded me to Angel's needs. I picked up the phone and called the therapist I had spoken with after my first encounter with Ian.

"I need to make an appointment. Please call me back at your earliest convenience." I didn't know if that would help, but it was all I could think to do.

TEN

ONE ADVANTAGE TO WORKING IN THE OR is there are always people who want to be off call or switch shifts. I spent the following days working and taking on-call shifts. I spent very little time at home, no time on the cold cases or talking to Frost, and I heard nothing from Angel. I refused to try to contact him, and my anger at his disappearance grew, but a small, terrified part of me wondered if he would come home at all.

I caught a faint whiff of his aftershave as I walked into our dark bedroom when I got home Tuesday at midnight. He was in bed, his back was to me, but he said nothing. I wasn't sure if he was even aware of me. I undressed and silently got into bed. How could you be glad someone had returned and furious that he had?

As I lay awake in the dark, my thoughts raced, bouncing around like a ping-pong ball. *He shouldn't have left. It was fine he left; he needed the space. It wasn't fine at all. He should have stayed up tonight until I got home, so we could have talked. I should have said something. He should have said something.* Thus, it continued until at some point my exhausted brain shut off and I fell asleep.

I woke up every couple of hours to check that he was still there, which infuriated me. I was up early the next morning, sitting at the kitchen table with a cup of coffee. He walked into the kitchen dressed for work and crossed to the coffeemaker.

"Nice of you to decide to come home," I said after a moment. I heard him exhale heavily, but he just poured a cup of coffee. "Nothing to say about being gone since Thursday or what prompted you to come home? I was worried about you."

"Annie, please don't. I have to go to work. We can talk later."

He made to move past the table, and I stood up in front of him. "No, I'm going to say what I need to say."

He drew his brows together and frowned. "Okay."

"I've had my head up my ass and ignored what you need. I'm sorry for that. But disappearing for days and having no contact with me is not the way to solve problems. I won't help Frost other than with the cold cases. I'll stay out of anything else. If that won't work, then tell me what you want me to do. Tell me what you need from me." He stared at me and said nothing, and my heart began to trip.

"Angel, I can't spend my life worrying about you disappearing on me temporarily or permanently, if I do something you don't like. I love you more than I've ever loved anyone, but we both need some help so we can reach some sort of compromise."

He watched me silently, then said, "Good to know." He set the cup of untouched coffee on the table and moved around me. I watched as he walked to the door, picked up his briefcase, and left.

We didn't talk when he returned that evening. As the days passed, it became impossible. Several nights he came home late, saying he had stayed at the office to work on an upcoming case. Other nights I would come home from work to find Angel had fixed dinner. We would eat in relative silence, he would help clean up, say he was exhausted, and go to bed early.

I would sit up late reading, or at least trying to, and go to bed around midnight. We didn't make love and he didn't turn to me in the night, pull me into an embrace, and whisper *Corazón*, as he always had. The distance between us in the bed seemed like miles rather than an arm's length, and neither of us tried to bridge the gap.

I had no intention of pushing the issue and trying to force Angel to talk, but his work schedule and mine effectively eliminated any opportunities to talk anyway.

The argument and his disappearance made me realize that neither one of us was dealing with the consequences of what had happened. It had prompted me to meet with my former therapist. We discussed how to deal with the dreams and the visions of Ian I was having periodically, but as she told me, I might dream about what had happened for some time. The conflict with Angel was like a storm cloud hanging over us. She urged me to talk with him, it just seemed impossible to do. I hadn't asked Frost about where he was with Laura's case, and Crispy's case was at a standstill.

At last, I reached my limit for waiting for Angel to talk to me. Sitting at the kitchen table after dinner, I decided to broach the subject.

"I can't live in this deep freeze any longer. We need to talk."

He nodded, assuming his trademark frown.

"I know you're struggling, and I know how hard it's been for you." I sighed. Now came the hard part. "I know you're unhappy about me working with Frost. I'd like to find a way to do that—eventually—without losing my husband."

He rubbed his forehead and closed his eyes for a long minute. Sighing, he leaned back in his chair. "Annie, I'm exhausted trying to work and worrying about what you're getting into. I'm tired of dealing with the consequences. We both have scars, *physical and emotional scars*, from what happened. Both of us nearly died, and we're still dealing with the aftereffects of what happened."

He fell silent again, staring at the tabletop. I was hesitant to say anything. After a moment, he looked up and gave me a half-hearted smile.

"I needed some space. When we're arguing, neither one of us gives in. I just wanted somewhere quiet to be able to think this through before one of us said something we couldn't take back."

"And did you?"

He nodded, casting his eyes around the room as if looking for a teleprompter. "What we went through changed everything for me."

The despair and resignation I could hear in his voice broke my heart. He laughed but there was no humor in it. "I thought I could handle what you get caught up in, and I used to be able to, but now? I flash back on being tied to that fucking chair, unable to move, knowing there was *nothing* I could do to save you. Knowing that he'd kill you and probably hurt you badly before he did. I've never been as afraid or as helpless. A man is supposed to protect his wife…and I couldn't."

He'd choked out the last sentence. I watched as he scrubbed a hand over his mouth, and we sat without speaking for a bit.

"Angel, we both need to see someone. So much has changed for you, the aftermath of the shooting, your job change…it's been too much. After things blew up between us, I realized I was trying to block out what happened and soldier on as if I was fine, ignoring you in the process. I think maybe that's what you've been trying to do, too. I've met several times with the woman I saw a couple years ago. She was an enormous help. I can give you her contact information, or you could see a male therapist if that'd be more comfortable for you."

I waited for him to respond, then said, "Or talk to Chip or Frost. Chip's a nurse; Frost has been through something like this himself. He was the one who insisted I see the therapist he'd seen. They care deeply about both of us, maybe they could help you. Father Giraldi even offered to talk with us, if we needed it. You could talk to Frost's wife, she might be able to help; she's been married to a cop for ages."

I walked around the table and pulled him to me. He wrapped his arms around my waist, pressing his head against me, and I ached for him.

"We've been through hell, but if we can get past what happened, things will be fine."

I wasn't sure he believed me, but I hugged him tightly and kissed the top of his head. "Listen to me, please. I'll be careful, I promise, or I'll stop working with Frost until he retires. I love you more than you'll ever know."

"I love you too; that's the problem." He pushed away from me. "I need for things to settle down, Annie. I need to be able to stop worrying about what you're getting into. And I'm…worried…that you can't give that to me. You can't seem to resist Frost's shit."

"So, what do we do?" I squeezed my lips together, tears stinging my eyes. The minutes ticked by as I waited for him to respond. When he didn't, I said, "I want you to get some help. I'll get some names for you, and you can pick one."

He didn't respond, didn't nod his head or indicate he'd follow through. Was it going to come down to giving up something important to me or losing the man I loved?

ELEVEN

I CALLED FROST THE NEXT DAY. "Can we go get lunch? I don't have to be at work until three. Can you leave for a bit?

"Yeah, what's up?"

"I want to talk to you where none of the other people in your department can listen in. How about we go to Cody's?"

At the restaurant, the waitress took our drink orders and disappeared. I wasn't sure how to ask him how he and Evie had navigated the bumps in their relationship he'd alluded to.

"So, what's up, kid?"

"I need to stop helping you…for a while, anyway. I'd like to hear what's going on with Laura's case, but I need to back out for now."

We stopped talking as the waitress delivered our drinks, took our lunch orders, and left.

"What's happened?"

"Angel and I had a major blowup. He doesn't want me involved with you right now because of…everything. I don't want any further complications over this." I took a sip of water. "He doesn't say much, but he's having a hard time. We both are." I peeled the paper wrap off the napkin and unrolled it, then lined up the silverware on the table.

I sighed. "He doesn't want me working with you at all. But I like this kind of work; I like working with you. He needs help, and I do, too. I suggested he see the therapist you sent me to, but I don't know if he'll see anyone. I'm seeing Donna and I'm going to get some names; hopefully he'll be willing to talk to one of them."

We sat in silence for several minutes. Frost always took his time responding. He watched me as he had done since I had first met him.

I began to squirm under his gaze. "Is everything okay between you two?" he finally asked.

"I don't know." Frost raised his eyebrows. I frowned, fisting my hands under the table and digging my nails into my palms.

"He scared me. I told him that I wanted to help you with Laura's investigation, and he lost it. He…he disappeared for several days after we fought about it. He's never been happy about me working with you, but he seemed to be okay with me reviewing the cold case files, probably because I'm not actively involved. Telling him about wanting to help with Laura's case blew up in my face. Right now, he's…" I shrugged. "I don't know how to resolve this, so I'm going to stop helping and hope we can come to some sort of compromise."

I gazed around the restaurant and frowned. "I want to help you find out what happened to Laura and work cold cases with you, but I don't want to push Angel over the edge."

"What the fuck does that mean?"

"Nothing, I just don't want to push him," I said. "I don't…I don't want to lose him."

Working with Frost was important to me. But if it came down to it, working with Frost wasn't worth jeopardizing my marriage. I hoped when we'd gotten to a better place, I could. Although he'd never mentioned it, the ghost of his potentially leaving me kept floating in and out of my mind. I didn't think he would, but people were unpredictable, and even Angel had his limits.

"I want to do this," I said at last. "But I can't right now. He needs some time for things to calm down a little." I looked away and sighed, putting my hands back onto the table.

Frost leaned forward and took my hand. "What happened to you two can't help but affect things."

"I know," I said miserably, pulling my hand away from his.

I leaned back against the booth. "I love Angel and he loves me. It's…he's struggling, we both are. I don't think our marriage is hanging in the balance, at least I hope it's not." I fisted my hand and rapped it on the table a couple of times. *Knock on wood*, I thought and sighed.

"We've never had a chance to settle into any kind of normal life after Ian. He's fucking with our lives even from the grave. He may be burning in hell, but he's probably enjoying watching us suffer."

"Most guys think a man should be able to handle shit; we don't share easily," Frost said.

I nodded. I took a sip of water. "He told me…" I wiped tears off my cheeks that had at last broken through. "He told me he's tired of worrying about me, that he can't do this anymore. I don't know what *this* means, and I'm afraid to ask."

I started to sob and tried my best to cut it off. Out of the corner of my eye I saw the waitress pull a U-turn with our lunches when she saw me crying. *Lunch will probably be cold*, I thought.

"I can't seem to get through to him that it would help if he'd talk to someone about it. I kept thinking that I knew how to deal with all that's happened, but I'm not managing very well. I told Angel I was seeing Donna, thinking it might encourage him to do the same."

"It's what guys do—not share, I mean." Frost frowned. "I'm like that; it drives Evie crazy. Seeing a therapist seems like…like weakness, I guess."

"But you saw her, you gave me her name and number. What made you see her?"

Frost winced and got this faraway look in his eyes, and I wished I hadn't asked.

"I killed a kid. He had a gun, he wouldn't drop it, and then he shot at my partner, and I shot him in the chest."

He looked lost for a moment. "He'd shot and killed his girlfriend, and before he died, he asked me if she'd forgive him, he said he hadn't meant to kill her. I told him yes, because I didn't know what else to say, he was dying. He was my oldest son's age." Frost paused.

"I couldn't shake it, couldn't stop thinking about him. I kept thinking maybe I could have done something to make shooting him unnecessary. I nearly killed myself over it. Evie found me in my office with my gun on the desk and forced me to see a therapist."

Finally, he looked me in the eye. "She threatened to leave me if I didn't, and she would have. I couldn't risk that, so I went, and it helped. On my own I never would have and probably would have killed myself." He shrugged and looked embarrassed.

I wiped the last of the tears off my face and took a deep breath. "I'm glad you didn't, and I'm grateful you pushed me to see Donna. I'm scared, Frost, scared I've crossed some sort of line in the sand with Angel that I didn't even realize was there. I'm afraid he'll leave me, and I feel like I'm walking through a minefield."

"I'll talk to him."

"*No!* Please don't, not unless he approaches you to talk. That'll only upset him further."

"Okay," he said resignedly.

We were quiet for several minutes. Frost had alluded to a "few bumps in the road" of his marriage, but I had never imagined anything like what he'd told me. Frost had always seemed to take what happened to people in his stride. He cared, especially about finding justice for the victims, but now I could see that most of how he felt was compartmentalized. Some things, though, couldn't be and this must haunt him. Not for the first time, I wished I could take the pain away from those I cared about.

"I'll try to talk to him again and see if he'll go to someone." I met Frost's eyes. "I want to be involved in the cold cases, and I'd really like to hear what you discover about Laura, but I don't want to upset Angel."

He frowned. "I'm glad you're seeing Donna. In the meantime, the cold cases aren't going anywhere. If it's any consolation, this job drove Evie crazy, too. She still worries about me. Eventually you learn how to handle the anxiety."

"Or you don't, and it destroys your marriage," I said.

TWELVE

ANGEL JOINED ME IN BED and, quite to my surprise, he spooned up against me. He slipped one arm under my neck and wrapped the other around me and pulled me tightly against him. We hadn't talked much for several days, and we hadn't made love since the argument. I both welcomed his holding me and worried about what it portended.

I had given him Donna's phone number and the name and phone number of the male therapist she had given me, and Father Giraldi's number. He'd taken them without comment, and I had no idea whether he'd contacted any of them.

He sighed. "Annie…it's taking me a while to get over what happened. If anyone knows what that's like, it's you." He kept his face pressed up against my shoulder, and I could feel the scruff of his beard.

"I do," I said, lacing my fingers through his and holding his hand against my heart.

I hoped he would see a therapist, any therapist, but I also knew that a person couldn't be forced to do it. Sometimes threats, like Evie had given Frost, were needed, but I had learned the hard way, never threaten anything you don't intend to follow through with.

"Give me some time to get back to normal," he said.

"I will, I promise." I could feel him nod against my back.

"I think, if you can do that for a bit, until things calm down for me, you could go back to helping Frost and it wouldn't make me so nuts."

"Okay. You'll…let me know how things are going for you?"

"I'll let you know."

We lay quietly enjoying the closeness. "You won't find someone less annoying?" I finally asked, remembering his girl-of-the-month days.

He kissed my neck. "No one could ever replace you. We'll figure it out."

I pulled his arm against me. "I love you. I hope you know that."

He gave me a reassuring squeeze and kissed my shoulder. "I know. I love you too; that's what makes this so hard."

I knew he loved me. That was a constant I had come to depend on and take for granted, and I also knew how easily that could change.

"I wish you'd shot him; you might feel better," I said pulling his arm tighter around me.

His breath was warm against my shoulder. "Yeah, I wish I'd been able to put at least one bullet in him. I'm just glad he's dead. I'm okay with you reviewing Frost's cold cases, just stay out of the active ones… for a while, please."

"Frost said not to worry about the cold cases, there's no hurry with them. I'm curious about how Laura's case will go, but other than getting updates from Frost, I won't get involved."

He pulled me over to face him and took my head in his hands. "I've missed you," he said, kissing me insistently as his hands began to roam.

"I've missed you, too," I said rolling him on top of me. I wrapped my legs around his waist and pulled him to me, feeling him slide into me, filling me, coming home.

Later, lying in his arms in the dark, listening to him breathe while he slept, I realized, despite this reconciliation, that I had broken something between us. We were not irreparably broken—not yet, maybe never—but the secure, unshakable foundation of our relationship had cracked. And cracks could open up unexpectedly and swallow every-thing nearby.

⌒Ɔ⌒

Frost yawned as he talked to me over the phone, giving me an update on Crispy's case. "I was out last night till late, cruising a couple of the bars that Crispy's friends said they frequented. No joy there. No one can remember seeing him leave with anyone in particular prior to his death.

"I passed out my cards with copies of his photo to anyone who'd take them, and I had the wait staff at the bars tape the flyers I made by the mirrors and in each stall in both the men's and women's restrooms."

I heard him yawn again and I heard his desk chair creak. "Someone may remember something and get in touch, but I'm not getting my hopes up. He could be dead for other reasons unrelated to his issues with women, and the bars could be a dead end, but it's worth a try. Who knows?"

"I think his death is related to the women he used," I said. "But this is one we may not be able to close. It happened eight months ago, and he was a creep who took lots of women home. He may have drugged all of them, which would make it hard for them to remember what happened, and we have no idea who any of them were. Like I said before, if it was one of the women he used like toilet paper, I hope we never figure out who killed him."

"I agree," Frost said. "But a murder's a murder. We don't get to decide who pays or who doesn't. It'd be nice to solve this and put the case to bed, but I'm stumped. And I'm gettin' old. Staying up till one in the morning is torture. I'm going to check out the last two bars on Friday and see if anything pops. Then, it'll stay as an open/unsolved case and I can move on."

"What's the plan for Laura's case?"

"I'm going to interview the parents."

"Will you interview them here?"

"No, not right now. I don't want to get their backs up. I'm going to interview them at home. I wanted to do the interview here, but Talbot talked me into doing it at their home. She said to tread softly. Maybe she's right. I think bringing people in pushes some important buttons, but soft-pedaling it now is probably better. Who knows? I gotta say she's got a real feel for interviewing people, even at the precinct."

"What does she do differently?"

"She says you can tell if someone is lying or at least holding something back by their unconscious body movements, their tells, like in poker."

He laughed. "You kinda get good at reading people, catching those tells, if you're any good at interviewing suspects. Knowing when to push them and when to back off is trickier, but she takes it a little further. She invades their personal space—you know, sitting closer than normal, walking behind them, touching them. I've seen her shake a suspect's hand and then not let go until they have to pull their hand away. That drives up their anxiety, which leads them to make mistakes."

"Interesting. I suppose you can do that at their home, too."

"Yeah, at least to some extent. But it's their home base; it's not the same as hauling someone into the police station to interview them. After what they went through when she was a kid, they'd probably arrive with a lawyer in tow."

My first contact with Frost had been in an interview room where I had come to give a statement about a friend's death. "My anxiety was pretty high when I first met you. Angel had me afraid to open my mouth."

"Fucking lawyers. He'll probably be a great defense attorney. Of course, that'll mean we'll lose cases. The rumor has made the rounds, and Roberts is getting a lot of flak because he's involved with Gabriela. I'm getting it, too."

"Nobody likes defense attorneys, until they need one," I grumbled.

I heard his desk chair creak again and I imagined he was leaning back in it. "True. I still don't like them."

"Angel could be a good source of cases when we become PIs, you know."

He cocked an eyebrow at me. "You're making me rethink that idea."

"You're not rethinking it; you're just being obstinate."

THIRTEEN

F ROST STOPPED BY THE APARTMENT on his lunch break and replayed the interview he'd recorded because Talbot hadn't been available to go with him. The Hutchinson's still lived in Evergreen, a town that lies in the foothills west of Denver. It began as a tiny town to which people often came to get away from the summer heat in the city. Evergreen is always about twenty degrees cooler because of its elevation. Snow started early there and stayed late in the season.

Evergreen had grown significantly over the last thirty years—most of the development being high-end homes and new businesses. A friend of mine calls the people who buy these homes "upscale transients"—CEOs and other executives who move to the area because of a job and then, a year or two later, are transferred somewhere else. Homes in these neighborhoods sold in the million-dollar-plus range and turned over regularly.

Frost had told me it was a comfortable, but rather imposing home. "It was impressive, lots of money there. The room I was shown into had a moss rock fireplace ran all the way to the twenty-foot ceiling and sported the mounted head of a six-point elk. Not sure if Hutchinson is a hunter or whether he bagged it himself, but impressive however he got it."

I'd had a lot of exposure to these kinds of trophies growing up in Texas. My father never hunted, but many of my friends' fathers did, and their trophies were always proudly on display. I avoided looking at them. Mounts of any animal, but especially elk, deer, and antelope, always looked sad to me. It was the eyes, I think, those big, brown, limpid eyes.

I'm a city girl and I like it that way. I'm also under no illusions about where meat comes from, and if you have to hunt to eat, I'm okay with that. I also understand about wildlife management. Some people, however, just like to kill things. I wondered if Andrew Hutchinson was one of them.

When Frost hit the play button on his phone's recording app, I heard him say, "Mr. and Mrs. Hutchinson, I'm Detective Frost from the Denver Police Department's Homicide unit."

"Can I get you anything to drink?" Mrs. Hutchinson asked.

"No, thank you," Frost said. "I'm one of the detectives investigating your daughter's murder and I'd like to ask you a few questions. I'm going to record this interview, if that's okay with you. It's a protection for me and both of you regarding what is said. If you're not comfortable with that, we can arrange to meet at the precinct for the interview and my partner can be present."

"That's fine." I heard Andrew Hutchinson say.

I heard paper rustle and the click of a pen. I figured Frost had retrieved the small notebook he carried to make notes. "When was the last time you saw your daughter?"

"Adopted daughter. I haven't seen Laura since she moved out at eighteen," Andrew Hutchinson answered. "I haven't had any conversations or meetings with her since then. She moved out right after graduation in 2016."

"Mrs. Hutchinson?"

"Pardon?" She seemed startled at hearing her name.

"When was the last time you saw or spoke with your daughter?"

"Oh…right after she moved out. She called to tell me not to worry, she had found a place to stay, and she'd keep in touch."

"You didn't help her move?"

"No...I...you see, she refused to go to college, and she was acting out, and...we...were upset with her. But I was glad she let me know she'd found a place."

"Did she say where it was?"

"No."

"And did she keep in touch? Did you have a way of contacting her?"

She hesitated as if uncertain whether to answer the question, and I wondered why. "I...received birthday, Christmas, and Mother's Day cards from her," she said at last. "I sent her cards and occasional letters and money on her birthday and at Christmas. I sent them to a PO box she had. I would hear from her at times, when she'd call. But I hadn't heard from her in more than a month.

"I had a phone number of a friend of hers. She said this friend would get in touch with her if I needed to contact her. She didn't want An—us—to have her phone number."

"Why was that?"

"I don't know, she just didn't."

"I had no idea, Elly. Why didn't you tell me?" Hutchinson asked, taken by surprise, clearly she'd kept it from him.

"She asked me not to." I heard her sniff. Laura had evidently wanted nothing to do with the man who'd adopted her. "Oh, Andy, you know the two of you didn't get along. Neither of you liked the other. She wanted a chance to be who she wanted to be, and she didn't want us to interfere."

"And look where that got her. She hasn't got a chance to be anything now."

What he'd said was unnecessarily cruel, and had I been in charge of the interview I'd have said so. But Frost didn't comment. I figured he was giving Hutchinson his unnerving cop stare.

"Why didn't you and Laura get along?" Frost asked after a minute of uncomfortable silence.

"I adopted her, but she never…she never accepted me as her father, never treated me as her father. Elly and I married when Laura was about four. I adopted her a year later. Her birth father was glad because it meant he didn't have to pay child support." I could hear the disdain in his voice. "I don't think she understood why her father abandoned her. She thought that her father had left because of me."

"Did he?"

"No, he did not," Hutchinson replied angrily. "He'd abandoned Elly and Laura sometime before Elly and I met, but logic has little effect on a child's thought processes. I did everything I could to be a good father, but it never worked. She was a pleasant child until after the incident when she was seven. Things changed drastically then. They had been gradually changing before she disappeared, but after…"

He paused and I heard him clear his throat. "She didn't want to come home with us and made a horrible scene at the hospital. There was some nurse who'd befriended her while she was hospitalized. She brought a teddy bear home with her that the nurse gave her and wouldn't let it out of her sight."

When he continued, his responses seemed aggravated at having to tell Frost about it. "When she finally began talking again, she said she didn't want to be with us. She had this ridiculous notion that the nurse would have kept her if we hadn't taken her home. She seemed to feel we were somehow responsible for what had happened. Maybe we were in some ways, we'd uprooted her and moved here, she had to leave her previous friends."

He paused and when he resumed his voice was subdued. "It's hard to know how to deal with something as horrific as what happened." He was silent for a bit then the anger was loud and clear when he began talking again. "When she was sixteen she found someone who'd do the tattoo on her wrist without a parent's consent. I wanted to prosecute the tattoo artist for tattooing an underage kid, but Laura would never say who it was. It didn't matter what we did to try to force her to tell us.

"I was sure she'd gone to someone here in Evergreen. Laura didn't have a car, but Jayden, her only close friend did. Jayden had a learner's permit and couldn't drive without a licensed adult in the car, so I figured she hadn't driven to Denver. I went to the two tattoo businesses up here, but of course they knew why I was asking and claimed they hadn't done the tattoo.

"The 'through adversity' bit seemed like she wanted to rub what had happened into our faces every time we saw the tattoo, remind us of what happened, and that she hadn't wanted to return home with us. It was one more way to torment us, and it worked."

He seemed hurt recalling Laura's aversion to him and what he saw as the reason for her tattoo. I wasn't sure what effect it had had on Eleanor. She hadn't commented.

Andrew continued. "It was never the same after she came home. She never told us, or anyone, who had done that to her. She wouldn't talk about it at all. She seemed to fight us at every turn. In high school she got into drugs and sleeping around."

I heard his wife began to cry in earnest then and I heard a sound like he was sitting down.

"Elly, I'm sorry, but it's true, you know that."

Eleanor didn't respond.

"You said things had been changing before she went missing. What do you mean?" Frost asked.

Eleanor spoke up at last. "She was withdrawn and had nightmares. When school started she didn't want to go, and she began acting out."

"Did you discuss it with anyone, try to find out why it was happening?"

"Of course we tried to find out," Hutchinson said, his voice breaking a little. "We didn't take her to anyone, but we talked to her and tried to find out what was bothering her. We did our best but, after the assault, everyone blamed us for what happened. We didn't do anything wrong!

"We were new to the area and that incident ostracized us. Do you know how many people refused to be associated with us? How many wouldn't allow their kids to come over or allow Laura to come to their houses? How people would look at us and talk behind our backs?"

"I imagine it was worse for Laura," Frost said evenly. The comment must have hit its mark but Hutchinson said nothing.

"Can you please tell me what you were doing the day before and the day Laura was murdered?" Frost asked.

"Are you implying we're suspects?" he snapped, his voice flaring in indignation.

"No, sir, I'm asking what you were doing that day. It's a routine question." Hutchinson didn't answer immediately, so Frost continued. "Mrs. Hutchinson, can you tell me where you were the day before and the day of her murder?"

Before she could reply, her husband said, "Elly, you don't have to answer that. We don't have to speak to him."

"You're not under arrest, but this is a murder investigation. If you won't talk to me here, voluntarily, then I will formally request that you to come into the Denver Police Department and answer my questions."

Neither said anything. "I'm going to need that contact information you mentioned, Mrs. Hutchinson. I'll need the PO box, the phone number, and the friend's name. I'll also need the names of everyone you asked to assess or treat Laura at the time of her childhood disappearance and any you know of recently. I'd appreciate your cooperation; it'll help us find who killed her."

I heard the sound of gradually diminishing footsteps on a hard surface. It sounded as if she'd gotten up to retrieve that information. "Who do you think abducted and assaulted her when she was a child?" Frost asked Hutchinson.

"I don't know. I've wondered about Elly's brother, but they couldn't pin it on him."

"And her murder?"

"I have no idea.

"What about you? You seem reluctant to provide an alibi."

"You think I killed my stepdaughter? It wasn't me," he said raising his voice in anger.

"Then where were you the day before and the day when Laura's body was found? I'll need your whereabouts and the names of anyone who can verify that."

"You bastard."

"Mr. Hutchinson," Frost said sounding tired, "as I said, we can finish this conversation here or we can do it at the station, your choice. Now, where were you?"

"I don't intend to answer any more questions without my lawyer present."

"Fine, ask him to meet you and your wife at the Denver Police Department tomorrow morning at nine. Here's my card. The precinct address is on it. We'll continue the conversation then."

Mrs. Hutchinson's footsteps could be heard again. "These are all the people I have contact information for," she sounded puzzled. "I… hope it helps." Perhaps she was baffled by the tension in the room. It came over loud and clear on the recording.

"Thank you, Mrs. Hutchinson," Frost said. "This is my card, it has my contact information. If you think of anything, please call me. We'll continue this interview at the police department tomorrow morning. I'm sorry for your loss. We'll do our best to find the person who killed Laura."

"Let's hope you do a better job finding her killer than they did finding out who assaulted her," Hutchinson said.

"FYI, if you don't show at nine, I'll send uniforms to pick you up and transport you to the precinct. If you want to avoid that, be there," Frost could be pretty intimidating when he was pissed, and I suspected he'd had his fill of Andrew Hutchinson.

Frost stopped the recording. "What'd you think?"

I blew out a breath. "I don't think Eleanor is afraid of him, but she's certainly concealed a lot of things from him, and his relationship with Laura was poor based on what both of them said. He acts like he wants to disassociate himself from Laura. He kept emphasizing that she was adopted; he wanted you to know that she wasn't his 'real' daughter, and he was completely unaware his wife stayed in contact with her. Obviously, she didn't share anything about Laura with him."

I paused for a moment. "The wife sounds stressed and grieving; he sounds embarrassed and angry at what's happened. Maybe that's how he is all the time. I'm not sure what I think about the whole situation, but I don't like him."

"Neither do I. It'll be interesting to see what he says tomorrow."

FOURTEEN

ANGEL HAD SPENT FORTY-FIVE MINUTES sitting on the couch after dinner that evening working on his laptop and muttering, probably swearing, in Spanish. I wasn't sure what was bothering him or what he was working on. I had learned early on that what he did was, for the most part, privileged information that legally he couldn't discuss with me, and I no longer asked. It was similar to me disclosing patient information, which was a violation of HIPAA regulations.

Frost, on the other hand, could talk about his cases at his discretion. When we first met, he didn't share information about my friend Libby's case, but gradually he began giving me what he called 'synopses.' Eventually he shared everything about cases I was interested or involved in.

"Put it away for tonight or you'll drive yourself nuts."

He sat back and ran his hands through his hair. If Frost tapped pencils when frustrated or annoyed, then my husband's frustration indicator was how messed up his hair was. It was all but standing on end at the moment.

The furor over our ill-fated discussion about helping Frost simmered away on the back burner of our relationship. We had yet to actually resolve anything long-term. We talked, hesitantly and superficially, about everything else, but it was easier to pretend our argument hadn't happened. That probably wasn't a good idea, but for the moment we both wanted peace, and this was one way to have it.

He nodded, saved whatever it was, and shut down his laptop, putting it on the coffee table. I brought the bottle of wine over from the kitchen table, refilled our wine glasses, and sat next to him.

"How'd your day go?" he asked.

I wasn't entirely sure why he asked, maybe it was just to make conversation. Maybe it was to check that I was honoring my promise to stay out of Frost's investigation

"I spent the day playing catch up around here." I took a deep breath and continued. "Frost told me he talked to Laura's parents at their home in Evergreen. He let me listen to the interview. He's going to interview the friend who was the go-between for Laura and her mother. Based on what I listened to, Laura was estranged from her parents but had limited contact with her mother. Her adoptive father—who repeatedly emphasized that fact—got angry and refused to talk to Frost, so he's making them come into the precinct."

Angel knew Frost was giving me information on the case. I hadn't done anything risky, and I wouldn't, but my uneasiness and uncertainty about our relationship hadn't disappeared. Our marriage was the equivalent of walking a tightrope over the Grand Canyon with no safety net right now.

"What have they found out so far?"

I started to feel as if he was cross-examining me in court. But he deserved an explanation, some reassurance I was not getting involved again.

"Apparently, her adoptive father had a terrible relationship with Laura, and it deteriorated after the assault. According to Hutchinson, she never accepted him as her father. He said he thought it was because Laura held him responsible for her parents' divorce. He thinks her acting out afterwards and as she got older was to punish him and her mother, but it's pretty classic for victims of sexual abuse. That's why he thinks she got her tattoo, to remind them about what had happened."

"All Frost is doing is updating you? You're staying out of it?"

I nodded and watched as he took a sip of wine and let the subject drop.

Frost planned to talk to the friend who supposedly relayed messages from Eleanor to her daughter.

"Can I listen in in the observation room when you talk to her?" I asked over the phone.

"Yeah, but keep your mouth shut about it. I arranged for her to meet me here at five. She works nearby and couldn't get over here until then."

That was good; my shift ended at three-thirty. "Okay, I'll get there before she arrives."

Jayden Byers was tall and blonde, her eyes a bright blue. Her hair was cut short—nearly shaved on the sides with the top long enough for her to be able to swing her head to get it out of her eyes, which she had to do on a regular basis. She wore half-inch gauges in her ears. She had an athlete's graceful physical presence and awareness of her surroundings and her body.

Frost had stationed me in the observation room. I watched the video feed as he ushered her into the interview room.

"Just so you're aware, we record all conversations that take place here," Frost said, indicating that she take a seat at the table with him.

She nodded. "That's fine."

"Ms. Byers, this is strictly an interview regarding Laura Hutchinson. You're in no trouble. However, you can have a lawyer present if you feel the need for one."

"I don't need a lawyer. I'll let you know if I change my mind."

Frost nodded. "Tell me about your friendship with Laura. I under-stand you were close."

"We were friends. I'm not sure about close. I'm not sure anyone was close to Laura." She fiddled with her right gauge and looked up at the ceiling for a moment.

"We began hanging out in middle school. Initially, it was curiosity on my part. I'd heard a little about what had happened to her as a kid. I was new to the school, and I'd hear people talk about her. She wasn't friendly or social; she didn't seem to have any friends."

Byers slumped back in the chair and watched Frost. "I was curious. When you're that age, you're drawn to weird shit, and the stories about her were the weirdest thing I'd ever heard. Some of it I learned later was just bullshitting on the kids' part. You know? Like that party game where a person whispers a message in another person's ear and by the time it gets whispered around the circle it bears no resemblance to the original message."

"What was being said?"

"Oh, all sorts of stuff. That she'd been kidnapped by Satanists was one of the stories." She laughed out loud at that. "People think devil worshippers are everywhere. I guess it's easier than believing that nice young man next door killed twelve people and has them in his freezer."

It was true, I thought. After an arrest or an incident, almost everyone said, "He seemed so normal." I could see a twitch of smile on Frost's face.

Jayden sighed. "Anyway, there was that, and some said her stepfather had molested her and had dumped her somewhere hoping she'd be found dead. I overheard some mothers who were chaperoning at a school function claim that it was an uncle who'd been living with the family.

"Laura had come to the dance and was actually dancing—by herself, which kids thought was weird. I guess that's what triggered the conversation I overheard. Laura's presence always caused gossip. I heard others speculate that some random pedophile had kidnapped her and then dumped her. I never really knew what the true story was, and Laura wouldn't talk about it."

"What did she talk about?"

"Pretty much anything but that or her mother and…well she always called him her stepfather, but I guess he'd adopted her. She hated him, never really said why, but she wouldn't have anything to do with him. If he showed up at some school function, she wouldn't say a word to him."

"Her father said she'd gotten her tattoo to rub in what had happened to her every time they saw it. She was underage. He also said he thought you helped her get it. Is that true?"

"Right on both counts. But she hoped for the stars, which was the other point that he never understood."

"Do you remember who the tattoo artist was?'

"No, I never knew his name and the tattoo place went out of business not long after that. My guess is he was doing a side business of underage kids and someone found out and had him shut down."

"Did she ever tell you about the assault or who did it?"

"No. If someone asked about what happened, she'd refuse to answer and leave. If she couldn't leave, she'd freeze them out. It was as if they ceased to exist for her. By the time we all reached high school everyone had learned not to bring it up."

She paused for a moment then resumed. "Honestly, I wondered whether she even knew who'd done it. If she did, once she hit her teens, wouldn't she have said something? I would have. I could have asked, I suppose; she might have talked to me about it. But I was afraid if I did, we wouldn't be friends anymore, and I liked her."

"She refused to tell her mother where she'd moved or what her phone number was because she was estranged from her adoptive father?" Frost asked.

Jayden stared at Frost for several moments. "She wasn't estranged from him; that implies that they once had a relationship. I don't think they ever did. Neither of them liked the other, and although she loved her mother, she once told me her mother had sold out and had put him first, even above her. She said she had no luck with fathers—that her real father had abandoned her and her 'stepfather' was an uptight, controlling prick."

Listening to the taped interview, Hutchinson hadn't struck me as a prick, more as someone who'd tried to parent Laura by controlling her and hadn't been successful.

"Laura didn't want to hurt her mother," Jayden went on, "but she didn't want her mother or Andrew having any direct access to her. That's why she had the PO box and gave her mom my number."

The woman flipped her hair out of her face and added, "She knew I wouldn't give them any information she didn't want them to have. I think she figured if she gave her mother her direct phone number, then Andrew would get involved."

"If they had no relationship, why would he get involved?"

"From what Laura said, he likes to control things. She thought he'd have tried to stop her mother from contacting her. I think that's why she acted out as much as she did in high school—because she knew that it would get to him and wasn't something he could control."

"When was the last time you heard from her? I take it she wasn't living with you?"

"No, she wasn't. She was living with a guy, not sure if they were an item or simply roommates, Laura never said. I heard from her probably three weeks before I found out that she'd died. I don't remember the exact date, but it was before Halloween."

"What did she want?"

"She asked to borrow some money."

"For what?"

"She just said she needed money. I didn't ask why, but I know she was working for a dealer, selling drugs. I think she may have owed him money. Rumor had it he was a nasty piece of work; I figured the money was to get him off her back. She looked as if things had been rough for her. Laura never handled anyone prying. If she didn't tell you, asking her got you nowhere. I gave her the five hundred bucks she'd asked for and didn't question her further. I wish I had; I never heard from her again."

"Any idea what she'd been doing?"

Jayden frowned and shrugged. "No, not really, I don't know what she wanted the money for. She sold drugs, like I said, but I don't think she ever used. When I last saw her, she looked stressed and anxious, so I could be wrong. I had heard rumors that she was into prostitution, but I seriously doubt it. That just wasn't Laura. I learned a long time ago, people like to bullshit, and the worse the story, the more they like to spread it around, whether it's true or not."

Frost dealt with that every day. "I need the names and contact information for anyone you know that she was friends with or was close to her, and the dealer if you know it." He handed her a sheet of paper and a pen and left the room. I knew Frost would follow up on the dealer if Jayden could provide a name or someway to contact him.

"I updated the lieutenant on Crispy." Frost chuckled. He'd stopped by on his way home the next day. "I had to get the case file and remind myself what his name was, thanks to you. Didn't want to call him Crispy in front of her."

"What'd she have to say?"

"Said to drop it. That it was wasted effort on something that's unlikely to be solved. So, that one's off the list of cases to review."

"Did you get anything important from the formal interview with the Hutchinsons?"

"It didn't produce much. They showed up with a lawyer, and it was Talbot and me playing games with the lawyer throughout the interview." Frost pulled on his ear. "We were able to get the names of the therapist they used and some other contacts and their alibis, which check out. Talbot doesn't like the husband, but based on his alibi, he wasn't the one who killed her.

"There's no real motive for him killing her," he said. "Talbot's trying to track down the mother's brother. And I'm in the process of tracking down the people whose names Byers gave me."

Frost leaned forward, resting his forearms on his thighs. "Her murder could have been as simple as her being in the wrong place at the wrong time, or she did something that pissed someone off, like that dealer Byers mentioned. If that's the case, then who that person might be is the question. And I gotta say, Hutchinson's a controlling jerk but, even without the DNA that cleared him, I wouldn't have pegged him for her assault."

"Why not?"

"A friend of mine worked sex crimes for a while. He didn't last long, but almost no one does. It's just too…ugly. Anyway, he always maintained that it wasn't the suspects who were angry or upset by questions who raised red flags with him. It was the careful, tightly alibied ones who never seemed worried that made him dig deeper.

"Besides, you don't stay married to someone as long as the Hutchinsons have and not know if your partner is up to no good. Wives, mothers, always know on some level that the husband is up to something, but for a number of reasons choose to ignore or deny it. If something like that's going on, you aren't as up-front about problems in front of the police as Eleanor Hutchinson was."

He waved a sheet of paper and frowned. "This is the list of friends that Laura's mother gave me. I'm gonna ask one of the uniforms to call and talk to them, but I gotta find one that isn't assigned to something else. With those gang slayings that Roberts and Adams caught most of the uniforms we use are occupied."

I hesitated, then barged ahead. "I could call them and at least arrange for them to come in to talk to you."

Frost gave me a calculating look. "That's not staying out of an investigation, like you promised Angel."

"It's just a few phone calls." I started to say more, then saw Frost absently rubbing his chest as he talked, and he still had that fatigued gray look to his face.

"Frost, when was the last time you saw a doctor?"

"Oh Christ, don't you start on me, Evie's driving me nuts."

"You look exhausted. I've seen you rubbing your chest a lot lately, and I don't like your color. Are you having chest pain?"

"It's indigestion," he said, giving me an indignant look.

"It might be, but you need to find out. I want you to see someone. I'll find someone if you don't have a doctor."

He sighed in exasperation. "For God's sake, don't hound me. I'll see our family doc. That make you happy?"

"If you'll actually go, yes. Call today and ask to be seen as soon as possible. Then I want to hear from you, d'you understand?"

"Fine. I'm going home. Here's the list, call them if you want, but I'd talk to Angel first."

He left muttering about interfering women making his life miserable. Over time, I had learned that with the people he cared about, Frost was crusty on the outside but soft as a marshmallow on the inside. Not that I'd tell him that; he'd probably never speak to me again.

FIFTEEN

IT TOOK ME ALMOST TWO DAYS to work up the courage to broach the phone calls to Angel. The last thing I wanted was to upset him, but… there was always a 'but.' Getting involved with Frost had triggered something in me that almost felt like an addiction.

After dinner as he relaxed on the couch I decided it might be an opportune time to talk to him. He'd eaten—Angel on an empty stomach was never a good time to upset him—he was relaxing with a beer, and trolling TV stations.

I took a deep breath. "I wanted to talk to you about Frost's case."

He looked up with eyebrows raised, at least the frown hadn't appeared yet. "What about it?"

"He has a list of people he wants to interview about Laura and the uniforms they use to call and set up interviews are busy with those gang shootings. Um…he wondered if I would call them. Normally, I'd just go ahead and do it, it's not dangerous, but I promised you not to get involved." The look on his face was pretty neutral so I pressed on. "I won't do it if it's going to cause problems for you."

He gave me a skeptical look. "Go ahead and call them. As long as that's all you're doing, I'll deal with it."

At home I worked my way down the list of people, setting up interviews for Frost and worrying about his health. I hoped he was making an appointment with his doctor. He'd always seemed healthy to me, ten or fifteen pounds heavier that he probably should be, but otherwise fine. His diet, at least when he was with me, was atrocious. What I thought was worrisome chest pain might be indigestion; some of the things I'd seen him eat would make my stomach hurt. But I would bet money it was cardiac-related pain.

By the end of the day, I had talked to three of the people on the list and made arrangements for them to come in and meet with Frost. They liked Laura, knew she was troubled, but had no idea who'd have done anything to hurt her.

One of them gave me the name and number of Bret Martin, the guy with whom Laura had been involved. I called and tried to set up an appointment for him to talk with Frost. He refused and said he wouldn't willingly come into the police station.

Assuming he'd perhaps tangled with the cops at some point, I offered to meet him at a coffee shop by the Auraria Campus, near Speer and Colfax. I shouldn't have. I should have insisted he come in and talk to Frost, or let Frost talk to him via phone, but I was worried that if I tried that, he'd disappear. I wanted to meet him first, hear what he had to say, and hope that I could cajole him into talking to Frost.

I got there early, took a seat, and watched the door. About fifteen minutes later, a skinny guy walked in, wearing jeans that had seen better days, a worn fleece-lined jean jacket, and a knit cap pulled down over his dark brown hair. I suspected he wasn't much past twenty. As he looked around, I saw part of a tattoo on his neck. It was partially concealed by his jacket collar, and I couldn't make out what it was. We made eye contact, and he walked over.

"Ms. Collins?"

"Annie, please," I said. "I'd like to buy you a coffee if you want one."

He nodded. I wondered whether he had enough money to buy one for himself. I handed him a twenty. "Why don't you go get them? I'll take a small latte. Get what you want and get a muffin or something for yourself."

He returned a few moments later, and I sipped my coffee while he inhaled the muffin he'd purchased.

Then he motioned with the coffee cup. "Thanks for this. I don't know what I can tell you, but I'm happy to help if I can. I just...don't like cop shops."

I nodded. "Talk to me about Laura. How did you meet her?"

"She moved into the studio apartment down the hall from me about a year ago. I'd meet her on the stairs, say hi. That evolved into conversations and finally we became friends."

He looked wistful. "Sometimes we'd pool our resources and go get something to eat. Fast food mostly, but it was nice."

"Were you romantically involved with her?"

"Yeah, after a while. A few months after we got together, she suggested we move in together to save on rent. I was crazy about her, and that seemed like a great idea. But I never knew whether what we had was as important to her as it was to me."

"Meaning what?"

He shrugged, sipping his coffee. "Laura was hard to know. There was this part of her that she never shared; it was locked away. She cared about me, I was a safe place for her, but I wasn't sure I could count on her staying."

"That must have been hard."

"It was, but I was in love with her." He indicated my wedding ring. "You're married, so you may not know what it's like to be in love with someone who doesn't feel the same about you. I took what I could get and was grateful. That probably seems pathetic to you."

"No, it doesn't. I've been there in the past."

I saw the sadness in his face, and I remembered how it was to be with someone you knew would eventually leave. It had been a while, and I thanked God for Angel, but I remembered the feeling all too clearly.

"You didn't file a missing person's report. Why is that?"

"I didn't think she was missing. Laura used to take off periodically for a few days. I never knew where. All of a sudden she would up and go, and then she'd come back. She said she needed to do that to clear her head. Once I knew what had happened, I was afraid to say anything. The cops always suspect husbands and boyfriends and if you haven't got an airtight alibi, then you're it. That's why I don't want to talk to that detective. My alibi isn't good enough, I don't need the trouble."

"Do you know anything about the circumstances that led up to her death? Anything you can tell me could help find her killer."

"I knew she was upset about something, had been for a week or so, but I couldn't get her to tell me what was wrong. It was why I didn't think she was missing. I figured whatever was bothering her had led to her taking off."

He took another drink of his coffee. "She'd been gone about four days, and I was getting worried. It was before I heard about her death on the news. I asked around, and my friend Eric told me he'd seen her talking to a guy in that little park between the City and County building and the Capitol. He said they'd been sitting on one of the benches for a while and that neither of them looked like it was a pleasant conversation."

"Any idea who he was or what they were talking about?"

"I have no idea who he was. Eric could probably describe him to you. He didn't know what they were talking about, but he said she got pretty upset at one point. She never said anything to me about meeting the guy. When Eric told me about it, I thought maybe…"

"Bret, I need you to be honest with me. The police can't find her killer if you aren't."

He sighed and looked uncomfortable. "Laura sold drugs from time to time to help make ends meet. I figured this guy was her supplier. She didn't like the supplier, said he was creepy and she didn't trust him. I don't know if that's who the guy was."

"Did she use?"

"No, I never saw her use drugs. Never."

"A friend of hers said Laura borrowed five hundred dollars from her but didn't say what it was for. Do you know what she needed it for?"

He looked taken a back. "I didn't know that. All I can think of is maybe it was to pay her supplier off. I had no idea she'd done that."

"Do you know the supplier's name?"

"Benny, something. I could ask around."

"That'd be great." I paused hesitant to bring it up, then went on. "There's a rumor she was involved in prostitution—"

Bret slammed his coffee cup on the table. "Who said that? Who? Whoever it was is a damn liar."

"Are you sure? Is it possible Laura was involved in that, and you didn't know?"

"Are you *kidding*? You can't live with someone, have sex with them, and not know that they're out turning tricks. Christ, you can smell it on them when they come home."

"Sounds like you have some experience there."

He glared at me. "I had a girlfriend once who started turning tricks behind my back. We lived together for a short while, and you know what they're doing; trust me, you know. It's why I left her."

I hesitated, then threw it out. "Did you know Laura was pregnant?"

He looked like I had punched him in the gut with a sledgehammer. "*What did you say?*"

"She was twelve weeks pregnant when she died."

"Ah God," he moaned, holding his head in his hands and covering his eyes as if doing so could make the news go away.

"Was it yours?"

He raised his head to look at me. "I don't know; I didn't know she was pregnant. Is there a way I can find out?"

"Yes. I'll find out what you need to do. If it wasn't yours, any idea whose it was?"

"No, things had been good for us. I'd have sworn she wasn't seeing anyone else. But things got weird before she disappeared. She was upset, jumpy; she wasn't sleeping. I couldn't get her to tell me what was going on, but I never thought it might be another guy."

He glanced out the window, lost in thought. "When I would ask her what was going on, all she would say was she was working on a way to get some money for us, enough to maybe move somewhere nice. She wouldn't say what she was up to. I kept telling her I didn't need a nice place, that we were fine where we were. Finally, I just told her to be careful, not to take any chances or put herself in danger." He winced at the memory. "And then she disappeared. I wasn't sure, this time, if it was temporary, if she'd come back. I hoped she would."

He stared at his hands, still wrapped around the empty cup. "I've wondered, since Eric told me about seeing her in conversation with that guy, if she wasn't trying to blackmail him or something. Maybe he owed her money."

"I'm going to need Eric's last name and a way to contact him." He nodded. I pushed a napkin toward him and pulled a pen out of my purse.

He scribbled on it and handed it back. "I want to know if it was my baby. I'll do whatever is needed to find out, but I want to know."

"Why?"

"I loved her. It may have been my kid. I'd like to know if it was… and I'd like to think she was faithful. If the baby was mine…"

"I'll let you know what you need to do to get a paternity test and get back to you. In return, I want you to tell Detective Frost what you've told me. He needs to hear it from you. Will you at least talk to him over the phone?" Bret nodded. "Good, I'll have him call you. It would help to know the name of her supplier, if you can find out."

I handed him the sixty dollars I had in my purse, and he pushed my hand away.

"I don't want to be paid for helping to find the bastard who killed her."

I held it out to him again. "How about you take it as a gift from me? It's not much, but it'll get you some food."

He nodded. "Thanks," he mumbled.

SIXTEEN

THE CONVERSATION WITH BRET MARTIN had upset me. Who we love is such a crap shoot. After first meeting Angel, if someone had asked me whether we would fall in love and marry, I'd have laughed.

He was full of himself, and women appeared and disappeared from his life as if there was a revolving door on his side of the duplex we lived in at the time. And yet, we became trusted friends, eventually lovers, and at last husband and wife. What we had was solid. Our relationship was limping a little at the moment, and that was unsettling, but I hoped that gradually we'd get back on track.

It sounded, despite Bret's insecurity about Laura, that what they'd had was a little shaky, but she'd told him she was making plans to get money so they could move somewhere nice. I hoped she hadn't double crossed her supplier or tried to blackmail anyone. I wanted to think she'd found someone who could love and cherish her. I wanted to think that her life had been on the mend, that she was near those stars to which her tat had alluded.

Angel had been working late the last few days and rather than drive home to an empty house, I detoured to Angel's parents' house to see Maria. Sophia was cooking dinner and insisted I stay to eat after I had seen her mother.

"And how are you and *Angelito*?" Maria asked. "I haven't seen much of him, does he like his new job?"

"I think so." I sighed. "It's a very different type of practice, and his decision has upset a lot of the people he used to work with. People in the DA's office and cops don't hold defense lawyers in very high regard. I worry that…well, he's a big boy, if he's not happy he'll do something about it."

"Do you think he's unhappy?"

"I don't know. I can't really tell. He always loved being an ADA and prosecuting cases. He hasn't gone to trial with anything yet, but what he's doing now seems tame. I hope he's happy."

She smiled. "I have never known *Angelito* to do anything he didn't want to. If he took this new job, it was his choice. He has always found a way to make things work for him."

I nodded and smiled at her. She'd known him far longer than I had, and I didn't want to worry her with our recent dilemma. She had lost weight, and I wondered how well her pain meds were working. She seemed her usual self, but I knew the cancer would catch up with her eventually.

"I don't want you to leave us," I said quietly.

"*Querida*, you know there's nothing either of us can do about that. I think, though, I will be here for a while yet."

She took my hand in hers and patted it. "I have always felt my mother close to me. I feel her now more than ever, and I look forward to seeing her again. I feel my husband too, he comes to me in dreams. He seems anxious to be with me."

She paused for several seconds. "What I mean is, I think we are always near those we love and, when I pass, I will be near all of you, too. I prayed the Lord would let me live to see you both safe, to know you were no longer in danger from that man. And God did. What happens now is not up to me."

It wasn't and that wasn't fair, but when was life ever fair?

❧

"My doc referred me to some heart guy who works at your hospital. I'm going to see him tomorrow, satisfied?" Frost grumbled when I talked to him by phone the following day.

"Who'd he refer you to?" The hospital I worked at had a world-class cardiac program, and I knew he'd be in good hands.

"Some guy named Simons. He any good?"

"Yes, he's really good. You'll tell me what he says, right?"

"Yeah, yeah, I will." I could hear him tapping a pencil on his desk, a sure sign of annoyance.

"Frost, if for some reason you need a cardiac cath or surgery, I want to be there, okay?"

"I'm not going to need either. I'm tired, and my stomach's been upset."

"I hope that's all it is." I didn't say that if his family doc had sent him to Simons, his symptoms weren't likely to be indigestion or that he was just tired. "But if you do need either, I want to be with you and Evie."

"Jesus, you and Evie are going to make me fucking nuts."

"We love you. Don't be a jerk."

"I'm going, aren't I?" The pencil tapping had ramped up a bit.

❧

Knowing Evie would call me if he didn't, Frost reluctantly called to report the results.

"He wants to do a cardiac catheterization. I told him I'd think about it. Evie's pissed and you probably will be, too, but I have better things to do."

"Like what? Have a heart attack?" I asked in exasperation.

"I'm not gonna have a—"

"Stop, right now. Simons wouldn't have suggested a cath if he wasn't worried about a blockage of one of your coronary arteries. If you have that, then you could have a heart attack at any time and probably will at some point."

Frustrated with trying to convince him, I resorted to scare tactics. "Do you realize that the most commonly blocked coronary artery is nicknamed the Widowmaker for a good reason? If that's the one that's causing the problems, you could just drop dead one of these days. Dammit, Frost, you're going to do this if Evie and I have to drag you to the hospital."

"Oh, for Christ's sake."

"You call his office right after you get off the phone with me and set it up. If I don't hear from you by the end of the day about when it's sched-uled, then I'll call Evie and we will schedule it. D'you understand me?"

"Jesus fucking Christ, okay, I'll call."

"You've got until five o'clock when the doc's office closes to get back to me."

He ended the call without saying goodbye.

Frost had asked me to meet him in the coffee shop across from the precinct on Monday. He hadn't said what the meeting was about, but I wasn't expecting it to be pleasant. He'd been in a foul mood, snarling and snapping at me and giving Evie hell. That mood had extended to the homicide department as a whole and to anyone who crossed him, asked him a question, or got within two feet of him.

He hadn't told anyone about the impending cath, and no one knew why he was being such a pain. As a result, Paul Roberts told me everyone in the department, including him and Talbot, were avoiding Frost if at all possible. Talbot let him interview the people I'd set up by himself, apparently figuring it was best to leave him be. I said nothing to Paul about the reason for Frost's behavior; if Frost wanted him to know, he'd tell him.

I had been holding down a table for about ten minutes, and my attention kept returning to a young woman sitting near the door. It was distracting. She repeatedly glanced up from her coffee and over at the main door to the police department in between nervously tearing up a napkin and looking at what appeared to be a business card.

She looked familiar, but I couldn't figure out why. When Frost walked across the street and into the coffee shop, shock registered on her face, and she abruptly got up and left.

Frost scowled at me after he got a coffee and sat down. "So, the damn thing's booked for seven a.m. on Friday, satisfied?"

"Good, I'm glad you scheduled it. Is that what this meet was all about?"

"Yeah."

"Why not tell me over the phone?"

"Because there's no privacy there and I don't want the whole *fucking* department to know. He's not going to find anything, and I don't want everybody thinking I'm getting old and can't handle the job. I don't want any more people on my case like you and Evie've been."

"You're impossible. If we didn't care, we wouldn't have pushed this."

"Yeah? Some days it'd be easier if you two didn't care."

"Well, you're out of luck." I sipped my coffee and told him about my conversation with Bret Martin. I gave Frost Bret's phone number; I had been able to convince him to talk to Frost. I relayed Bret's information about the person who saw Laura talking to an unidentified man and that he would try to get the name of her supplier.

"This Eric guy needs to come in and work with a sketch artist. He saw Laura with someone before her death and, according to Bret, she was upset and jumpy afterward. Maybe Eric can give us an idea what the person looked like." I handed him the napkin with Eric Abrams's information on it. "And Bret wants to know if he's the father. How would he go about finding out?"

"They'll have collected DNA and fetal tissue during the autopsy. He needs to get a buccal swab for DNA. When I talk to him I'll have him come in and give us a sample or I'll meet him somewhere and get it myself."

Frost's eyebrows were scrunched together, and he looked even more upset than usual, if that was possible. "You weren't supposed to go and talk to her boyfriend in person, ya know."

I started to respond, and he jabbed his finger at me in exasperation. "All you were supposed to do was talk by phone to the people on the list I gave you and arrange for them to come in and talk to me. I was supposed to do the interviewing. That was to keep me out of trouble with my lieutenant and you out of trouble with Angel."

He looked exhausted. "If you keep overstepping like this, doing things on your own, I'm gonna can you. You're not a cop, Annie. You shouldn't even be involved in this. On top of that, you're going behind Angel's back and doing what you said you weren't going to do."

I flushed, knowing he was right, but my defensive hackles rose. "Frost, I wanted to talk to him face-to-face. I thought I could get more from him that way. We met in public at a coffee shop. He refused to come into the precinct, but I finally got him to agree to talk to you over the phone. My talking to him helped."

"I don't give a damn what your reasons were," he said whacking the table. "You need to do what ask you to do and keep your promise to Angel."

He stopped, frowned, and rubbed at his chest; his face had taken on an alarming shade of gray.

"Frost? What's wrong?"

"*Nothing's fucking wrong!* Do as you're told, or you're out of here!" He stood up and stormed out of the coffee shop.

SEVENTEEN

I SAW THE YOUNG WOMAN standing outside the coffee shop. She watched Frost as he stomped across the street. She stood there for a few moments, then seemed to make up her mind about something and returned to the coffee shop and walked over to me.

"That's Detective Frost, right?" she asked nervously.

"Yes, did you need to talk to him?"

She held a business card, turning it over and over in her hand. "I…um…I guess I do. *Yes, I know*," She whispered, to whom I didn't know. "He seems a little upset."

"He is at the moment, but mostly with me. I work with him. Can I help?"

She closed her eyes and continued to flip the card over and over, her lips moving silently. "My name's Annie Collins, what's yours?" I said, when it seemed she wasn't going to continue.

"Janet Casey."

"Janet, have a seat. Maybe it'd be easier to talk to me first."

She nodded and sat down. "I don't know if coming here was…I don't know what else to do."

"How did you get Frost's card?"

She looked at the card she held as if seeing it for the first time. Her hair was stringy and unkempt; her clothes looked as if she'd slept in them. I doubted whether she had showered in days. Something was clearly wrong.

It hit me all at once, where I had seen her. It had been here, three or four times over the last month or six weeks, sitting at a table by the window with a cup in front of her that she never drank from, staring at the precinct building across the street. I had assumed she worked either at the precinct or knew someone who did or worked somewhere near the coffee shop. I'd noticed her but hadn't given her much thought.

"He…he handed them out a while back at a bar I'd gone to with friends. They'd insisted on taking me there to try to cheer me up. I didn't want to go…but they insisted." She continued to twist the card over and over with her fingers.

"And you wanted to talk to Detective Frost in regard to what?"

"The man…the man who died in the house fire a while ago," she said. Her voice was barely above a whisper, and I had a hard time hearing her.

"Do you know something about that?"

At that she began to cry and finger a gold cross on a chain at her throat.

"Janet, talk to me." She shook her head, got up abruptly, and walked out of the shop. I snatched up Frost's card that she had dropped on the table and followed her, shoving the card into my coat pocket. I grabbed a couple of napkins. She'd left crying, and I figured if I got her to talk to me she'd need them.

"Janet!" I called and then caught up with her. I linked my arm with hers and continued to walk down the sidewalk.

"Tell me what you know. I promise I won't say anything to anyone. If you still want to talk to Frost, I'll take you to him." She had made repeated trips to the coffee shop. Something had been weighing on her mind even before getting Frost's card. I waited, hoping she'd talk to me.

"They told me I had to. They said, *an eye for an eye,*" she managed to say between sobs.

She continued to mumble almost to herself, fingering the cross, until she said, "He raped me. He slipped me something. I remember talking to him. He…he came over to the table where I was sitting. I thought he was nice and then, when I came back from the restroom, he'd bought me another drink. We talked for a bit and drank, and I started to feel funny. He suggested taking me out for some air. I don't remember much after that."

Her hands shook and I pulled her into the doorway of an empty storefront to get out of the wind. "Tell me what happened. What do you remember?"

"They said I had been deceived. *Whosoever is deceived is not wise.* He deceived me," she said, shaking her head a couple times.

It sounded like she was quoting sayings from the Bible. I had no idea who "they" might be. Members of a congregation, perhaps?

"I went there to meet a friend, but she never showed up. He came over and started talking to me. He was nice looking. He was *nice* to me, he bought me a drink. *Be careful that you are not deceived. I know, I know that,*" she whispered as if talking to someone. "I'm so stupid."

She took a hitching breath. "I woke up the next morning in a crummy hotel room. I was sore and terribly sick. I didn't remember how I'd gotten there or what had happened, but I remembered him. He put something in that drink when I went to the restroom, I'm sure of it."

"I don't think you're the only woman he did that to. Would you be willing to talk to Detective Frost and give him a statement?" I rested my hand on her arm.

"About the murder?" she asked, her eyes wide with fright.

That hit me between the eyes. The *murder?* That information hadn't been released to the media. The police had said he'd died in a house fire.

"I shouldn't have come." She frowned and shook her head again, then said in a whisper, "*I told you I shouldn't.*"

She started to pull away from me, but I stopped her. "Janet, if you know something about this, please tell me."

She began to cry again. "I thought what I did was right, they told me it was, they told me he had to pay. But then God told me I had to atone for what I'd done. I didn't know who to talk to. Then I thought I should talk to the police. I came here many times, trying to decide what to do, but they wouldn't tell me what to do."

They? Who the hell was she talking about?

"Then Detective Frost handed out his cards at the bar the night my friends took me there. It was a sign." She wiped at her face and looked at me with a pained expression.

"Janet, tell me what happened, and I will help you as best I can."

She nodded and took a deep breath. "*The wages of sin are death.* I don't understand, they said he needed to pay," she said looking at me earnestly. I wasn't sure what was happening with her. I was worried she was having some sort of breakdown or psychosis. I nodded, hoping to encourage her to continue.

"I followed him home from the bar several weeks after what happened."

Tears continued to run down her face, and I pulled the paper napkins from my coat pocket and pressed them into her hand.

"He didn't recognize me when he answered the door. He pretended to, but I could tell he didn't. He didn't know my name. I reminded him who I was. They said to tell him I wanted to have another night with him. He was so sure of himself...it never occurred to him I might be lying. *Lying lips are an abomination to the Lord.*"

I had never heard as many biblical quotes in one setting in my life, and it worried me. She seemed to be hearing voices that were coming from some sort of religious ideology.

She wiped her face and looked up from the napkin. "He smiled and let me in. He asked if I wanted a drink. I said yes. He got one for both of us and said he was glad that I wasn't upset, that he'd enjoyed his time with me."

Her voice shook and her face was so pale I was afraid she'd pass out. "He said he'd put some music on for us to enjoy. While he was doing that, he had his back to me, and I dosed his drink with that date rape drug. I offered to get him another drink when he'd finished the first, and I dosed that, too."

She swiped at her eyes with a napkin and wrung her hands looking at me with confusion written all over her face. "He'd gotten pretty sleepy, and I suggested he lie down on the couch. He did. I waited a bit, until he looked like he was almost asleep. I shook him and told him I was going to make him pay for what he did. He tried to get up but couldn't, then he passed out. I…I'd brought lighter fluid in my backpack, like they told me to," she said indicating the bag slung over her shoulder. "I got it out and poured it on him and the couch and set fire to it."

She reached out and took my hand, crushing it in hers, as if the harder she held on, the more likely I was to side with her. "*I killed him.* They said he deserved it, that he'd tricked me. I thought God would approve of what I did, but *the cowardly, the unbelieving, the vile, the murderers, the sexually immoral—they will be consigned to the fiery lake of burning sulfur.* He'll burn, but I will, too, unless I repent, unless I atone for my sins. That's what God said. Why didn't he tell me that it was a sin before it happened? Why didn't he tell me not to listen to them?" She began to sob, her breaths coming in gasps. She let go of my hand and covered her mouth as if to stifle her sobs.

"I thought…I thought I'd feel better when he was dead…when he'd paid for what he did to me. I knew no one would believe me about what had happened. I thought God wanted him to pay, that he *needed* to pay."

She gripped my hand hard again and searched my face looking for something, absolution perhaps.

I said, "I think he did the same thing to a lot of other women," hoping she'd keep talking to me.

"But…I can't keep from seeing him on the couch, the flames growing, setting his clothes on fire, his hair catching fire." She squeezed her eyes shut tightly as if to erase the sight of him. "He…he struggled for a bit. I was afraid he'd survive, but he stopped…at last. When the fire started to spread, I took off.

"I don't know what to do," she cried. "I thought I was doing the right thing, but I can't live with it anymore. They won't leave me alone. I thought maybe coming here, talking to Detective Frost and confessing, would help. What should I do?"

Jesus—no offense intended if you're listening, I thought, *I'm not sure what to do—maybe take her to the ER and get a psych hold to give me time to think?* I frowned. *If I do that she'd most likely confess to the ER staff, and they would have to call the cops.*

I wanted to tell her to leave and say nothing to anyone about it, that I would say nothing about what she'd told me. I wanted to tell her she was right, he'd deserved what had happened, whether God had sanctioned it or not, but she was haunted by the memory and the guilt. Most alarming to me were her references to what "they" had told her. I was worried that with her level of distress, "they" or God, would tell her to kill herself. The question here was, what was right?

I put my arm around her shoulder and gave it a squeeze. "Come back to the coffee shop and sit down; let me think for a bit."

When Angel showed up, I met him at the door of the coffee shop. He shook his head and stared at me.

"How the fuck do you do it? I swear to God, it's like you're some kind of disaster magnet."

"Angel, I didn't know what to do," I said, quietly. "I could have taken her to the ER for a psych assessment, she certainly needs one, but once she told them what she'd done, they'd be obligated to call the police, and she'd have no protection."

I gripped his forearm. "She confessed to me. There's some weird religious theme to it all and she keeps talking about how "they" told her what to do. I think she may be schizophrenic and hearing voices. I think the voices told her to do what she did, that it was the right thing to do and that God approved, then suddenly God didn't approve, at least that's what I think she's saying. I can't blame her for her actions, the guy deserved it. But she needs someone to represent her. I hoped…I hoped you could help her."

He shook his head again and blew out a breath. "Introduce me, then go home. After I've had a chance to talk to her, I'll take her to see Frost."

He started toward the woman and then turned back to me, leaned in, and whispered, "I don't care what she said to you, you forget you heard it. If you want to help her, introduce us and leave."

I nodded, introduced him, and left.

I saw Angel lead her to his car and help her in, but he didn't drive off. I assumed he was talking to her there; it certainly was more private than the coffee shop. I hadn't gone home. I'd waited in my car that was parked down the street from the coffee shop. At last, they emerged from the car, and I watched as he led her to the precinct, a guiding arm around her shoulders, head bent talking to her as they walked. If I knew Angel, he was soothing her and reassuring her. It was as if he was holding her upright, and perhaps he was.

I had said nothing to Frost about Janet, as Angel had instructed. Regardless of that, my guess was I would have some explaining to do about how Angel had gotten involved. I knew Angel wouldn't talk to me about his conversation with her or what had transpired during the interview, but I hoped he'd thought of something that would help Janet and keep me out of it. I hoped he hadn't mentioned me at all.

Whether Angel said anything or not, I knew Frost would put two and two together rapidly.

"How the hell did Angel get involved with this?" Frost demanded over the phone several hours after I got home. "This Casey woman can no more afford his representation than fly to the moon. That means you were involved."

I sighed. "She was in the coffee shop, had been there for a while, staring at the precinct doors and fiddling with what turned out to be your card. The one you gave her at one of the bars you visited."

I could hear him tapping a pencil on his desk; he was clearly upset with me. "When she saw you walk in, she looked terrified, and she bolted outside," I went on. "After you left, she came back in and told me she needed to talk to you. When she told me she wanted to speak to you about Crispy's death, she was really upset. I know how it feels to talk to you when you're scared, and you were in a terrible mood when you left the coffee shop. She needed representation, and I called Angel."

"What did she tell you?"

I hedged. "That she had information about the death. Based on how upset she was, I figured she might know who'd killed him. That's all."

The line was silent for several minutes, just long enough for me to begin to squirm. Frost was good at that, but I had gotten good at waiting him out.

"Fine. I don't believe that's everything she told you, but I'm not going to hassle you about it. At least he'll protect her, if possible."

"What happened?"

"None of your goddamn business," he said.

❧

It was quiet throughout dinner. Angel said next to nothing, and I finally couldn't take it any longer.

"Can you at least tell me what's going to happen to her?"

He looked up from his plate and set his fork down. "I don't know at this point. I knew you'd ask and, unless she gave me permission, I couldn't talk to you about it. I explained that to her. She says she trusts you and said I could talk about it with you."

He huffed out a breath. "She confessed, and it's clear it was premeditated. There are extenuating circumstances—I think you're right about her having some serious mental health issues. That's the only saving grace…"—he grimaced at the term—"She seems to be on the edge of a breakdown, but you can't plead down murder one."

He sighed and shook his head. "I talked with Rick Chamberlain, the ADA who caught the case. I'll ask the court to have her evaluated for competency, and I'll get a private psychiatrist to evaluate her as well. Rick's not unsympathetic to what happened to her."

He sat back and ran a hand over his face. "If she's deemed competent, then I've got my work cut out for me. She'll be tried for first degree murder, which, if convicted, gets you life. Her mental state, however, is pretty shaky at the moment. Honestly, I'm hoping she isn't competent and she can be sent to a psych facility instead of prison."

He shrugged. "It's not prison, but it's not a great solution. She could be in there for years. They evaluate patients every six months and if she's deemed competent and isn't deemed a danger to herself or others, then she would be released to step-down monitoring, but the court still has jurisdiction over her. Other than that, I can't tell you. I won't know how it shakes out until it does."

He continued. "She has no prior convictions or offenses, but she has no ties to the community, family, or a support system. There's no bail for murder one, so she'll be in the Denver Detention Center until the eval is arranged, then she'll be taken to the state psych hospital in Pueblo. The good news is I was able to expedite her being evaluated by a private psychiatrist, which will help move things along."

He hesitated, then said, "She asked me to thank you. She said that you'd helped her." He shrugged his shoulders, as if it wasn't important, but I could see his eyes glisten. "She said I was lucky to have you…and I am, *Corazón.*"

I smiled and reached for his hand. "I'm lucky to have you, too. I wanted to help her. I thought about telling her to forget about it, that the case was dead in the water, but she was clearly racked with guilt. I thought…I thought, since she'd intended to talk to Frost, that turning herself in might relieve some of her distress."

"Maybe it will." He returned to his food, then stopped and looked at me. "That was kind of you to call me. I'll take her on *pro bono*, and I hope it works out for her. I'm glad you called me rather than telling her to forget about it."

I rolled my eyes. "I thought about it long and hard, believe me. Crispy deserved what he got."

"*Crispy?*" he asked with a look of disbelief on his face. "Jesus, *that's* what you call him?"

I nodded, and he began to laugh, a deep belly laugh that turned his face red and made his eyes water. He shook his head at me when it subsided.

"*Chica,* you scare me sometimes."

EIGHTEEN

IT WAS AS IF I WAS IN THE MIDDLE of the perfect storm—one of the people I loved dearly was dying, another was facing the possibility of serious surgery and, while there were no overt signs of trouble, life felt fragile around Angel.

I couldn't do anything about Maria; she'd already survived longer than her oncologist had predicted. And I couldn't do more than I already had for Frost. Evie and I had pushed and cajoled and then threatened Frost until he'd scheduled the cardiac cath. I didn't want to harass him, but I didn't want to lose him. He was pushing both of us away. He was irritable and angry, and he didn't look good.

Angel had asked the night of Janet's arrest why I had been in the coffee shop with Frost. The moment of truth had arrived.

"He asked me to meet him to tell me what he'd decided to do about his chest pain. He also gave me an update on Laura's case. I've been calling people for him and arranging interviews over the phone."

Angel had a slight frown on his face as we cleaned up after supper, but he didn't look upset. "What d'you think is going on with Frost? He looked like hell when he was interviewing Janet Casey."

I rubbed my temples, hoping to ease the headache I had. "He's probably got a coronary artery blockage of some sort. I've seen him rubbing his chest a lot lately, and I know he's having angina—chest pain—but he denies it. His color isn't great, and he's tired all the time. He says it's indigestion, but that's wishful thinking. His primary care doc would never have referred him to a cardiac doc if he wasn't worried."

"Or maybe the doc is just being cautious," Angel said.

"Maybe," I said.

"But you don't believe that."

"No, I don't."

Frost's cardiac cath would be performed the following morning at seven. I was waiting for a call from Simons. Although Frost was barely talking to either of us, Evie had convinced him to list me as an alternate person with whom the doc could discuss his current status and the outcome of the cath. She'd asked Simons to call me before the surgery and let me know what he thought was going on and what he planned to do.

When Simons finally called, my worry escalated. "I'm pretty sure he's got at least one significant blockage. I won't know which coronary artery it is or if more than one is involved until we do the cath and angiogram. If it's the left anterior descending then he'll need surgery, if it's one of the others I can probably stent it during the cath. If I stent him, he can go home later in the day. He can go back to work in a couple of days. If it's the LAD, he'll need surgery, and the recovery is quite a bit longer."

"Okay, thanks for calling. I'll be there tomorrow with his wife. Between the two of us, we can probably make him do what he's told to do. Might have to get him a shock collar."

Simons laughed. "I'd say that was a sure thing. He's pretty crusty and bullheaded. I'm glad you and his wife forced him to do this."

"I'm not having goddamn heart surgery!" Frost shouted in the outpatient post-op unit where he'd been taken after the cardiac cath.

The unit nurse came over to his cubicle with a frown on her face. "Mr. Frost—"

"DETECTIVE Frost," he snarled at her.

"Detective Frost," she began again, a frown line appearing between her brows. "Please try to relax; you're going to raise your blood pressure, which could cause bleeding at the catheter insertion site."

"I don't need to…"

I nodded at the nurse, who returned to the unit's desk area, and cut off his obviously annoyed response. "Listen to me, Frost. Do you want to leave Evie a widow? Do you want to leave your boys? I sure as hell don't want you to drop dead, and you will at some point. People don't usually survive an infarct of the LAD. You *need* this surgery."

"I got a right to decide what I'm going to do or not do." He'd lowered his voice, to avoid attracting the nurse's attention, but he hadn't calmed down by any means.

"Yeah, you do, but you've also got a lot of people who love you and need you alive, not buried in some damn cemetery."

Evie had talked to him until she'd lost it and stormed out a few minutes earlier, leaving me to deal with an angry, bullheaded cop used to being in the driver's seat. I watched the frown on his face and then noticed something I'd been too frustrated with him to see—he was afraid.

"Talk to me, Frost, *please*. Help me understand why you don't want to do this."

He folded his arms over his chest and glared at me, saying nothing.

"I'm staying until you talk to me," I said.

He raised his hands and held them against the sides of his head as if trying to keep it from exploding. "I can't be laid up for six weeks. I've got cases, responsibilities," he said.

"All of which would be reassigned until you're back. What's really bugging you?"

"Fuck you, Annie." He rarely called me by name, and I knew he was on edge.

"You can't, Angel's in charge of that. Besides, Evie'd kill you."

That got a laugh at last. "Jesus, you make me nuts."

"So, what's new? Tell me, Frost, please?"

He covered his eyes with the heels of his hands, lowered them to cover his face briefly, before dropping them into his lap. He stared at me, brows knit together, and said, "They'll force me to retire. They don't need some cardiac cripple dead weight on the team."

He closed his eyes, but not before I glimpsed the desperation. "They'll wait until I get back, let me have a few months, and then my lieutenant will diplomatically suggest it's time for me to retire and enjoy my pension."

I knew what the job meant to him, but I wanted him to know what he meant to all of us.

"Frost." I reached out and gripped his hand. "You won't be a cardiac cripple after the surgery; it'll fix the problem. You'll need to recover, and then you'll be back to normal."

He shook his head in irritation, and I tried another approach. "You were talking about retiring anyway. I know how important this job is to you, but you're more important. Evie needs you, your kids need you, and I need you."

He looked away from me but let me continue to hold his hand. "I'll help Evie take care of you when you get home and help get you back on your feet. While we're doing that, let's work out the bugs for this private investigation business."

He turned back to me. "You don't get it."

"Then help me get it."

"You can't...I can't...cops can't be..."

"Human? Vulnerable?"

He scowled. "They won't want me back, especially since it'd be open heart surgery. Six weeks, *nobody* is gone for six weeks. And it's not like this is a line-of-duty injury. That at least has some integrity to it. This"—he gestured angrily at his chest—"this is just getting old and falling apart."

I sighed, not really knowing if I was having any effect or making matters worse. "You're imagining all sorts of things that might not happen. You're a valuable detective. Your lieutenant isn't going to throw you out. My guess is she'll welcome you back."

"They won't want me back." He looked away from me and said, "Fine, let 'em do whatever they want. Maybe I won't wake up."

I pulled my hand out of his, grabbed his chin, and forced him to look at me. "If you go into surgery with that attitude you might not wake up." He said nothing. "Fine," I snapped. "Don't have the surgery, and when you drop dead, I will *never* forgive you."

I turned around and left him lying in the bed, alone. I made it to my car before I broke down and sobbed.

I had managed to stop crying by the time I got home. Now I was mad. When Angel got home, he brought the takeout he'd offered to pick up into the kitchen, where I was chopping salad veggies into minuscule pieces to keep from taking my frustrations out on glassware I wanted to smash.

After a few attempts at conversation that got him one-word replies, he took the knife out of my hand and leaned against the counter. "Annie, what's wrong?" Then, his eyes widening, he said, "Jesus, Frost didn't die, did he?"

"No, but he probably will," I snapped. "The *stupid*, bullheaded, pain in the ass doesn't want surgery—which he needs—and he says if Evie and I force him to have it, he…he hopes…he hopes he doesn't wake up."

I pounded my fists on the counter in frustration. Everyone has a right to make their own health decisions, but it was hard when it was someone close to you making a bad decision out of fear. I had worked in the OR long enough to be superstitious. If someone believed they were going to die or didn't want to wake up, they often didn't survive. I didn't want that to happen, but I knew Frost needed surgery.

"I talked to Evie a while ago." I made a face. "The doc decided to keep Frost overnight because he's been angry with Evie, me, and the staff, which has elevated his blood pressure enough that the doc wants to monitor him for bleeding at the incision site. Evie told the surgeon to schedule the procedure and she hopes to get Frost to agree to it."

I took a deep breath. "But I don't want him to have the surgery if that's how he feels about it. I don't know what to do."

Angel took me in his arms and held me as he talked and I cried. "Let's go over and I'll talk to him. Maybe I can knock some sense into him. Then I'll take you out for dinner."

"What about the takeout?" I asked, wiping tears off my face and blowing my nose with a soggy tissue as I watched him scoop the destroyed veggies into the garbage.

"We can have it tomorrow. It's Indian food, it's better the next day anyway, and you need a night out."

I gave him a watery smile. "Okay. Let me go wash my face." I got up and headed toward the bedroom.

"Where do you want to go for dinner, *chica*?" he asked, trying to lighten the mood as we headed out the door.

"I want Italian. Somewhere that serves wine, pasta, and tiramisu. Lots of all of it."

"You got it."

We arrived at the hospital's twenty-four-hour-stay unit, and I stood outside the door to Frost's room to eavesdrop while Angel talked to him alone. I listened to him tell Angel all the reasons why he didn't want to have the surgery.

There was silence when he finished. A few moments later, I heard

Angel's voice. I had to smile. The pause was the lawyer thinking before he spoke, planning his attack on an unsuspecting witness.

"That's understandable, but you're not thinking this through clearly."

I heard Frost snort.

"You're not. Think about it. If I know Annie at all, she's going to march into your lieutenant's office and talk your boss into threatening to fire you if you *don't* have surgery. You know how bullheaded she is, she's as bad as you are."

Silence was Frost's response, and Angel continued. "If that doesn't worry you—and it would me—I'd like you to think about how not having the surgery will affect the people who love you. I'm going to be selfish here and not even address how painful it will be for your kids and your wife when you drop dead. My concern is for Annie."

Silence reigned.

"She loves you, Frost, you're like her father now, that's how much she cares about you. There are two important people in her life, aside from me, and that's you and my grandmother."

I heard Angel clear his throat and knew talking about his grandmother was hard.

"*Abuelita* is dying and there's nothing we can do about it," he said. "But you, *you* can have surgery and be there for your family and Annie. You think about that, you stubborn bastard, and you make the right decision."

I heard a chair pushed back and assumed it was Angel getting up.

"Think about it overnight; then let the doctor know what your decision is. If you continue this bullshit about having surgery and not waking up, I swear I'll come over and tear your heart out for putting Annie and your family through this, and it'll be a moot point whether you have surgery or not."

I heard Angel's footsteps approaching the door when Frost said, "That'd be killing a police officer, dipshit. Not something you want to do."

"It'd be payback for getting Annie involved in *your* shit, and it'd be justifiable homicide. No one who knows you would arrest me," Angel said.

NINETEEN

DON'T KNOW WHAT CONVINCED FROST, being badgered by his wife and me or Angel's talk, but he agreed to the surgery. The doc had scheduled the procedure in the hope that he'd agree to it. A week later I stood in the pre-op area with Evie, his boys, and Angel. I waited until his family had had a chance to hug him and Angel herded them to the waiting area. He glanced back at me.

"I'll be there shortly." I took Frost's hand and said, "You swear to me that you intend to wake up."

"I plan to wake up. I'm tired of listening to you people. Let's get this over with. I'll see you when it's done."

He looked a little frail in the hospital gown with the IV hanging at the head of the gurney, but hospital gowns tend to diminish people. I hadn't been this apprehensive since Maria's surgery.

"Swear to me, say it and mean it."

"I swear, Annie, I swear. Stop worrying."

"Okay, then. See you later." I leaned over and kissed his forehead, which made him blush, and motioned for the nurse to come and get him.

The surgery was a success according to Simons. Frost had a few minor setbacks post-op, and he went home almost a week later than planned, but all in all, he did well. He was glad to get home. He didn't feel good yet and was depressed; for him the setbacks and his postoperative weakness were a death knell for his career.

"The first few weeks are rough," I said. We were sitting in his living room. I'd come over to relieve Evie and allow her some time off. "The doc told you to expect that, and you had a few issues post-op. You're getting better."

"Not as far as I can see. Hell, when Evie makes me walk and do the exercises, it wears me out," he grumbled. "I wish I hadn't had the surgery. It would've been better to drop dead of a heart attack than feel like this."

I sighed and shook my head. The man could drive a saint to drink, but I understood why he felt the way he did. "It'll get better, I promise. And in a few more weeks, you'll be ready to go back to work."

He glared at me. "Yeah, right."

Three weeks after his discharge from the hospital Frost was feeling better and was more optimistic. I wasn't stopping by or calling daily, but I came over on my days off, mostly to give Evie a break. Because he was feeling better, he had more to gripe about, and Evie took the brunt of his frustration. I remembered being in that position when Angel had been recovering. On bad days, you tended to fantasize about killing them in creative, painful ways.

"Look, Paul Roberts told me he's been updating you on where Talbot is with the Laura Hutchinson investigation," I told Frost. "He's taken over your other cases and he'll help on this one, if needed. You're covered, relax."

"I guess."

"Alex, stop, you need to take it easy and not get all wound up," Evie said. She'd handled him thus far, but her patience was running out.

He glared in her direction, then lowered his voice. "I want out of the house, I'm going nuts," he said. "The surgeon won't let me drive, and I need your help. If the doc doesn't tell her it's okay for me to do something, she won't even discuss it." He looked at me with utter disbelief and whispered, *"She hides the car keys, for God's sake!"*

I wasn't very successful smothering a laugh.

"Wipe that smile off your face. It's like having Nurse Ratched taking care of me."

"I heard that," Evie said with an annoyed expression on her face. Frost glared at her.

"How are you feeling?" I asked.

"Fine. Up walking around like normal now, the doc says I'm doing good." He frowned and pointed in Evie's direction. "She's supervising the exercise program and the cooking. You wouldn't believe the food I have to eat."

He rolled his eyes. "I've never had as many fucking vegetables in my life, and it's all low salt, for God's sake—who eats food with *no salt*? And decaf coffee, Christ Almighty, that's cruel and unusual punishment. I can't wait to get my hands on a burger and fries."

I shook my head. "I think you like upsetting me and Evie. You're such a pain in the ass."

He glowered at me and then assumed a pleading look that would have put a puppy's best efforts to shame. "Could you at least take me out for a drive?"

I looked at Evie and raised my eyebrows. "Okay with you?"

"As long as you don't take him somewhere he can get a burger and you don't take him by the precinct."

"Jesus, Evie, you're killing me here."

"When you're back to work you can do that for yourself. I'm not doing it for you."

"See what I mean?" he asked. The incredulous expression on his face was priceless.

"It's cold out, so bundle up," I said, standing up and putting my coat on. They both needed a break.

Sure enough, despite what Evie had said, he tried his best to talk me into driving to McDonald's or Burger King, and when that didn't work, he begged to be taken by the precinct.

"No, Frost, I'm not doing it. You can talk to Roberts and Talbot over the phone if you need to."

Frost frowned. "I talked to Talbot," he admitted at last. "She finally connected with Eric, the friend of Bret's who saw Laura with that guy in the park. He's working with a sketch artist to create a drawing of the guy. Once she has it, she's going to talk to the parents again and see if they recognize the person in the drawing.

"Paul's finishing up the interviews with the people on my list, but he and Adams got hit with a couple new cases, so he's been pretty busy. I don't know, it feels like everything's stalled, and I can't ride herd on it. I don't like being out of the loop."

"I know you don't, but Paul and Talbot are filling you in."

"I still don't see why going by the precinct would be such a big deal. I swear, between you and Evie…I was going to say there's no point in living, but I don't want you all jacked out of shape."

"That's good to hear." I drove to a coffee shop near their home and parked. "Tell you what, I'll buy you one small cup of regular coffee and let you check in with Paul while we sit here. One cup of regular coffee won't kill you. Will that appease you?"

His eyes lit up. "That'll do it kid, thanks."

We got out of the car, and he added, "Don't tell Evie, okay?"

TWENTY

IT WAS OUR THIRD CHRISTMAS AS A COUPLE. In Angel's family, Christmas was a big event—make that a huge event. No one escaped and everyone was expected to participate. Angel's mother, Sophia, always laid claim to Christmas Eve. She spent days cooking and cleaning and wrapping gifts and fussing about how much work there was left to do. I'm hopeless as a cook. I can intubate a patient and probably take your appendix out, if there is no one more qualified to do it, but I can't cook to save my soul. And still, she managed to rope me into helping.

The day before the big Christmas Eve celebration, she insisted I come over and pitch in. I was family now; the honeymoon period had expired. No excuse would get me off the hook. By the end of the day, I was very glad to get home. I hadn't let anything burn, I hadn't burned myself, and the packages I'd helped wrap met with Sophia's approval. That seemed like a win to me.

"How'd things go, *chica*?" Angel asked when he came home that night. He looked a bit guilty. He'd managed to escape his mother all week long and had left me to deal with her.

"I didn't kill her, she didn't kill me, no cookies burned, and none of the stuff I was asked to stir or help with was ruined. Not bad, all things considered."

He grinned and joined me on the couch as I offered him a glass of wine.

"You owe me big time, dude. It was like being in the Marines. She's a real drill sergeant."

"Yeah, she loses her mind over Christmas."

"You managed to escape today, but she has plans for you tomorrow."

He groaned. "Now what?"

"Moving furniture, setting up tables, making liquor runs, that kind of stuff."

He blew out a breath and ran his hand through his hair. "No escaping it. When are we supposed to arrive?"

I told him, and we cuddled on the couch for a while before I heated up some of the tamales and green chili Sophia had sent home. She sent food over regularly, fearing her firstborn would starve if he had to survive on my cooking. He wouldn't starve, it just wouldn't taste as good as what she sent.

We put off going over to Angel's parents' place until mid-afternoon, spending the morning with Frost and his family. Frost was feeling better but was bored and driving everyone nuts. Going back to work couldn't come soon enough for Evie.

Christmas Eve was in full swing by the time Angel and his brother, Martín, had carried card tables in from the garage and his sister Gabriela and I got them decorated. Kids were running around like maniacs, and Angel's father had roped several of the older men into a poker game liberally lubricated with alcohol. It was a Christmas Eve tradition. Angel had warned me not to let his father talk me into playing. Sophia was in her element, harassing everyone, and running the kitchen like Gordon Ramsey minus the profanity.

I was happy to see Paul arrive. It gave me an excuse to escape Sophia's clutches. I wasn't sure Paul would make it. We'd brought Gabriela with us because he'd been called to a crime scene early that morning, and it was anyone's guess how long he'd be occupied with that. A smile lighted her face from across the room when she saw him. He tossed her an air kiss and mouthed, "Hi, beautiful."

"Hey, Annie, how's Frost?" Paul asked, giving me a hug.

"How do you think he is? He's like a caged bear."

He grinned and took a drink from the beer Angel's brother had handed him in passing. "He's been on the phone with me or Talbot at least a couple times a day. He might as well not be on sick leave; he's working from home."

"Yeah, he's driving his wife nuts, too. But that's Frost."

Paul took a swig of beer and said, "I'm not sure if you know Blake Halloran, he consulted with Frost about a case that's pretty bizarre. Multiple murders of prostitutes and a woman he thinks may have been assaulted by the killer. She survived, but is amnesic. The case depends on her remembering, so it's stalled for all intents and purposes. That should give Frost something to do."

"At least he's nearly ready to return to work. It can't happen too soon. It'd be a shame if Evie kills him, kind of a waste of surgery," I said.

Paul snorted a laugh. "Yeah, I'd like to kill him, so I imagine it's worse for her. Half the time I don't answer my phone when he calls. If I answered every call, I wouldn't get anything done."

He took another drink of beer and caught Gabriela's eye across the room, smiling at her. "Frost filled me in on the Hutchinson case he and Talbot caught. I've been touching base with her, helping out where I can. Weird case."

"Yeah, it's odd all around," I said.

"She got the drawing of the guy supposedly talking to the victim and has been showing it around to the people Laura knew; but so far, no one knows him or will admit to it and no one's seen him around lately."

"They never solved the original assault case." I took a drink of my wine. "I think the two cases are related. I think Frost does too, but you know him, he doesn't jump to conclusions."

"That's not a bad thing; it keeps you from making mistakes." He took a sip of beer. "Heard you got the person responsible for the arson murder case."

"I didn't get her; she found me. But it's solved, so that's good."

I looked at all the smiling faces, Angel's frazzled mother, the sugar-crazed kids, half-tipsy male relatives slapping down cards and hooting when they won a hand, and said, "It's Christmas. Let's talk about all this later."

He nodded and let the topic drop beaming a smile as Gabriela made her way across the room to join us. His mind was clearly on more pleasant subjects than murder.

We declined going to midnight mass, and I saw Sophia trap Angel in the kitchen, speaking rapidly in Spanish and waving an index finger in his face. She nearly stuck it up his nose at one point, causing him to rear back and catch her hand in his. No doubt a lecture about church.

"Are we in the doghouse for not going to mass?" I asked on the way home.

Angel huffed out a breath and frowned. "To paraphrase, she said that if I wanted to go to hell, that was my choice, although it would break her heart. In her opinion, now that I'm married and children will be coming, I need to get in the habit of going to church to set a good example for them."

He shook his head in exasperation. "I pointed out that there were no children on the way and might not be for a while, or ever, but that didn't stop her."

I could see the frown settle on his face. Angel had always had a strained relationship with his mother, for good reason. As far as her children were concerned, their lives were hers to orchestrate. Her eldest son had never taken to that.

"She told me I should be in church, thanking God he saved me and that I was alive. I told her that I was alive because of you, and God had nothing to do with it."

I cringed. "That was probably the wrong thing to say to your mother. And if it weren't for me, you wouldn't have been shot in the first place."

Angel snorted. "That's true." He reached over and stroked my face. "I will always regret that I couldn't protect you."

I held his hand to my face and smiled. "I know you would have if it had been possible. Don't take that on, Angel."

He returned his hand to the steering wheel. "She kept going on and on about kids—why weren't you pregnant, when were we going to give her grandchildren, the usual—so I told her that as far as babies were concerned, when or if we had them wasn't up to her and she needed to back off. That's when I almost got the finger lobotomy."

"Yeah, I bet that went over like a lead balloon."

"I don't care. She's on my case about kids every time I talk to her. I told her the other day to give it a rest. We'd have kids when it suited us, or not, and it wasn't any of her business. She's not happy with me."

"My guess is, we're both in the doghouse now." If I knew anything about Sophia, now that Angel had proven uncooperative, she'd start in on me.

He made a face and drove in silence for a few moments. "Being in the doghouse might not be a bad thing," he said at last. "Maybe she'll leave us alone. She wears on me, and I'm fed up with her pushing and pestering and trying to run our lives. She badgered Martín and Claudia into having kids sooner than I think they would have if she'd left them alone. I'm not letting her do that to us."

"She probably won't let up. She thinks we have an obligation to give her grandkids."

"Too bad. If we have kids, that's going to be our decision, not hers." He drove up to the triplex and parked.

We'd talked about kids. Sort of. He knew I wasn't altogether sold on the idea—not opposed to it, I liked kids, I just wasn't sure I was mother material. I worried that my hesitation was putting as much pressure on him as his mother was, just in the opposite direction.

"We've never really talked about kids, not seriously. Do you want them?"

He shrugged his shoulders. "I don't know what I want right now except a chance to actually enjoy being alive and not have to worry about that lunatic Patterson killing one of us. Or something happening to you," he added, glancing in my direction.

He pulled the keys out of the ignition and then turned to me. "I'd love to have kids with you one of these days, but if I had to choose between you and kids? I'd choose you every time. I'm in no hurry to share you with anyone, not even a baby, so relax."

Getting out of the car and gathering up the presents and the food that we'd been sent home with, we made our way carefully toward our front door over the icy sidewalk.

"We may have to move somewhere far away. You know how your mother is when she's got an agenda."

"You could shoot her, I suppose," he said. I glanced at him and saw the grin on his face.

"For God's sake, don't say that to anyone likely to repeat it to your mother."

I waited as he maneuvered the key into the lock and opened the door. He held it open and allowed me to pass with the bags I was carrying as he brought his in off the front porch. After he'd abandoned the gift bags by our tiny tree in the living room, he shrugged out his coat and removed mine dropping both on the nearest chair.

Carrying the food containers to the kitchen, I said, "She hasn't said anything about kids to me, at least not directly. A few unsubtle hints about babysitting for our kids someday, but nothing overt."

"She's scared of you, *chica*."

"Oh, she is not. Your mother isn't scared of anyone," I said as I put the food packages in the fridge.

"She's scared of you. You're a nurse, you got me to marry you, and you saved me from dying twice. She can't compete with that. You're a scary lady, *Corazón*."

I laughed. "And you're full of it. Besides, I didn't get you to marry me, you talked me into marrying you."

He walked up behind me in the kitchen and wrapped his arms around me, drawing me against him as he nuzzled my neck.

I squirmed a little, laughing. "Your nose is cold, Santa."

"Wait till you feel my hands," he said, and began undoing buttons on my shirt. "Are you sorry I talked you into marrying me?"

Jesus, his hands were cold as he slid them down my belly and into the waistband of my slacks. He was doing knee-melting things to my neck with his lips and teeth and those talented, cold hands were warming up elsewhere. I had a hard time answering. "Uh…God, that feels good…no, I…don't stop…no, I'm not…sweet Jesus…not sorry."

He had magic fingers, and I realized that my shirt was unbuttoned, my bra undone, and somehow his shirt was lying on the floor.

"I want you," he whispered.

"I'm all yours," I said turning to him. He picked me up in his arms, cradled me against his warm chest, and carried me to our bedroom.

"Yes, you are," he whispered as we quickly shed the rest our clothes and he lowered me to our bed. "*Siempre mia, mi amor.*"

Maybe I should be the one in church thanking God that he's alive, I thought, treasuring the warm, contented weight of him on top of me. The reassuring beat of his heart comforted me as we moved together.

TWENTY-ONE

FROST HAD TALKED TO TALBOT and relayed what she told him. I was as curious as he was about what was happening. Based on photos the Hutchinsons had provided of Eleanor's brother, the sketch artist's drawing didn't look like him, and Talbot was convinced that whomever Laura had been talking to, it wasn't anyone associated with her earlier abduction or her death.

According to the report Paul gave him, despite not believing that Laura's earlier assault was connected, Talbot was being thorough and spending time interviewing the therapist who'd cared for her after the original abduction. That hadn't netted much as the therapist said Laura refused to talk about what had happened. It was her opinion that Laura might not have known who had been responsible.

Talbot was also tracking down and interviewing people currently associated with Laura, hoping that either someone would look like the guy she'd been talking to or knew who he was, or that someone would identify the supplier.

Frost had forwarded the email Talbot had sent him with the drawing attached to it, and I had printed a copy to keep. I mentioned to Angel the idea of calling Eleanor Hutchinson and meeting her for lunch in Evergreen, and he surprised me by not objecting. I wasn't sure what had or was changing, but I was grateful. Maybe knowing that I would talk to him about the case was reassuring.

The restaurant was in the original downtown Evergreen and said it offered comfort food. I got there early and staked out a table. It was a funky little restaurant, but the food on the menu sounded good. Eleanor arrived on time, and we ordered.

"Thank you for agreeing to meet me."

"My husband won't be happy if he hears about it. He thinks neither of us should speak to the police without a lawyer."

"Mrs. Hutchinson, I'm not a police officer, I just help Detective Frost periodically. Nothing you tell me could be used against you."

She frowned but nodded. "I want to know what happened to Laura. She was my only child, and she was carrying my only grandchild. I need to know."

I waited until the waitress had deposited our lunches and left. Then I pulled the copy of the drawing out of my purse and showed it to her. I wanted her to have a chance to speak up without her husband present. I didn't want him influencing her to conceal anything she might know about the man in the drawing.

"I know Detective Talbot showed this to you and your husband, but is there any chance he could be someone you know or used to know?"

She stared at it for a long time, her eyes tracking over the drawing. Drawings made from witnesses' memories never looked exactly like the person, but they can be surprisingly close depending on the witness. At last, she shook her head.

"I'm sorry, I don't. The detective wouldn't say, but is this the person who killed her?"

"Detectives Talbot and Frost don't know. It's a man Laura was seen talking to before her death. They're trying to identify him."

"When she showed it to us, I was relieved it wasn't Andrew or my brother."

"Did you think it might be either of them?"

She took a quick sip of her iced tea. "I'm ashamed to say that before I saw the drawing, I was worried it might be." She picked up her fork, looked at her food, and put it back down.

"I didn't *think* it would be Andrew, not really, but there was this tiny bit of doubt because of his relationship with Laura. Not for the original assault—he would never do anything like that. But I...I wondered if he'd run into her and...I don't know what I thought. I was just glad it wasn't him.

"I was more worried that it was my brother. He'd been in trouble in the past. Not for sexual assault," she hastened to say. "He managed to get into trouble a lot, but again, I don't know why he'd come back now or why he'd kill her." She took a tiny sip of tea. "I haven't seen or heard from Jim since he left. That was right before Laura disappeared. I don't know where he is or whether he's even alive."

She stared at her food. "I shouldn't have ordered anything, I'm not really hungry."

She looked thinner than the last time I had seen her, and I could only imagine the distress she was in.

"Mrs. Hutchinson, what you've gone through, is hard for me to imagine. It must be horrible, but Laura's friend stressed that your daughter loved you. She wouldn't want you to make yourself sick."

She began to cry silently. I reached out cautiously and laid my hand over hers. "Do you have anyone to talk to?"

"Not really. Andrew is upset about all of this and doesn't want to talk about her. Laura never liked him. He won't admit it, but that hurt him. We couldn't convince her that he hadn't somehow caused the divorce between me and her father. He felt that was the cause of her rejection of him and for her behavior later on. At that point he withdrew and distanced himself from her and the embarrassment." She slipped her hand out from under mine and dabbed at her face with her napkin.

"I can get contact numbers for a support group for parents of murdered children. You'd have a group of people to talk to who know what you've been through. It might help."

She nodded and without looking up at me said, "Maybe the support group would help. I doubt anyone who hasn't lost someone to murder, especially a child, could understand."

"I'm sure that's true. I'll get the information for you."

I could relate to having someone you cared about murdered, but I had never lost a child. I couldn't begin to imagine what that would feel like. I hoped I'd never have to.

"Laura disappeared from your yard. That makes me wonder if it was a neighbor or someone nearby who abducted her. Does that drawing remind you of anyone in the neighborhood, even vaguely?"

"No, but the lots in our subdivision are pretty large, and neighbors aren't close. It's not like a normal neighborhood; people aren't all that friendly. We've lived here since Laura was seven, and I only know a couple of them, plus many of them move in and then move out. Andrew and I aren't overly social."

I was out of questions, and she was out of answers. She picked at her food for a while and then pushed back from the table and fumbled with her purse, pulling out a twenty.

I held up my hand. "Please, I'll pay for lunch, it's the least I can do."

She offered a strained smile and made her way out of the restaurant. I watched through the window as she walked up the sidewalk and disappeared around the corner of the building. After finishing my lunch, I sat in the car and called Paul Roberts.

"Paul, is it possible for you or Talbot to find out who lived in the subdivision where Laura's parents live when she first disappeared as a child, and whether they still live there?"

"Probably. It'll take some work. Why do you want to know?"

"The drawing of the guy Bret Martin's friend described to the sketch artist doesn't look like either Laura's stepfather or her uncle, and from what Talbot told Frost, none of Laura's friends look like him or recognize him. I'm wondering if he could be a neighbor."

I turned the car on to get the heater running and continued, "Laura never identified her abuser, but her parents said her behavior had changed in the months before her abduction. You know pedophiles, they often groom their victims and her behavior makes me wonder if she wasn't being abused before she was abducted. If so, whoever was abusing her had to be someone close, maybe someone her parents or she knew, maybe the father or brother of one of her friends at the time. Her mother said that people move in and out of the subdivision a lot. We'd have to find the neighbors who lived there back then. I don't know how to do that."

I heard him sigh. "We've been pretty overwhelmed with Frost out. We've prioritized the urgent stuff; everything else is kinda on the back burner."

"It was just an idea. If I knew how to do it, I wouldn't ask."

"It's okay, I'll see if I can find somebody to at least get started on it. If something comes up, though, the person will get pulled."

"How about asking Frost? He's bored out of his mind."

"That's not a bad idea. I'll give him a call."

I had a brief flash of inspiration and returned home. I Googled support groups and came up with a phone number for a parents of murdered children group. I called Eleanor Hutchinson.

"Mrs. Hutchinson, I have that support group contact information," I said. "I hope you'll at least go to one meeting and see if it would help."

"I will. I appreciate the information."

"While I have you on the phone, can you to give me the names of Laura's friends at the time of her abduction? It'd be helpful to speak with them and their parents. They may know who the man in the photo is."

I hesitated. "He could be a sibling who might know something about what happened."

She was silent for a few seconds. "We'd only lived in the house six, maybe seven months. Laura hadn't made more than one or two friends. It'll take me some time to gather that. Can I call you back?"

"Of course. Thank you for helping."

"She's my daughter. I would do anything to help find the person who killed her."

The original detectives probably had interviewed a lot of people; certainly they would have canvassed the neighbors. Maybe they couldn't find anything incriminating back then, but they didn't have the drawing that we had now. Even if Laura's death wasn't connected to her abduction, I was sure that finding the guy in the drawing was the key to what had resulted in her death.

TWENTY-TWO

THE PRIVATE PSYCHIATRIST ANGEL RECRUITED had finalized her evaluation and ruled Janet incompetent. She'd diagnosed her with schizophrenia with hallucinations and psychosis. Janet had been diagnosed with schizophrenia several years before but had stopped taking her meds and the rape had triggered the psychosis. The psychiatrist wasn't convinced Janet could understand her culpability or the legal process.

The Judge remanded Janet to the state psych hospital in Pueblo for the court evaluation. The psychiatrists at the hospital would send a report to the court and, if they declared Janet incompetent, she'd stay there until they believed she was no longer a danger to herself or others. Angel didn't discuss the particulars, but he seemed at least somewhat hopeful.

Several weeks later, the evaluation period for Janet ended and the court had ordered that she be kept at the hospital for treatment. It seemed like the best situation, but it was a sentence that could last as long as a prison term. Angel reminded me of John Hinckley, who had only been released after a stay of thirty-five years and was still under court jurisdiction, meaning the court could send him back if he violated the conditions of his release. The only redeeming feature was the possibility Janet would be released at some point, and she was getting the psych care she needed.

I sat at my desk in the bedroom we used as an office and stared at a copy of the police artist's sketch. The drawing was not a guy you'd remember—average features, nothing to attract attention—like a chameleon, he'd be able to blend in and go unnoticed. The guy in the sketch was late twenties, early thirties. At the time of Laura's abduction, he would have been high school age, old enough to sexually assault her, and now old enough to murder her.

Frost called to say he was working on finding the people who had lived near Laura's parents and that he'd let Paul know what he found. "Thanks for asking him to give it to me. It's keeping me out of Evie's hair."

"I'm sure that's a relief for her. Maybe these people might recognize the guy if Paul shows them the photo."

Maybe.

It had been several days since I had talked to Eleanor Hutchinson, and I had heard nothing. I hoped she'd come through. The abduction case file listed the names of neighbors and school friends' families and the interviews the police had conducted, but there were no photos of them. I sent Frost the original list of names, hoping he could find out who still lived in the subdivision; maybe some of the people originally interviewed would still be around. If so, it might be possible to eliminate or establish a connection to Laura's abduction, and, if we were lucky, help identify the guy in the drawing.

I had Googled the names of those on the original list of interviews. I looked specifically for those who no longer lived in Colorado. I checked out their social media accounts, if they had them. Some were private, but most of the women's accounts were public and allowed me to view photos of family members. None of the photos matched the drawing.

"Who are you?" I asked aloud, studying the drawing. "And what did you say to upset her?"

The ringing of my phone jarred me out of my thoughts. "What's up, Paul?" I asked, seeing Roberts's name on the caller ID.

"Frost found a few of the people still living in that subdivision when Laura first went missing—one lives a mile or so from the parents. I talked to Talbot, but she's tied up on another case. I'm going to head up there and talk to them. Are you free to come?"

"You're asking me to go with you? I'm surprised."

"I'm not taking you with me on the interview. You'll have to sit in the car. I'd like your company, though. I've got some things— personal stuff—I wanted to talk to you about. I've been so busy I haven't seen much of Gabriela, or anyone else outside of work, so I figured this would give us some time to talk."

"I'll come."

The ride was quiet until we got on westbound I-70. "What did you want to talk to me. about?"

Paul rubbed at his eye, pushing his sunglasses up as he did. "How's Frost doing? I mean, is he going to be able to come back?"

"Yeah, why?"

"I wanted to know. I heard a couple of the crew talking about his surgery and the setbacks he had. The rumor is he won't be fit enough to come back. I talked to Halloran. He said Frost looked okay to him when he was there. I wondered what you thought, being a nurse and all."

So, Frost's fears about his job had been real. I shook my head and bit back the angry response I was thinking. "He'll be fine. He's feeling good, and when he comes back, he'll be good as new."

"Really? You're not just saying that?"

"Paul, what're you worried about? Whether he comes back or not is up to his doc and the lieutenant, not public opinion."

He shook his head. "Public opinion can make a big difference around the department, around police in general. They'll watch him and anything that goes wrong, any screw-ups, will be attributed to him not being able to do the job because of his heart."

He took the Evergreen exit off I-70 and continued. "Nobody wants to be unsure of a partner or fellow detective who's supposed to have your back. It's a macho culture—you have to man up whether you're a man or woman on the force. Men don't get sick; they take care of business. It's a stupid attitude, but it's real."

He drove for a few miles, then said, "I'm worried about him coming back too soon. I don't want him coming back until he's a hundred percent. Maybe a hundred and fifty percent. Halloran's comments have helped, but…" He shrugged. "You know how it is."

I watched him while my temper went from simmer to boil. "So, his fellow officers are going to decide if he stays or not, based on their medically uneducated opinions and prejudices. What bullshit."

"It is, but I'd like to be able to counter that with some positive news about him, maybe put a stop to the speculation. That's why I asked."

"You can tell any jerk who suggests Frost isn't up to the job that he's fine. His recovery is on schedule, and he feels good—better than before, actually, because his heart is getting the blood flow it needs to work properly. There's no reason he won't come back or be able to do the job. Or send them to me, and I'll tell them."

"Yeah, that's probably not a good idea. I don't want them getting hurt."

I gave him a tight smile. "It'd be over quickly, and OR nurses know how to deal with dead bodies."

"Please, let me handle it." He glanced over at me with a worried look on his face. "Please?"

TWENTY-THREE

WE MADE OUR WAY THROUGH BERGEN PARK and turned into the Hutchinson's subdivision. There were three homes on the list to visit. Paul drove up the long drive to the first house and parked in the turnaround area.

"Promise me you'll tell me what they said?" I asked as he shrugged into his jacket and grabbed his briefcase from the back seat of the car.

"I told Talbot I'd record the interview since I'd be there solo. You can listen to it when I get back."

I watched as he walked up the sidewalk to the huge front double door. The home was made of stone and stucco. It reminded me of Frank Lloyd Wright's Fallingwater, minus the waterfall. It was modern and spare lined, yet completely at home in the mountain subdivision. I saw Paul press the doorbell, and it took a few moments before a heavy, unhappy-looking woman opened the door.

She frowned and pointed to a sign near the doorbell, which I assumed was a "No Solicitation" notice and said something. She started to close the door, but Paul stopped it with his hand, then pulled his shield off his belt and held it out to her. She continued to frown but held the door open for him to enter and closed it, shutting off my view.

Thirty minutes later Paul returned to the car, a thoughtful look on his face. A tall, thin, expensively dressed man had walked Paul out the front door and shook his hand. He smiled and waved as Paul got in the car. He looked surprised when he saw me as Paul turned the car around and drove down the driveway.

"I don't think he expected to see me sitting in the car," I said, watching the man go back inside as Paul pulled out onto the road. "You don't look happy. How'd it go?"

Paul shrugged. "He was pleasant and cooperative. I don't know… take a listen," he said, activating his recording app.

"Mr. and Mrs. Lewis, I'm Detective Paul Roberts from the Denver Police Department, and I'd like to ask you some questions regarding a case we're handling. Because my partner couldn't come with me, I'm going to record this interview. If you object to that, or feel you need or want a lawyer present, then we can conduct a more formal interview at the precinct. Recording the interview is a precaution that protects me and both of you. Are you okay with that?"

"Go ahead, officer," said a man, who I assumed was the one I'd seen watch as we left. He sounded friendly enough.

"It's detective," Paul corrected him. "Here's my card. If you have questions or concerns after we're done today, you can reach me at that number."

"Is this about our son?" a woman asked. "He's an adult now, nearly thirty, and it's past time for him to grow up and stop expecting us to bail him out."

"I'm not here about your son's legal problems, Mrs. Lewis, I'm from homicide."

"Has he been killed?" she asked, anxiously.

"Not as far as we know."

"You scared me to death. What's this about then?"

"Your family lived here when Laura Hutchinson was abducted as a child. Your property isn't too far from her parents' home."

"Hutchinson?" she asked sounding puzzled.

"He's talking about the seven-year-old who went missing when

Mike was in high school and Kathy was in grade school," said the man. "Surely you remember the hullabaloo that went on, dear? They interviewed us."

"Oh yes, now I remember. The name didn't register. Is that what this is about? That was years ago."

I heard the man let out a sigh. "Really, darling, you need to watch the news. She's a young woman now, was a young woman. She was found dead recently. Is that what you're here about?" Lewis asked.

"Yes," Paul replied. "What d'you remember about her original disappearance?"

"It was terribly intrusive and chaotic for a while. Police showed up several times, interviewed all of us, including the children, and nothing came of it. The child returned home, but the family was essentially ostracized."

There was a pause, before he continued. "It was unfortunate, really. But because no one was charged, the speculation was rife. If memory serves, the papers said suspicion fell on the stepfather and the wife's brother, although according to the papers, he was no longer living with them. I seem to remember that the stepfather was cleared somehow. I don't remember all the details.

"Nonetheless," he continued, "parents didn't want their children going over to the house anymore and didn't want the girl in their homes to prevent her saying something to their children about what had happened. Although I don't believe she ever said anything about the experience."

"Regardless of what the girl remembered," said the woman, "keeping the family at arm's length was warranted in my opinion." Her voice grated on the ear.

"Why was that?" Paul asked.

"Who knew what might have gone on in that home? She and our daughter, Kathy, were classmates. Kathy had made friends with her before the previous school year ended, and she came over for playdates.

Kathy had been at their house several times as well. I put a stop to all of that after what happened. I didn't want Kathy in that house. I think other parents felt the same way." She paused. "Honestly, I don't know why the family didn't move. I would have. Why stay somewhere if everyone thinks you molested your stepdaughter?"

It angered me that she wouldn't call Laura by her name. Laura was just "the girl." I didn't think Mrs. Lewis was very bright, but perhaps she was just narrow-minded. I wondered how the man could stand being married to her. He sounded intelligent. A bit condescending to his wife, but I could see why.

Takes all types, I thought. No one knows what goes on behind the closed doors of a marriage, or what attracts people. Perhaps, when not being interviewed by a homicide detective, the Lewises were more compatible. Some pairings didn't make sense to anyone but those involved.

It occurred to me that perhaps she was the one with the money and leaving her wasn't an option he wanted to exercise. Once you're used to a certain lifestyle, the idea of halving it via divorce is unappealing.

"Was there any suspicion about other neighbors or anyone else in the community?"

"Not that I was aware of," the man said.

"I'd like you to take a look at this drawing." I heard Paul open his briefcase. "Do you recognize this person?"

There was a moment of silence during which I assumed he was showing them the drawing.

"No, it doesn't look like anyone we know, does it Charlotte?"

"I don't recognize him," she replied. "Who is it?"

"We don't know; he's a person of interest we'd like to talk to. We're trying to determine if Laura Hutchinson's abduction is connected in any way to her murder. We're interviewing everyone who was living in the neighborhood at the time to see if anyone can identify him."

I heard a rustle of paper and the snap of the closures on Paul's briefcase. "I'd like to speak to your son and daughter," he said. "If you'd provide their contact information, I'd appreciate it."

"Mike is out of town at the moment, he has been for a couple of weeks. I can give you his phone number. Our daughter lives in Denver," the wife said.

"I doubt if either our son or daughter can give you much information." Lewis said. "Kathy was the same age as the Hutchinson girl, and Mike was in high school. He rarely paid any attention to his sister or her friends." He sounded annoyed, though whether that was with Paul or his wife I couldn't tell.

"That's a fairly large age gap between siblings."

"My wife and I went through a period of infertility before Kathy came along." I could feel the deep freeze in his voice through the recording.

"Your wife said he was out of town now. Do you know where he is?"

There was a brief silence. "No. Neither of us knows where he is now; we had a serious falling out recently."

"So, you can't really be sure he's out of town, can you?"

"As I said, we don't know where he is."

The recording picked up sounds of people standing. "Thank you for your time, Mr. and Mrs. Lewis."

"Happy to help, detective," Lewis said.

"You have my card. If you think of anything or you talk to your son and daughter, please ask them to call me." The recording ended.

"What d'you think?" Paul asked.

"Lord, where do I start? He seemed helpful, pleasant, but he really didn't like the questions about the age gap between his kids. I don't think he likes talking about his son at all. And his wife? She just sounds narrow-minded and snotty."

Paul laughed. "Tell me how you really feel."

"From what I could see when he stood on the porch, he doesn't look like the drawing. That lets him off the hook for being the guy seen talking to Laura, but he's an odd duck—cooperative, but not warm and friendly. The way he looked at me as you were coming back to the car made me uncomfortable."

"I wouldn't worry, he probably just didn't like being questioned and wondered who you were."

I thought for a moment about what had bothered me most. "She never called Laura by her name, and he called her 'that Hutchinson girl.' Seems to me both of them wanted to distance themselves from her. He was cooperative but he sounded…I don't know cautious, I guess, when he answered your questions."

"Most people are when talking to cops. It was interesting," Paul said. "He gave her one of those little shoulder rubs when he first sat down next to her. He might have been doing it to reassure her or to signal her to let him do the talking. I think the wife lied about the son being out of town. He seemed irritated with her and then made sure I understood they didn't know where he was. I don't think they want me talking to either kid. I'm just not sure why."

"It'd be a good idea to talk to both of the kids, for that reason alone. They may be more willing to talk about the incident and may know more. They might know who the guy in the drawing is."

"Yeah, I'll talk to Talbot and let her know what I found out and see what she wants to do. I'm also going to investigate what kind of trouble the son has been into. Sounds like whatever it is, it's a chronic problem."

We'd been traveling down the subdivision's main road to our next destination, but instead of pulling into a driveway, Paul pulled over to the side of the road.

"Why are we stopping?"

"I wanted to talk to you about Gabriela."

"Are there problems?"

"No, not really."

"You're not going to break up with her, I hope. If so, you should put in for a transfer before Angel finds out about it."

He laughed. "No. Although to be honest, he wouldn't be able to come into the precinct and punch my lights out these days. No one would let him in the door now that he's defected to the defense side of things."

"You and Frost." I scowled at him. "You *know* Angel, he's family. He's a good man. You two need to stop thinking he's sold his soul to the devil. Not every client of a defense attorney is guilty."

Paul shifted uncomfortably. "A lot of them are, though. Dislike of defense attorneys is pretty ingrained in cops. It feels like they undo everything we work our asses off to do. I know Angel's a good guy. I just liked it better when he was on our side."

"Oh, for God's sake. Both of you want the bad guys punished and put away. He's just making sure people don't get railroaded." At least that's what Angel's goal would be. The problem for me, and apparently Frost and Roberts, was Angel would have to defend guilty people as well and try to get them acquitted. I hadn't adjusted to that yet, but I would defend Angel always.

"If you can't accept that or what he's doing then…never mind." He and Frost were family by now so they'd either accept the change or keep their opinions to themselves. He made no move to drive on. "What about Gabriela?" I finally asked.

"I want to marry her," he said.

"Why are you telling me? You should be asking her."

His voice faltered. "I don't know. . ." he said, tapping his fingers on the steering wheel. "I'm not sure if it's a good idea. She's eight years younger than I am. She's got a lot of years ahead of her to play and have a good time. I don't know if it's right to ask her."

"Do you love her?" He nodded. "Does she love you?"

"She says she does, but she's twenty-three. What does a twenty-three-year-old know?"

"What do any of us know, Paul?" I looked at him, exasperated. "But if there's anyone who knows what she wants or can take care of herself, it's Gabriela. She's grounded and mature for her age. Sometimes I think overly so."

I sat back in the car seat. "Now Marisol, she may be older chronologically, but she's incredibly immature and spoiled. It's funny; in the Cisneros family, Angel was the first boy and was badly spoiled, and Marisol was the first girl, and she was spoiled, too. Angel grew out of it, sort of. He still has a bit of that entitled attitude at times. But Marisol hasn't grown up or grown out of the sense of entitlement at all."

I paused. "If you were asking about proposing to Marisol, I'd tell you to wait a year at least, because by then, she'd be long gone. Gabriela won't be. If you love her, ask her. Life goes by too quickly to miss an opportunity to be with someone you love."

"Will Angel come after me?"

I laughed. "If you ask her to marry you and she says yes, he'll be fine with it. He mostly figures you'll screw around with her and then move on."

I watched him nod, a faint frown on his face, and I turned toward him. "I think that's because he behaved that way with women before we got together. To be fair, he had a reputation, so it seems to me women should have counted on him not sticking around. It's why I refused to get involved with him for as long as I did. He was never mean about it or cruel. From what I know, he was always honest about his intentions, or lack of them. But there were bound to have been some broken hearts. He doesn't want to see his sister hurt."

Paul nodded, and talking as if to himself, he said, "Okay. Okay, good to know. Thanks."

"If she says no and you break up? Transfer city, dude."

TWENTY-FOUR

PAUL GOT CALLED BACK TO THE STATION while we had been talking, and he wasn't able to interview the two remaining people in the subdivision. Talbot and Paul completed the interviews the following day. According to Frost, no one looked like the guy in the drawing, and no one remembered much more than the Lewises had or could identify the man in the drawing.

I was beginning to think the guy in the drawing or what the conversation had been about wouldn't be identified. I was trying hard to connect Laura's childhood abduction and her death, and it was probably wasted effort. Frost was most likely right; she'd been in the wrong place at the wrong time, and probably for the wrong reasons.

"Kid, it takes time to get to the bottom of these things. TV's made it hard for real cops 'cause everybody expects cases to be solved in a couple days. The first forty-eight hours are crucial, but a lot of them take longer. Sometimes a lot longer, and some never are solved."

Frost and I sat at the coffee shop near Frost's home. It had become my habit on my days off to give Evie a break and get Frost out of the house. The lure of a cup of caffeinated coffee never failed to cheer him up. He looked good to me, his color was back to normal, and he looked rested and healthy.

The cardiac surgeon would clear him to return to work in another week. He'd dropped some excess weight and, according to the doc, his cholesterol had returned to normal. Both Evie and I had tried our best to convince him it was the lack of fried foods and eliminating red meat that had done it, but he didn't believe it. I figured once he was out from under Evie's eagle eye he'd be back to cheeseburgers and fries. The man was perverse.

"Have Talbot or Roberts managed to find the Lewises' son?" I asked.

"They haven't had time, either of them. Paul was going to follow up on the son's arrest record, but both have had other cases dumped on them, so that's on hold. I don't know how much help finding him would be. He probably has no connection to the case. His parents said they didn't recognize the guy in the drawing. The case is kinda at a dead end at the moment."

I rubbed my eyes wearily; I was exhausted. The anxiety about Frost that'd I'd been carrying since his diagnosis and surgery had eased, but I'd been having weird dreams about Ian again. I'd dream he was standing at the foot of our bed watching me or sitting on the bed next to me, and I would jerk awake to find the room empty. Getting back to sleep after one wasn't easy.

The dreams seemed to come in waves, retreating until I figured they were a thing of the past, then roaring back and crashing over me. What I was experiencing was common with PTSD, my therapist, Donna, told me, and it might be some time before the dreams disappeared.

What had really unsettled me was that I kept thinking I saw Ian when I'd walk past the living room on my side of the joined apartments to get to my office area. A fleeting glimpse and then nothing. Once, I thought I could smell the aftershave he'd always worn. Sometimes the thick, coppery stench of blood hit me. I hadn't said anything to anyone, not even Donna, because I was afraid it was some sort of psychosis.

"Everything okay, kid?"

"I'm tired. I haven't been sleeping," I said automatically, as I had to Angel when he'd asked the same thing that morning. I took a sip of coffee. "This whole case is frustrating. I offered to talk to the Lewis girl over the phone for Paul and she wasn't much help. She didn't really want to talk to me at all. She said her mother cut off all her contact with Laura other than at school."

The story made me angry and sad, and as tired as I was, I was afraid I would burst into tears telling it. I was on a thin edge; it wouldn't take much to push me over it. By contrast, Angel seemed to be returning to normal. He was sleeping better, and the nights he prowled the house were infrequent now.

"The kids at school were wary of Laura, and basically did what the grownups did, they stopped having anything to do with her. Her kidnapper was never caught, now it looks as if her killer won't be either. At the moment, no one looks like the guy in the drawing," I said and yawned.

"The Lewises are odd, the oldest son is nowhere to be found, but the daughter had little to say about her brother. In fact, she didn't seem to want to talk about him or her family at all. I got the impression she was estranged from all of them, although she didn't say so. I texted a photo of the drawing to her, and she said she didn't recognize the guy. Then she said not to call her again."

"If you'd take me by the precinct for an hour or two, I could log into the system and research Mike Lewis's arrest records," Frost offered.

I frowned. I wanted to take him up on the offer, but I remembered Paul's comments and hesitated. I didn't want Frost going in until he was cleared to return. Even a small lag in his physical status might be seen by others as some confirmation that he wasn't going to cut it once back to work. And I didn't want him to know about Roberts's concerns.

Like any good investigator, though, he picked up on my unease. "What's up, kid?"

"Nothing, it's like I said, I'm discouraged. I don't want to screw up your recovery. I'm not taking you into the precinct until your doc clears you. Could you give me your log-in password so I could look up the arrest record?"

"No. They know I'm not there; I can't log in unless I am, and they'd know something was up. 'Sides, it'd be illegal, you're not a cop. Yet."

I made a face at him. "And I'm not going to be, I love my husband and I don't want him going postal on me. The PI angle is going to be a hard sell as it is. I guess I'll have to wait until Paul or Talbot get around to looking it up."

Frost watched me and then patted me on the arm. "Stop worrying, kid. I know what I'm up against at work. I haven't come up through the ranks all these years not knowing what goes on."

"What are you talking about?"

He cocked his head and raised his eyebrows. "There's talk, there always is when something like this happens to a cop. They're speculating about whether I'll be back to work or put out to pasture, like I told you before surgery."

I closed my eyes, fighting the urge to cry. "Yeah, there is. Paul talked to me. He was worried about you. I know you're doing fine, and Paul and Blake Halloran will put the word out, but I guess the rest of the department doesn't really."

"I feel good, better than before, and I'm glad you pushed me to do it," Frost said. "I'll be fine, and who knows? I might decide to retire anyway."

He finished his coffee. "I could take some time off, take Evie on some trips, have some fun. Then when you're ready to go into business with me, we'll do the PI thing."

"Is that what you want to do?"

"No, not right now. But if it shakes out that I have to, it'd be fine."

I looked dejectedly at him. "I wonder if Angel isn't right. He accused me of being a disaster magnet. Things never work out the way I figure they will, and somebody I love always gets caught in the mess. I'm sorry, Frost."

"Sorry? For what? You didn't cause the coronary occlusion." He laughed at that. "Been around docs so much lately I'm talking like them now."

He patted my hand. "It's not your fault, any of it. You helped Evie and me enormously. I don't think she'd have gotten through all this without you, and I probably would have refused the surgery and dropped dead on her. All in all, you did good."

"I guess. I hope your doc releases you to come back soon."

"Me too, I'm so fucking bored I could scream."

I laughed and it felt good. "I imagine you are."

"I can't tell you how relieved I was when Halloran brought that case of his for me to review."

"Paul told me a little bit about it."

"Interesting case. I'll let you read the file he brought me and see what you think. He's got an amnesic assault victim who he's pretty sure is connected to a string of homicides, only she can't remember squat. He asked me to read the file and give him some suggestions about where to go with it. I'm curious how that pans out."

"I'd love to see it."

We stood up and headed for the door. He held it open for me, grinned, and said, "Disaster magnet, huh? Never heard a better description of you."

TWENTY-FIVE

ELEANOR HUTCHINSON FINALLY CALLED WITH NAMES and contact information for Laura's grade school friends. It wasn't a long list.

"Laura was never good at making friends, even before she disappeared. After? She had no control over that. Children are both perceptive and cruel. Their parents, on the other hand, they were just cruel."

I heard her sigh. "The children knew that something 'bad' had happened to her. It might have been different if she hadn't been sexually assaulted, then perhaps they'd have seen her as someone who needed their support. I think they picked up on their parents' discomfort talking about it with them and probably overheard what had actually happened. You never know what kids hear. The result was they abandoned her, like the parents ostracized us."

"I'm curious why you didn't move. It can't have been easy enduring all the gossip and the isolation."

"It wasn't, but we stayed because Andrew refused to move. He had a good job— that's why we moved here originally—and he refused to allow the community to push us out. At least that's what he said. In actuality it had already happened. We were shunned. I wish we had moved. I think Laura would have been better off; perhaps we could have survived intact. Perhaps she'd still be alive."

"Have you been to the support group yet?"

She was silent. "Once," she said at last. "I told Andrew about it, I thought it might help him, too, but he doesn't want to talk about what happened or have anyone else know about it. He refused to go. In all honesty, it was torture listening to the other parents. My grief over Laura is too fresh. I probably won't go back, and I don't want to upset Andrew. He's grieving, too; he just handles it by not talking about it."

I blew out a breath and then decided what the hell. "Mrs. Hutchinson, I can understand why the support group might be too much right now; give yourself some time. I think it would help you, please give it another try when you're up for it. If it's that upsetting to him, he doesn't have to go. Take care of yourself, please."

"It's complicated. I don't know how long you've been married, sometimes it's hard for others to understand."

"I've been married and in relationships with others long enough to know that totally abdicating your needs for those of your partner's never works."

I found myself tapping the pen I held in my hand in frustration. Frost had really rubbed off on me. "Allowing one person to have control of the entire relationship isn't healthy or, in my experience, successful."

I wasn't really in a position to give marital advice, seeing as my marriage had been a bit precarious for a while. Angel and I were working things out, but it takes time. Regardless, my comment was met with silence. I knew this probably was falling on deaf ears, but I persisted.

"Mrs. Hutchinson—Eleanor—you need someone who understands what you've lost, this support group would provide that. He doesn't have to go. Please consider it, when you're ready."

"I will. I appreciate you wanting to help." She disconnected.

If she'd countermanded some of those decisions, I thought, *Laura might still be alive.* Then I sighed. *Or maybe not.*

Laura wasn't alive, and neither Andrew nor Eleanor Hutchinson was likely to change, not at this late date.

⁓

The talk with Eleanor Hutchinson had revived my anxiety over Angel. Life had settled down, but I spent my days taking deep breaths periodically, hoping to ease the weight on my chest and relieve that sinking feeling that wanting to work with Frost would cost me my marriage. Was I forcing my needs on Angel just as Andrew Hutchinson had forced his on Eleanor? I hoped not.

Angel seemed okay with what I was doing recently. I wasn't sure, though, that we had permanently resolved anything. For all the unsolicited advice I'd given Eleanor Hutchinson, Angel and I hadn't talked about what that resolution might be. We'd just allowed things to settle.

I had given him the names of several therapists after I first brought the subject up. He'd taken the list, nodded, and stuffed it in his jeans pocket without comment. I had no idea what that meant, but my mind kept providing explanations that only increased my anxiety.

"I've been thinking," Angel said that evening after coming to bed.

"What about?"

He spooned up against me. It was the first real contact we'd had in nearly two weeks. He'd been busy, and I'd been working late nights at the hospital. My heart began to race and not from arousal. Curled up against me as he was, it was clear sex wasn't on his mind, either. The recent loss of that easy, mutual sexual connection had left a hole in my heart. The attraction was still there, but the "easy" had disappeared. What if that couldn't be repaired? When that question arose, I ruthlessly shoved it underground again, hoping we'd find our way.

"Have you ever thought about moving?" he asked.

"Moving? Moving to another house?" This was not what I had imagined he had been thinking about.

"Yeah." He kissed my shoulder and pulled me closer.

"What brought that on?"

"I've been talking to that therapist, the referral you got from your therapist."

I closed my eyes and said a silent thank-you, not sure who I was thanking, but grateful, nonetheless. "I'm glad to hear that," I said softly, my eyes pricking with tears.

He was quiet for a bit, then said, "I think my...concern for you is because I can't stop thinking about what happened, how close we both came to dying. Sometimes, when I walk past the living room on your side of the apartment? I see Ian, pointing that gun at you, knowing that he would hurt you, that there was nothing I could do about it."

They were frightening memories that we both tried unsuccessfully to suppress. Suppressing things like that was never good, as Donna frequently reminded me, but remembering them left me drenched in cold sweat, my heart hammering.

"His energy, or whatever, is still here. There are too many reminders here."

"So, you want to move?" I wasn't sure what I thought of that idea.

"I've given it some time, thinking that maybe all that shit would ease or go away. It's eased, but it hasn't gone away. I dream about him and...things replay for me, sometimes when I least expect it. The therapist is teaching me how to deal with it, but things trigger me."

He tightened his arms around me. "Maybe the flashbacks have nothing to do with being here; maybe we'd both have them regardless of where we live. I don't know."

"What does the therapist think about our moving?"

"He's a therapist, you know how that goes. He thought it might help, but he also suggested that it might not, that it might be better to try to work it out first." Angel sighed. "Hell, who knows? It's just an idea."

"Moving might help." We were quiet for a few moments. "Would we have to sell the triplex to move?" I asked at last.

"We might. I'm not sure. Depends on what a bank thinks. If keeping it was doable, I could have my cousins take out the door between my old unit and yours; make them two separate ones again. We could rent them after we move out. If all three were rented, that'd pay the triplex's mortgage and I could up the rent a bit to be more like the current market. It'd be income property. But who knows?"

I turned toward him as he rolled onto his back. I lay my head on his shoulder and stretched my arm across his belly, feeling the scar as the sensitive skin of my arm brushed across it. *War wounds,* I thought.

"Another option would be for us to live on your side for a while and see if it helped," I said. "If it did, then we could have your cousin turn my side into a one-bedroom and your side would give us three bedrooms. If it didn't help, we could move."

"It's a thought," he said, absently playing with a lock of my hair that lay on his shoulder. It didn't sound as if he was totally on board with the idea, and the thought of Andrew Hutchinson refusing to move flitted through my mind.

Several minutes went by before he said, "I'm making good money now, and there's money in our savings account we could use for a down payment. Plus, there's that money that my parents gave us as a wedding gift. I'm going to talk to the agent who helped me find this place and see what's out there."

I sighed. "I like it here, but what happened preys on my mind, too." I thought about it in the silence that lay between us. "I see him," I said. "Just glimpses when I least expect it. It might help both of us to move."

"We don't have to decide right now, but I wanted to see what you thought about it."

"Look into it and then let's talk about it more seriously." I rubbed my cheek on his chest and let my hand drift down his belly. "Is seeing the therapist helping?"

"I don't know, mostly we just talk. Although he's given me some tips to short-circuit the flashbacks and taught me this weird tapping routine for the anxiety. I think it's helping. I'd prefer not to think about what happened at all, but I can't seem to stop."

"I don't think trying to stop the memories helps. Sometimes you just have to let them come and deal with it, but it's exhausting. If we moved, there wouldn't be that continual memory trigger."

He stroked my back and kissed the top of my head. "Just think about it, *Corazón*."

I dropped my hand lower and stroked him. "I will."

"Mmm, that feels good," he said.

I kissed him and nuzzled my face against his chest and took in the scent of him that I loved. I could feel the soft dusting of his chest hair under my cheek. I continued to stroke him and heard him sigh as he began to run his hands over me and started to roll me onto my back.

"No, let me," I said softly, as I straddled him.

I wished more than anything that I could erase what had happened to us; erase it and have a chance to enjoy our lives without the effects of Ian's chaos. I hoped we would be able to move past what had happened, eventually.

I leaned over and kissed him softly. He ran his hands through my hair and held my head as he opened his mouth to me and our kiss deepened. He let his hands drift down my neck and caressed my breasts as we continued to kiss and I lowered myself onto him. I moved slowly and surely as he gripped my hips and moved in rhythm with me.

"I will always love you," I said.

"*Siempre mia, mi amor.*"

Always mine, my love, he'd said. And he was always mine.

When the orgasm overtook us and had subsided, a sob welled up in me, and I broke down and cried in huge racking sobs against his chest.

He wrapped his arms around me tightly. "I've got you," he whispered into my hair. "I've got you, *Corazón*. We'll figure this out."

TWENTY-SIX

I TOOK IT UPON MYSELF to call the young women on the list that Eleanor Hutchinson had given me. Before his surgery, Frost had talked to Jayden Byers. Paul wasn't involved with Laura's case now because he'd been reassigned. I had no idea what Talbot was doing and couldn't ask. Neither she nor Frost knew about the list.

"I don't remember much. Gosh, I haven't thought about Laura in years."

"I assume you heard on the news about her death?"

Tiffany Blake was silent for several seconds. "No, I hadn't. I don't watch the news, it's too depressing. I'm sorry to hear that, though."

"Tell me what you do remember."

"We met in grade school. I think it was second grade. She came to the school after we returned from the holiday break. We weren't close friends—like you are at that age, friends one moment and then not for some stupid reason. Laura was shy, and it got worse after what happened to her. It happened pretty early in the new school year. We hadn't had a chance to become good friends before the end of the previous year, and we weren't after that."

She paused for few moments. "I don't think anyone handled it well. My folks wouldn't let me go over to her house or have her over. At school she was completely withdrawn, never spoke unless the teacher asked her a direct question. At that age you avoid kids like that, and we did. I didn't know until I was older what exactly had happened. By then there was no way to repair how we'd treated her."

"She ever talk about it?"

"No, she never talked about it to anyone that I'm aware of. She never really talked much at all after that, especially in grade school. By middle school, she refused to even acknowledge that it had happened."

"Did you have any idea who might have done that to her?"

"I didn't know what had happened other than her disappearance. And now? I can't even guess."

"I want to text you a photo of a drawing and see if you recognize the man in it."

She hesitated. "Okay," she said at last.

I sent the photo and waited. "Does it ring any bells?"

"Not really, I'm sorry, I don't remember anyone like that."

"We're trying to identify him. You don't recognize him at all?"

"No, I'm sorry." She paused then said, "Is this the guy who killed her?"

"We don't know, but it's possible."

"I'm deleting it. I don't want to see it again. It creates too much negativity."

"Well, thanks. If you remember anything, please let me know." I sighed. Too much negativity indeed.

"I can't put my finger on it, but he reminds me of someone," Kelsey Connors said after I sent her the photo.

"Someone you knew at the time, or someone you know now?"

"I can't say, honestly. And I don't know who he reminds me of, he just looks vaguely familiar."

"Would you think about it for a few days, maybe show it to your parents, see if they might recognize him?"

"Sure. Maybe my folks will know."

"I really appreciate your help. If you think of anything or they do, please call me right away."

"I will." There was silence on the line. "I liked her then. I was sorry for what happened to her, but I was a kid. I didn't know how to bridge the gap that my folks had caused by refusing to let me hang out with her, and I didn't want to make them mad by defying them. Later, when we were older, I was afraid to befriend her for fear I'd be treated like she was. Sounds pretty lame and selfish to me now."

"At that age, parents who are just trying to protect their kids make the decisions. And when we get older, we're heavily influenced by our peer group. There's no point in judging yourself for what you did as a kid. It can't be changed."

I wasn't sure whether Kelsey would call back with any other information, but it was encouraging that the drawing had sparked some recognition, vague as it was. Maybe there was a connection between this man and Laura's childhood assault. Now all we had to do was identify and find the guy in the drawing.

I met Frost at the precinct the following Monday to help celebrate his return. He'd brought donuts for the group. Donuts might be a cliché, but they were never turned down. The detectives present greeted him with back slaps and jokes, and it angered me because I knew that underneath all that happy horseshit, they were watching him and judging him. But he knew that, too, and had worked with these people for years. It might be okay in the end. He looked good and was happy to be back, and I was glad he was back.

"I've been talking to these girls that used to know Laura—"

"You what?"

"I…Eleanor Hutchinson gave me a list of Laura's friends from grade school."

"And you called them."

"Yeah," I said. The look on his face worried me, he didn't look happy. "Roberts and his partner have been totally overwhelmed with the cases they caught, and Talbot doesn't know I've been helping you with the cold cases, and you weren't here. I thought I could help."

"I should never have left you unsupervised."

"I don't need supervision. I just talked with them on the phone."

"How the hell did you get the list from Laura's mother?"

My face must have looked guilty based on the scowl on Frost's face. "I…um…met her for lunch, and we talked. She called me and gave me the names."

"Jesus fucking Christ. I don't know why you didn't become a cop years ago, but you're not. You need to let me or Roberts or Talbot handle this shit."

"None of you were available or able to help and I thought you didn't want Talbot knowing I was involved."

Frost sighed and rubbed a hand over his face. "What's done is done. What'd you find out?"

"Kelsey Connors thought he reminded her of someone, but she couldn't say who it was. She was going to show the drawing to her parents to see if they recognize him. Part of the problem is the drawing is of an adult. If he was involved in the abduction, he was quite a bit younger. He probably looked a lot different."

I huffed out a breath. "And we have no idea if he's connected to either the original incident or her murder. He could be someone she was selling drugs to and nothing more. He could be her supplier. Bret's trying to find out who the guy is, but I haven't heard from him."

Frost pinched the bridge of his nose. "Okay, let me know if he finds the guy. I'll talk to Talbot and tell her I talked to these women to keep both our butts from getting chewed. Gimme their names and numbers, and I'll follow up with them." He frowned at me and absently began rubbing his chest and my anxiety spiked.

"What's wrong? You're not having chest pain, are you?"

He grinned and stopped rubbing. "No, I'm not. That was payback for you being a pain in the ass."

"You...you..." I couldn't think of a word that was adequate. "Don't pull that again, Frost, or I swear to God if you drop in front of me, I'll walk away."

He laughed out loud at that. "Then behave yourself for a change."

TWENTY-SEVEN

THE FOLLOWING DAY, Frost came by the hospital. He'd texted and asked me if I could meet him in the cafeteria. When I got there, he waved some sheets of paper at me as I approached the table he'd claimed.

"Look what I found."

I took the papers and looked at the face staring up at me from an arrest sheet, the same face as on the drawing. "It's Mike Lewis," I said, reading the name on the arrest record.

"Yes, it is. Now all we have to do is find him." He had that look in his eye, like a dog who'd picked up a scent. If he'd had a tail, it'd be pointing straight up in the air, and he'd be staring in the direction of what he'd scented.

I thought back to the interview Paul Roberts had with the Lewises. "Frost, his parents must have known it was him the minute they saw the drawing—it's actually pretty spot on—yet they denied they knew who it was."

"I take it you went with Roberts when he talked to them, eh?"

I frowned. "I rode up with him, he wanted to talk to me about Gabriela. I didn't sit in on the interview, but he let me listen to the recording—in the car."

He rolled his eyes. "I'll talk to Roberts first, and then I'm going to call Talbot, and we'll bring the Lewises in for a formal interview. I don't like it when people lie during an investigation."

"Are you going to interview them together?"

He cocked his head at me and raised his eyebrows. "Yeah. I want to see the interplay between them. I suppose you want in on it?"

"I'd like to watch in an observation room, if possible."

"Yeah, you can do that. I gotta arrange the interview."

"They'll show up with legal representation, you know that. They'd be stupid if they didn't, and from what you say, the husband isn't stupid," Angel said. "It may be a struggle to get much out of them if their lawyer's any good."

"I'm sure they'll show up with an attorney. But Frost tells me Talbot has the magic touch in interrogations, he's going to let her take the lead. Maybe she'll get them to give the son up. That assumes they know where he is. They may not be lying about not knowing."

Angel and I were finishing dinner when I told him what was planned. I had kept him up to date about the case. I had decided to take a more cautious approach and try to stay on the periphery of Frost's investigation. At least for now.

Marriage isn't easy; there's no happily ever after, except in fairy tales. But it's worth it, I thought, as I watched him gather the dishes and carry them to the dishwasher. That doesn't mean it isn't hard at times.

"I talked to the realtor; he's got a couple places he wants to show us on Saturday if you're up for it," he said, rinsing dishes and loading them into the dishwasher.

"Where are they?" I had let Angel handle all the discussions and arrangements with the realtor.

"There's one near Wash Park, but I'm hesitant to go see it. It's quite a bit more expensive, and I don't want to fall in love with it and then not be able to buy it. He's found one in the Highlands. Not sure about the Highlands; that's awfully close to my parents. I don't want *Mamá* thinking our house is her second home."

"Yeah, neither would I. She'd probably be over every chance she got pestering us about something. I mean, I love your mother, but there are times…"

"A lot of times," Angel agreed. "The realtor said there was one near DU, but he hadn't been able to set up a viewing yet. He's got a couple more he wants to show us."

"I'd be okay with you handling this. You picked out the triplex."

"No, I want you involved in choosing. I can handle the rest. I want this to be our final home. I don't want to move anymore. I want it to be a home where our kids can grow up."

"Kids? Now? Jesus, Angel, did your mother finally—"

He grinned at me. "Relax, Annie. Not right this minute. Although I'm always up for practicing." That made me roll my eyes, but it seemed we were finding our way back to normal, at least in that respect. I must have had a deer-in-the-headlights look on my face, though, because he hastened to add, "I meant eventually, if it seems right."

I responded with a rather weak laugh. "Right. Eventually."

Watching on the video feed, I was surprised to see what Charlotte Lewis looked like. When she'd opened the door to Paul, I had caught a brief glimpse, but seeing her and her husband seated together was a surprise. As tall and thin and impeccably dressed as Tom Lewis was, Charlotte was his polar opposite. She wore expensive but ill-fitting clothes, and nervously smoothed the tight pants that encased her rather large, sausage-like thighs. A pinched, disapproving look seemed at home on her face.

Lewis looked calm despite sitting in a police interrogation room waiting to be interviewed. Interrogation rooms made most people nervous, whether they were innocent or not. He listened to the attorney who had accompanied them, and made a few comments to his wife, but, if anything, he acted as if he was simply being inconvenienced rather than questioned by the police. I noticed, though, that he kept rubbing one thumb over the other as he sat with his clasped hands on the table. Was he nervous or was this just a habitual tic?

Talbot was good. As I watched her on the video feed in the observation room, she came across as friendly, female, and harmless as she began the interview with the Lewises. She wasn't. I had heard some of Frost's tales about her and knew she wasn't a pushover. It would be interesting to see what happened.

Talbot had been asking them questions that Paul had asked during his interview about Laura's original abduction and what they remembered. Lewis was as helpful as he'd been previously, smiling at Talbot and mostly repeating the same things he'd said during Paul's interview.

Frost hadn't said anything, but his presence as he watched both of them across the interrogation room table seemed to rattle the wife, if her frequent quick glances at him implied anything. It wasn't unwarranted. He could be unnerving at times.

"I'd like to know why," Talbot asked, suddenly changing focus, "when Detective Roberts asked you to look at a police sketch of a man seen with Laura, you lied and both of you denied that it was your son?"

"My clients did not lie to the officer who interviewed them. They failed to recognize their son based on a police artist's sketch," the attorney said before either of the Lewises could respond. "They can hardly be held responsible for that."

"That surprises me," Talbot said, opening a folder, pulling out first the sketch and laying it on the table, then pulling out the latest arrest record photo of their son and placing it next to the sketch.

She let the lawyer and the Lewises stare at the two for several uncomfortable moments. It was clear that the sketch matched the photo of their son. "Looks like the same person to me, and I'm not his parent. Do you have trouble recognizing your own son?"

She stared at the couple and their lawyer, waiting for them to respond. They didn't.

"Mr. and Mrs. Lewis, I'd like to know why, when this clearly looks like your son, you denied it was to Detective Roberts."

Based on the frown on the lawyer's face, the Lewises hadn't mentioned how much the drawing actually looked like their son. Their lawyer adjusted the knot of his tie, cleared his throat, and said, "I'd like a moment to confer with my clients, please."

Talbot shut off the audio recording and left the interview room with Frost in tow. I cracked the door to the observation room and eavesdropped. Frost had threatened me with death if Talbot, or anyone else, discovered I was there.

"They can't deny it's him. It'll be interesting to hear the story they cook up for lying about it," Frost said.

"I'm pretty sure they know where he is or can point us to someone who does. But I need to get them to cough it up," she said. "They'll give us something—they have to—or I can charge them with obstruction, and their lawyer knows that. The drawing and the mug shot make it obvious they lied."

The lawyer opened the interview room door and indicated they were ready for Frost and Talbot to return. Once seated, the lawyer cleared his throat again and began to try to explain.

"My clients' son has had a number of run-ins with the police, and they didn't want to—"

Talbot held up a hand and interrupted. "Counselor, your clients lied to Detective Roberts who was quite clear he was conducting a homicide investigation. If you and your clients would like to listen to the taped interview, I'd be happy to play it for you. They lied about this," she said tapping her finger on the drawing for emphasis. "They said they didn't know who it was. Their son could have valuable information about Laura Hutchinson's murder or could, in fact, be responsible for it. That's obstruction, and you know it, regardless of what their reasons were for doing it."

She paused and stared the lawyer down. "I want information about where their son is, or I charge them now."

"That's ridiculous." Tom Lewis looked surprised by that possibility.

"No sir, it's not. If you'd like a few minutes alone with your lawyer, I'm sure he can explain exactly how serious this is."

The lawyer nodded and Frost and Talbot left. I waited in the observation room and wondered what the Lewises would eventually say. There was a lot of silent arguing going on from what I could see. I saw the lawyer open the interview room door and motion Frost and Talbot back inside, where she resumed the audio feed.

"My clients have a statement to make."

"Okay, let's hear it. Then I have more questions, and I expect answers."

Tom Lewis stared at her. "I apologize for denying it was Mike. We chose not to identify our son out of concern that the police would arrest him and charge him with something because of his past record. It wasn't to obstruct your investigation; it was to protect him."

"Which, in effect, obstructs our investigation," Talbot said staring back at him. I saw a flush rise up his neck. "Mr. and Mrs. Lewis, you have one opportunity—now—to tell me where your son is, or tell me who might know, or provide me with a way to contact him. I really don't care why you lied, only that you did. So, it's in your best interests to talk to me."

"My clients need some guarantee that they won't be charged if they provide you with the information you want."

"Counselor, your clients are in no position to bargain for anything. I will, however, consider not filing obstruction charges if they provide the information I need, and," she said staring straight at Tom Lewis, "the information turns out to be accurate."

All parties sat silently. Talbot and Frost were good at waiting. It appeared that Lewis was not. He waved his hand irritably in the air in front of his face. "Fine, fine. What do you want to know?"

"First of all, where is your son and how do we contact him?" Talbot pushed a small notepad across the table to Lewis.

"I don't routinely contact him, but here is the phone number we have," Lewis said. He scribbled down a number and pushed the pad back to her. He sat staring at her, his former affability now gone as he waited for the next questions.

"Is he in fact out of town as you told Detective Roberts?"

"No. And I don't currently know where he's living. He doesn't share that with us."

"Did your son know or have any contact with Laura Hutchinson around the time of her original abduction?"

"I have no idea. He may have. Our daughter knew her in grade school."

"Kathy spent time at their house, and the girl spent time at our—" Charlotte Lewis looked as if she intended to continue when her husband cut her off.

"It doesn't matter what Kathy did, Charlotte, for God's sake, shut up and let me handle this!"

"If your wife has something to say Mr. Lewis, let her speak."

"I...no, I really have nothing to add." Charlotte quickly said.

"Did your son have any ongoing contact with Laura Hutchinson?" Talbot asked Lewis.

"Not that I'm aware of."

I saw Talbot's eyes narrow as Charlotte Lewis shifted away from her husband, moving her buttocks from one side of the chair to the other and resettling herself. Talbot had picked up on something, but I had no idea what it was.

"Will I find out differently when I interview him? Will I find out you lied about this too?"

"Detective Talbot, that's uncalled for," the lawyer said.

"No, it isn't. He's lied before; they both have. He could be lying now. Mr. Lewis, if your son had ongoing contact with Laura Hutchinson and it turns out he killed her, you'll be charged as an accessory for lying about it and trying to shield him from us."

"Look, I have no idea who he fraternizes with, and I no longer care. He's gone off the rails since he was a teenager. Drugs, alcohol, DUIs, bar fights—I disassociated from him a long time ago."

I saw Talbot glance at Charlotte Lewis. "Mrs. Lewis, how about you?"

"What?" She looked taken aback that she'd been asked a question. "What about me?"

"Do you know whether your son had ongoing contact with Laura Hutchinson? Think carefully before you reply."

"I...I don't know. I can't imagine why he would have."

Talbot stood up and stretched. "Gets tiring sitting in here after a while; these chairs aren't very comfortable." She walked around the table and over to the door and then behind the Lewises. As she approached Charlotte, she placed her hand on the woman's shoulder, making her jump. Talbot kept her hand there and leaned in.

"It's hard, isn't it? Being a mom, watching a kid grow up, cause problems, get in trouble. Takes a lot out of a person."

"I never minded," Charlotte said, wetting her lips nervously.

"Were you close to Mike?"

Charlotte glanced at her husband who scowled at her. "To some extent. But boys, after a certain age, they're not as close to their mothers."

"Did he confide in you?"

"No."

"What sort of relationship did he have with Laura?"

"I don't think he had one. She was Kathy's friend. She visited our house multiple times, and Kathy visited her house, until all that happened."

"'All that' meaning her abduction and rape?"

Charlotte blanched. "Yes. Why do we have to talk about that? It's been over and done with for years."

"Did your son have anything to do with what happened at that time?"

"No! Why would you say such a thing?"

"It's a legitimate question. Your daughter knew Laura, she was around your house frequently, your son must have known her, too."

"Well, of course he knew who she was, but he wasn't friends with her. She was a child, and he was in high school."

Talbot returned to her seat letting the statement hang in the air. Frost remained silent taking turns staring at the husband, his wife, and the attorney. Talbot rifled through the file on Mike Lewis, pausing periodically to peruse a page more closely, letting the silence drag on. I could almost smell the flop sweat coming off Charlotte Lewis. The underarms of her blouse were visibly wet, and she continued shifting in her chair. Jesus, Talbot would scare the hell out of me if I were the one she was questioning.

"His legal troubles started his senior year in high school," Talbot said at last. "That was the year Laura was abducted. Interesting that he'd 'go off the rails,' as your husband called it at that time. Any idea why?"

"That's asking my clients to speculate, detective, and they're not going to do that. If you wish to speak to them again, you'll arrange for it through me. We're leaving."

"One thing before you leave. Mr. and Mrs. Lewis, under no circumstances are you to contact your son and let him know we're looking for him. If he flees the state after this meeting, I will get an arrest warrant charging you both with obstruction. If we can prove he had anything to do with either Laura's original assault, or her murder, you'll be charged as an accessory to the crimes. You don't want to go there, I assure you."

The lawyer nodded and escorted the couple out of the interview room.

Talbot stood up, holding the file against her chest. "All we have to do now is find Mike Lewis."

"I'm going to start with the phone number and see what that nets me. See if I can locate where its signals are coming from," Frost said. "If I find out he's holed up here in Denver, and I can't connect with him by phone, I'll make arrangements for some plainclothes cops to watch the place and talk to any neighbors in the building. If he shows up, I'll have them pick him up."

"Okay, keep me posted. Let's talk before we leave today."

Frost nodded and waited until she'd left before coming into the observation room. "Damn, that woman is good. Christ, I was almost ready to confess." Frost laughed.

"It seemed like she picked up on something with the wife, right before she walked around and got in her face. Do you know what it was?"

"Talbot calls it the butt swipe. She learned it in a seminar she took from a former LAPD detective who teaches interrogation techniques."

"What does it tell you?"

"That Charlotte Lewis was nervous, that she might be preparing to lie about something, or was uncomfortable with what was happening. Going around, putting her hand on the woman's shoulder, and getting in her face jacked up the wife's anxiety, which gets people to make mistakes. You saw how she kept shifting her position, and she was sweating like crazy. She knows something, and she's nowhere near as skilled at hiding her discomfort as her husband. She's the weak link and he doesn't want her talking. Whatever she knows, we weren't going to get it today, but we will eventually."

"Huh, interesting."

He laughed. "Ain't it just?"

"The husband, though, other than getting pissed at being forced to admit they lied, is relatively controlled, but Talbot got under his skin. He doesn't like women being in control."

Frost nodded. "I think they both know something about Mike being involved with Laura. Not sure what, but they bear watching. I'd like to know what set the kid off and got him into drugs and alcohol, but unless Mike tells us, it'll be like pulling teeth to get it out of the father. That assumes he knows."

TWENTY-EIGHT

YEAH, I'VE HEARD ABOUT THAT COP," Angel said later that evening when I told him about what Frost had said. "He had one of the highest solve and confession rates when he was in the LAPD. He goes around and gives interrogation technique seminars now that he's retired."

"I've never heard anyone talk about what Frost told me." We were sitting on the couch, and Angel was rubbing my feet. If I'd been a cat, I'd have been purring loudly.

"That's because most PDs don't have the budgets to send detectives to his seminars, cops often have to pay out of pocket, and it isn't cheap. As an ADA, I sort of wished they'd been required to go. It would have made my life easier. Now that I'm doing defense work, it's probably good that they don't."

"Are you happy working on the other side?"

"It's different but interesting, from a strategy point of view. I've taken some flack over it from people in the DA's office. Frost isn't keen on it either, but he'll get over it. The money's good, and I don't have to deal with the DA keeping me sidelined," he said, smiling at me. "I'm okay with the change."

"Okay's not happy, though."

"I doubt anyone is completely happy with where they work. It's good to try new things and I'm content, that's enough."

I frowned at him. Regardless of what he said, I knew he'd been happy as an ADA. Prosecuting cases, going up against defense lawyers, winning cases fueled him, made him happy. Now I wasn't sure.

"I don't want you doing something that doesn't make you happy."

He studied me for a moment. "I can't go back to the DA's office, and I don't want to," he said at last. "This job has its rewards, including the money. It's also opened my eyes to the other side, to some of the things that the DA's office has tried to slide by.

"It's funny, it felt like a game when I was at the DA's office, but it felt like it was for a good cause. There's this attitude of being a good guy, no matter what it takes, because you're taking criminals off the streets. Now I'm seeing how that affects defendants. Everybody should have to play fair, and really no one does.

"I've decided to do some *pro bono* work, like with Janet Casey. That makes me feel good. I'll be helping people who can't afford anything other than a public defender. Not saying they're bad, but they're overworked and underpaid, and they lean heavily toward plea bargaining. People like Janet often need more than that. It's important to me to feel like I'm helping them."

He ran his thumb up my arch and I sighed. The man really knew his way around foot rubs. "I appreciate you taking her on. She ought to be given a medal instead of being prosecuted."

"I'd agree, but murder is murder, *chica*. Because of the court's ruling, she's in the state psych hospital until further notice. What happened doesn't excuse her killing him, but at least it's not prison. It should be less traumatizing, at least I hope so."

"She seemed terribly alone. Defending her is a good thing, you're watching out for her, but what about other clients who don't deserve that? Who are guilty?"

We sat quietly for a while until he said, "I'd never ask a client if they were guilty. Everyone is entitled to representation, but I've spent too long on the prosecutorial side to feel great about defending someone who's guilty, and I'd have to defend them. Owen said to assume they were innocent and not to ask. But if it was obvious, because of the evidence the prosecution had, that they were guilty, and the DA's office offered a plea bargain that was to their advantage, I'd push for the client to take it. If not, then I'll defend them as best I can, that's my job."

"That's what I mean. It's a great job, but it puts you in a compromising position. The DA's office didn't."

"*Chica*, some of the people I had to deal with during the cases I picked up at the DA's office were scum. They might have been a victim of the crime we were handling, but they weren't innocent by any means." He yawned. The shadows under his eyes were back and he was slumped against the back of the couch. He'd been putting in ten- and twelve-hour days—not unusual before his injuries, but I wondered if he'd taken on this new job too soon.

"Sometimes, though, I felt like the police had put blinders on. You know, they had a theory, and once they had someone who fit their theory, they quit looking. It was my job to try to convince a jury beyond a reasonable doubt that the person was guilty. That wasn't always easy to do, but then convincing a jury someone is innocent isn't easy to do either.

"In the law, there's always something that isn't fun. I'm sure the OR is the same way. It's life. Don't worry about me. I have you and our life together, that's enough." He gave my foot a squeeze and grinned. "We use investigators. Maybe some someday my wife and her partner in crime could help out from time to time."

"Seriously? You'd be okay with that?"

"I'd at least be willing to give it a try."

"I don't deserve you."

He laughed. "No, you don't, but you're stuck with me."

Therapy was evidently working for both of us.

"Talbot says she hasn't been able to find Mike Lewis. I haven't been able to reach him by phone or locate the phone. I think he's got it turned off or is using a burner. You talked to his sister. Do you want to see if she'll tell you where he is?" Frost said when I checked in with him the next day.

"I can try, but she wasn't happy that I called the first time. She denied the drawing was him like her parents did. I'm not sure she'll talk to me."

"Give it a shot. I got an address from the DMV, but it's nearly a year old, and he may not even live there anymore. God help the Lewises if they tipped him off; Talbot will come down on them like a ton of bricks."

"Do you think he was involved in either incident?"

"He's involved in some way, if only because he was seen talking to her shortly before she was killed. I wanna know why. It may have had nothing to do with either her original abduction or her murder, but it's curious. Curious things make me want to dig."

That was Frost in a nutshell. He kept digging until he got an answer. It might not be the answer he hoped for, but he got one. I hung up and rifled through my desk drawer until I found Kathy Lewis's phone number.

"I thought I told you not to call me again."

"You did, but please don't hang up." She didn't, so I hurried on. "I'd really appreciate it if you'd answer some questions for me."

"I am not going to add to my brother's problems. I'm not going to help you put him in jail."

"I'm not asking you to, I'm asking you to talk to me and help sort out why he was talking to Laura Hutchinson before she was killed. It may have nothing to do with what happened to her."

I was treading a thin line—she didn't want to talk to me, and I had no way to force her to—but I continued. "When pressed by Detective Talbot, your parents finally identified him as the man in the police sketch. I'm wondering why you didn't say you recognized him?"

She said nothing, and I figured she'd hang up on me. At last, she said, "Mike has had a hard time, for a long time. I didn't want to add to it. My father claims he cut him off, but Mike told me they were still giving him money. He said they owed it to him but wouldn't say why."

She blew her nose, and I wondered if she was crying. "My mother doesn't want any hint of scandal touching her perfect marriage. Mike's an embarrassment to her, no matter what she says to the contrary. And my father? He's so self-involved he barely notices either of us. Mike might be his son, but I don't think he cares about him at all.

"Mom's fine with him being out of their house. To be fair, Mike wasn't easy to live with. I'm not surprised they denied knowing him; neither of them really wants to have anything to do with him."

I could hear the disgust in her voice, and it seemed that she was the only one who was trying to protect him, not an image or a status.

"Talk to me about the trouble he's been in."

She exhaled abruptly. "It started in high school. Drugs and alcohol, his grades dropped after that started, and he barely graduated. It drove my father crazy. Status again—his only son had turned into a dirtball. Those were his words during an argument he had with Mike that I overheard.

"I'm not sure what changed for Mike. As I said, he frustrated my mother growing up. He was never an easy kid, I guess, but it got worse when he went to high school and started getting into real trouble. She put on a good front to the public about caring for him, but in private, her anger and frustration was hard to miss."

She paused, then continued, "It might be why they give him money. I always thought it was to control what he did, you know, behave a certain way or the gravy train stops. If that was the case, it never worked. Mike seemed intent on self-destructing, and they never cut him off. Maybe giving him the money meant he'd stay away and not bring the trouble to their house."

"And you have no idea what caused the self-destructive behavior?"

"Something changed. His attitude…I don't even know how to describe it. I was pretty young, but I could feel it. He was challenging, argumentative, then withdrawn and depressed. I guess those are the words I'd use. It could have been normal teenage rebellion. My father is such a control freak, Mike rebelled against that. But whatever the reason, the drugs and alcohol made it worse."

"When did it begin, do you know? Can you identify a timeframe or anything that set it off?"

"It seemed to start up the fall of his senior year, that's as close as I can call it. My folks sent me to a boarding school around that time, so I wasn't around."

That was also when Laura had been abducted and raped. The timing was interesting to say the least.

"Can you tell me where he is? The detectives on the case need to interview him."

"Interview him or arrest him?" she demanded.

I closed my eyes. I'd probably lost her with that comment.

"Interview him. The police have no idea why he was talking to Laura, or if it in any way relates to her murder or abduction. All they want to do is talk to him, Kathy."

"Right. I know how cops work; he's in their sights. He's had numerous arrests, so he'll be their scapegoat," she said angrily. "In any event, I have no idea where he is. I hope he's left the state. I hope he never comes back here."

I called Frost and relayed the conversation. "The timing of him 'going off the rails,' as his father called it, coincides with the time Laura was abducted."

"He seems to have gone to ground. I've put out an APB on him, but not sure whether that'll produce anything." I could hear him tapping his pencil. "Talbot talked to the DA about charging the Lewises with obstruction. She's convinced they alerted the kid about us wanting to talk to him. DA said if we got proof of that, to let him know, otherwise forget it. Fucking lawyers."

The line went dead. He might feel better after his surgery, but his phone manners could stand some improvement.

TWENTY-NINE

RET, THIS IS ANNIE COLLINS. You gave me the name of your friend Eric, who'd seen the guy talking to Laura. I tried the phone number you gave me, and he doesn't answer. Do you have any way to get in touch with him?"

"His phone probably ran out of minutes, and he can't afford to reload it. I'll see if I can find him and have him get in touch. Why do you want to talk to him?"

"The police have identified the guy Eric saw, but he's disappeared. I hoped maybe your friend would know where he might be."

"I doubt it. But I can ask." He paused. "If you'll send me a copy of the photo, I can ask around, see if I can find anyone who knows him."

"That would be great, I'll text you a photo of the drawing. Before I forget, did you turn up anything about Laura's supplier? A name or some way to contact him?"

"I checked with several people and found out his name is Benny Tulio. I put out the word that I needed to talk to him, so I'll let you know if I hear from him."

That worried me. "Do you think that was a good idea? What did you say?"

"That I needed to talk to him about one of his dealers."

"Just...be careful, I don't want you getting hurt.""

"I'll be fine. You should be careful, too. People know I've been helping you."

"I will." I remembered the look on his face when I'd told him about Laura being pregnant. "Did you take the paternity test?"

"Yeah, I did." He was quiet.

I was sorry I had asked. It would be hard for him whatever the results. Either he'd lost someone he loved and their child, or Laura had cheated on him and gotten pregnant. I wished at times I'd learn to stop asking intrusive questions, but it was an occupational hazard of nurses and cops, and I lived in the no man's land between the two.

He cleared his throat, and his voice sounded rough, as if he was on the verge of tears. "The baby was mine."

"I'm so sorry."

"Yeah, well, at least I know she wasn't screwing around on me. That's something. But in a way it makes it harder. If she had been, I could be angry with her. Maybe it wouldn't hurt as much that she and the baby are gone."

His voice wavered, and he cleared his throat again. "But she wasn't cheating, and I lost both of them. Life's just shit sometimes."

"It is, but Laura cared for you and would want you to take care of yourself."

He laughed ruefully. "Don't worry, I'm too scared of dying to do anything to myself. Life goes on. Sometimes you wish it didn't, but it does. Probably a good thing."

"Probably. Bret, if you need anything, please let me know."

"I'll see what I can find out about this Tulio for you. He's not a great guy from what I've heard, so be careful," he said ignoring my comment.

"I will. You, too. If you find the guy in the drawing, don't do anything stupid. We have no idea what his connection to Laura was. He could simply have been someone buying drugs from her. Promise me you'll let me know where to find him and not do anything that could get you into trouble. Same goes for the supplier."

The line was silent. "Bret, promise me."

He sighed. "I promise. If either of them had anything to do with her death, I want them in a prison cell for the rest of their lives. I'll be in touch."

We stood on the sidewalk in front of a ranch-style house in the Highlands area a bit west of downtown Denver and listened to the realtor drone on about the area, property values, resale value, and improvements that had been done. I had tuned him out, but Angel was listening attentively.

It was a nice house. It had what realtors called curb appeal—light-gray paint with white trim and a bright blue front door, a wide front porch with a pillared overhanging roof, a well-maintained yard. Neighboring houses were tidy, too.

Boy, I thought, *we're on our way to becoming a boring suburban couple.*

It was bigger than our combined apartments at the triplex, and there were four bedrooms. Based on what I had seen in the listing information, it had a lovely back patio and privacy-fenced backyard. A surge of anger welled in me at the thought that Ian, once again, was forcing us to move from a place we liked and had settled into.

"Everything okay?" Angel asked. Apparently, I hadn't been able to keep the frown off my face.

I forced a smile. "Yeah, let's go take a look inside."

"Bob, can you open up and give us a minute here?" After a nod from the realtor Angel pulled me aside. "What's wrong? If you don't like it, we can go."

I shrugged. "I like it, it's cute. I just...I...I hate what Ian's done to us. He's forcing us to do things we don't really want to do. It makes me angry, that's all."

Angel stroked my back. "I know, it upsets me. too. A move, though, maybe it'd be better for both of us. Seeing that living room, I don't think it's good for either of us. I guess I'm the one forcing us to move."

I reached up and touched his cheek. "No, you're not forcing anything. It's a good idea. You know me. It takes me a while to adjust to change. There've been too many changes the last few years. I want to find a place to live that's not temporary. Let's look and see what it's like."

By the end of the weekend, we had seen ten properties, and they were all starting to blur for me. Most were in and around Denver or at least in a nearby suburb, which would make getting to work easy for both of us.

Angel had been talking about the places we'd seen, asking what I thought. Figuring there probably was no better time, I said, "If we could figure out a way to avoid seeing the room where he died, how would you feel about it? Would you be willing to see if it made the flashbacks any less intrusive?"

He rubbed a hand over his mouth and chin. "I guess it would depend on what the solution was. Have you thought of something?"

"When you added the door between our units, it gave us extra room. But it also gave us two kitchens and two living rooms, which was fine, but unnecessary. I think we could have your cousin divide the two units and make my side a one-bedroom unit. That'd give us three bedrooms on your side, and we wouldn't have the duplicated kitchen and living room space."

He had listened and now, in his usual lawyer-like fashion, he was mulling over things in his head. I got up from the couch, walked into the kitchen, and refilled our wine glasses. I brought along a pad of paper. I flipped it open to a drawing I had made.

"This is what I was thinking," I said, showing him my rough sketch of how the units could be divided.

I sipped my wine as he looked carefully at the drawing. "It's an idea for sure. Is this what you want to do instead of moving?"

"I want to do whatever is best for you, for us. I think closing off my unit would work, at least temporarily, and it would let us see if it solved the problem." I watched as he studied the drawing. "In the meantime, we could keep looking at houses."

He frowned as he drank his wine and guilt washed over me. "Angel, we don't have to do this." I took his hand. "If you need to move, then we'll move."

He leaned over and kissed me. "It might work." He cupped my cheek in his hand running his thumb over my lips. "Let's close the door between the units and live on this side for a while and see how it feels."

I nodded. "I want you to tell me if it doesn't work. If you need to move, don't agree with me, tell me."

"I have an address for you," Bret said, rattling off a street address in Denver. "As of yesterday, that's where he was. I can't guarantee he's still there. Eric was showing the drawing around, and friends of his happened to know the guy. They said he was moving around a lot, couch surfing for a day or two then moving on. I haven't heard much about the supplier, but I'll let you know if I do."

I wrote quickly as he spoke. "Bret, thank you, this is a big help. I'll let the detectives know. I meant what I said, if you need anything, please let me know."

"Yeah, thanks. I appreciate it, but what you and the detectives are doing to find out who killed Laura is enough." He paused. "I guess, if you can, when they find who did it, can you let me know? Can you explain why they did it?"

"I will if I can. I doubt whether knowing will make sense of it or make it easier to live with."

"I don't expect it to. But…I would like to know, and I want to know the person responsible will pay for it."

⁓

"I got the name of Laura's supplier from Bret. It's Benny Tulio, I don't know anything else about him," I told Frost the next day.

"Good, I'll let Talbot know, and we can round him up. We've got the address Bret gave you for Mike Lewis staked out, watching for him. I didn't want to be obvious and spook him," Frost said. "Tell your buddy thanks for the info."

"I did." I sat quietly at his desk for a few moments. "Frost, do the reasons that result in someone being killed ever get you down?"

"I try not to think about it. It doesn't help and rarely makes sense. We're not a peaceful species, and it doesn't take much for a person to think that killing someone is the answer to their problems."

He sat back in his chair, his hands folded over his chest, and watched me. "'Sides, if people didn't kill each other I wouldn't have a job, your hubby wouldn't have a job, and you wouldn't have a hobby."

He laughed when he saw the indignant expression on my face. "It's not a hobby, I get pulled into these things. And you brought me into this," I replied.

THIRTY

I **WAS ON MY WAY HOME FROM WORK** the following day when my cell rang, and I hit the accept on my steering wheel button.

"Guess who just showed up?" Frost said.

"Mike Lewis?"

"You ruined my surprise, you're no fun at all. Yeah, he showed up a little bit ago—lawyer in tow mind you—and said he wanted to clear up any misunderstandings about his contact with Laura."

"How did he find out about Talbot wanting to interview him?" I turned the car around and headed in the direction of the precinct, hoping Frost would let me listen.

"My guess is his sister told him we were looking for him after you talked to her. She probably told him we had a sketch too, which may be why he was moving from place to place."

"I suppose. Although I would have expected her to tell him to take off rather than come in."

"She probably did, but he figured it'd be better to come in."

I frowned at him. "Odd that he'd avoid his apartment, move from one friend's place to another's, then show up out of the blue and volunteer to be interviewed."

"Sometimes avoiding us for a bit gives a person a chance to think about it or talk to someone who knocks some sense into them. If they're not guilty, they realize it's better to come in voluntarily."

Frost was silent for several moments. "The suit looked pretty high priced for a kid who hasn't got a pot to piss in. My guess is his parents are paying for it."

"Based on what his sister told me, they were giving him money, but according to them, they'd washed their hands of him and his legal problems."

"Guess not. Maybe they hired the lawyer so the kid could come in and reassure us he's not involved, which would let them off the hook for obstruction and potential accessory to murder charges. Who knows?"

"Has Talbot had a chance to interview him?"

"She's got him waiting in the interview room. She's gonna let him sit and contemplate his predicament for a while." Frost laughed. "And run up a bigger bill for whoever's paying for this. She'll let me know when she's ready, if you wanna listen in get your butt over here. I'm gonna let her handle this alone. She always looks like a pushover."

"I'm on my way. You sound excited, what's going on?"

"Just curious about what he'll have to say. Let's see what Talbot comes up with," he said. "Heard you and the boy are looking for a house."

"Yeah, we're looking," I said as I looked for a parking spot near the precinct. "Angel wants to move. Seeing the room every day where all that went down bothers him. A lot."

I rubbed my forehead and frowned. "It'd be nice not to have that reminder every time I walk past my old living room, or make a point to avoid it, but I like the triplex. I didn't plan on moving." I snorted. "But then, I didn't plan on a lot of things the last couple years."

"It'd be a new start. It'd let you get away from the memories."

"Yeah, it probably would. I came up with an idea about dividing up both units until we decide what to do. Angel's thinking about it. We're going to try staying on his side for a few weeks before we decide."

I heard a brief conversation in the background before Frost said, "If you want to listen in, hurry up, but be discreet when you get here."

In the observation room, we listened to Talbot. Her frustration came through loud and clear.

"Mr. Lewis, we've been trying to track you down to interview you for quite some time. You seem to have been avoiding us. I'm surprised, considering the efforts you've made to avoid the interview, that you decided to show up. But you're here, so let's get down to business. What were you talking to Laura Hutchinson about in the days before her murder on the twelfth of September?"

Before Lewis could reply, the lawyer said, "First we need to have your assurance that my client will be given immunity from prosecution for the information he provides."

"Mr. Connor, you know I can't grant immunity especially if it involves a felony. If that's what your client is involved in, then I can speak to the DA and see what he's willing to offer, but I can't do that if I don't know what your client knows."

"What my client has to tell you concerns a drug-related felony, but nothing more serious. Talk to the DA and see what he says. We'll wait to hear the outcome."

Talbot frowned, turned off the audio feed, and left the room. When she returned half an hour later, she was clearly annoyed. "The DA says that if what your client tells me is information that is a drug-related felony involving *buying* a controlled substance, then he is prepared to overlook it in exchange for information about the meeting with Laura Hutchinson.

"If your client aided or abetted anyone committing any other type of felony, or committed one himself, and he emphasized that meant *anything* other than a drug buy from Laura, then the offer is off the table."

"At least the DA didn't give him blanket immunity," Frost muttered in the observation room.

The lawyer nodded and indicated Mike Lewis should begin.

"I met Laura by accident. It was a drug buy. My usual dealer had been arrested, but a friend turned me on to her. We met in the park between the City and County building and the Capitol. I didn't recognize her, from before—you know, before when she was a kid, 'cause all she told me was her first name. But she recognized me and told me who she was, then it kinda came back to me.

"I made the buy. Everything went fine until I said how sorry I was about what happened to her. She got upset, told me she didn't want my pity and to mind my own business, and she took off.

"I never saw her again, and when I heard about her death, and my sister told me about the sketch, I was worried I'd be a suspect, and I made myself scarce."

Talbot stared at him for several minutes. "You didn't talk about what had happened regarding her abduction and rape in detail?"

His eyes went wide. "No, we didn't. I only know what was being talked about at school at the time and what I heard my parents say. When I offered my sympathy, she got mad and left."

"Did you have any contact with her before or after the abduction?"

"No, I was a senior in high school. She was at our house a lot that spring after her family moved into the subdivision, and throughout the summer, before, you know, but it's not like we hung out together. She was a little kid."

"And you didn't see her to buy drugs again, after your first drug buy from her?"

"No. She left angry. I figured she wouldn't have anything to do with me after that."

"Who is paying for your legal representation? Mr. Connor doesn't come cheap, are your parents paying the bill?"

"Detective Talbot, my client is not required to divulge information about my representation. Do you have any further questions about his meeting with Laura Hutchinson?"

"I may, but for now, no."

He handed her a business card. "If you have further questions, please contact me."

Talbot stood. "I believe you and your client can find your way out on your own?"

She watched them leave and walked out in the hallway where Frost met her near the observation room while I eavesdropped.

"His parents and his sister have been obstructing things since day one. I think his involvement was more serious than a chance encounter," Frost said.

"I'm sure it was," Talbot said sounding annoyed.

"Do you believe him?" Frost asked.

"Not entirely. You heard when I asked who'd provided him with his representation, the representation told me that was none of my business. Who else but his parents would do that? His parents claimed that they weren't going to bail him out of his legal problems anymore."

"With kids, you can say you cut them loose, but when it comes down to the wire, you're their parent. You help, if you can," Frost said "At least the kid came in instead of making us drag him in."

"For all the good it did us. I doubt he's telling the truth. Some of it's true, at least part of it, but not all of it. He was nervous, and his story sounded liked he'd rehearsed it. With the lawyer there, I couldn't push like I would have."

"Plans?"

"None at the moment other than to keep an eye on him and see if I can find a way to talk to him alone." Talbot pushed her hair off her forehead. "I'm going to ask a couple of the undercover vice guys to keep an eye on the kid. If anything looks odd, or he makes another buy—which won't be covered by the deal with the DA—I'll have them pull him in."

Frost crossed his arms over his chest. "Good plan. If they catch him buying, my guess is he won't want the parents to know that, and he's less likely to call the lawyer. The parents said they wouldn't intervene if it's arrest related; we might be able to pressure him for more information. No telling if they meant what they said. I'd like to know what made them arrange for the lawyer for this interview. Seems odd to me."

"Yeah, I'd like to know the reason behind it, too. Makes you wonder what they're protecting him—or themselves—from. I'm going to head over to Vice and set something up."

THIRTY-ONE

I TOLD ANGEL THAT NIGHT ABOUT MIKE LEWIS showing up with a high-priced lawyer in tow when he spoke with Talbot and wondered what had prompted his parents to provide that.

"His parents claimed they'd washed their hands of him, and his sister backed that up. She said they were giving him money, but they told him they weren't going to bail him out anymore. Then he shows up with a lawyer he couldn't possibly afford. I don't understand that."

"Depends on the parents, I suppose. Some parents try to rescue their kids. My folks got me a lawyer, but they let me take my knocks. Turned out it was a good thing, too."

"*What?* Why did you need a lawyer?"

Angel's grandmother had alluded to him being a worry to them and misbehaving and getting into trouble growing up, but trouble requiring a lawyer had never entered my head.

"Sure you want to hear this?"

"I think I need to."

Angel picked up his beer and settled back against the couch as if the telling would take a while. That was worrisome. How complicated was the story?

"I was thirteen, when you think you know it all and don't have the common sense to realize you don't. You know my family, we're solid middle class, no weirdness, no excitement, no trouble," he said, as if this was a bad thing.

"I made friends with a classmate when I went to middle school. Tomás Rodriguez's family was different. A couple of his uncles had served time, and his older brother was in prison. At thirteen, that seemed…glamorous, I guess.

"My parents didn't like his family, but he was a nice kid around adults. He was respectful and polite; parents can get taken in by that. I think they thought maybe I'd be a good influence on him, or our family would be."

"Like Eddie Haskell in *Leave It To Beaver*."

"Leave it to what?"

I smiled remembering the show and how archaic it had seemed to me. "It was a show my mom and dad had watched as kids. They found it on a channel that runs old TV shows and let us watch it. There were two brothers, Wally and the Beaver…"

Angel cocked an eyebrow and grinned. I gave him an annoyed look. "Get your mind out of the gutter. This was a fifties sitcom. The parents slept in twin beds—so no suggestive talk or behavior—which was why we were allowed to watch it.

"Anyway, Eddie was the friend of the older brother, and he was a real sleaze, but super polite to the parents. It was that 'Yes, Mrs. Cleaver,' 'You're looking nice today, Mrs. Cleaver,' kind of brown-nosing. The parents thought he was okay, when actually he was the troublemaker. Is that what Tomás was?"

"No, not a troublemaker. He was a kid without any boundaries or supervision."

"What'd he drag you into?"

"He started hanging around a gang. He wasn't a member, just a wannabe. They never took him seriously as far as I knew. Tomás said his oldest brother, the one in prison, had told the gang to leave him alone, which made it much more attractive. He'd talk to me about it, and it sounded cool. Sounded exciting. There was nothing exciting at my house. School, homework, chores, church, *Abuelita* monitoring everything." Angel shuddered a little.

"Anyway, unbeknownst to my parents, at night I'd sneak out of the house every now and then, and go with him, and we'd watch from the sidelines. Their parties were out of control, and they scared me. I'd never have admitted it, though. One night, I snuck out of the house to go with Tomás. I had no idea where we were going, all he would say was the gang was going to have some fun."

He frowned and took a sip of beer. "The gang was harassing an older guy. He'd already called the cops on them once that week according to Tomás. I don't know what else they'd been doing to him that prompted the call, but unfortunately, they went back to harass him. He came out with a gun in hand, which surprised them, and yelled that he'd called the cops—again. Shots on both sides were fired, and when the gang members heard the sirens in the distance, they took off. Tomás and I did, too, but I tripped and fell in the street.

"I'd have probably been fine, the guy would have caught me and turned me in to the police, but Tomás saw me fall and came running back toward me yelling at the guy. The guy thought he was coming back to cause trouble, and he shot him."

"Oh my God." I laid my hand on his arm, and he reached over and squeezed it.

He sighed and nodded. "The cops came, I was sitting in the middle of the street holding Tomás, crying my eyes out. It was quite the scene, an ambulance, the coroner, the cops, neighbors standing all around watching. The coroner took Tomás to the morgue, and the cops took me to the station and called my folks."

He shook his head. "Didn't matter that I'd lost a friend, my parents and *Abuelita* were furious. They called a lawyer to prevent things from getting out of hand, but they let the cops interrogate me and send me to juvie for the night. They refused to intervene."

He smiled at me. "I think my mother would have, but between *Papá* and *Abuelita*, that wasn't happening. Juvie is a scary place, especially for a middle-class kid who'd never been in trouble before.

"At the hearing, the judge was lenient. With my background and no record, he sentenced me to six months of community service. I was underage, I couldn't go to a business and volunteer, but my parents worked out a deal with our priest. I had to work at the church doing whatever the priest decided needed doing and go through family counseling. If I completed it without issue, then my record would be expunged."

"What about the gang members?"

"Hell, they didn't even know who I was. Tomás wasn't an actual member, and his older brother had promised retribution for Tomás's death. They said nothing. I couldn't tell the police anything, and Tomás was dead."

He took a long drink of beer. "I didn't really need the counseling, but it was court mandated. That infuriated my parents. And *Abuelita*? Christ Almighty she made my life a misery. I couldn't breathe without asking permission. The good thing was, it's part of the reason I became a lawyer. I wanted to prevent people from being hurt or getting lost in the system."

"Mike's parents should have stayed out of it."

"My guess, based on what I saw through the DA's office, is that they've been bailing him out his whole life. People don't learn their lessons when they get bailed out. If that's what they've been doing, it's not surprising they'd step in again."

I wondered about that. Why get involved now? What had worried them or triggered enough guilt to make them get involved? If you weren't going to step in if a kid got arrested, why support him financially, and why provide a lawyer for a simple interview? Maybe it was Talbot's threat of charging them with obstruction or being an accessory if he was guilty of Laura's murder that had changed their minds.

"Lord, I hope if we ever have kids they're better behaved."

Angel laughed. "I don't think we have to worry about that until they hit their teens, then we'll lock them in the basement until they turn twenty-one."

"We don't have a basement," I said.

THIRTY-TWO

H EY, ERIC TALKED TO ME YESTERDAY and said that Mike Lewis wanted to talk to you," Bret said when he called two days later. I was at work and in the middle of setting up a room for the next procedure.

"I'll be right outside the door, just wave at me if you need anything. I have to take this call," I said to my scrub nurse as she set out supplies.

Out in the hall, I said, "How did he know about me?"

"I guess he'd found out that Eric described him to the sketch artist and after he'd been to the police he confronted Eric. Eric told him you were the one who'd been trying to find him and told him to talk to me."

"Why does he want to talk to me? He's talked to the police already."

"Not sure, but when we connected, he told me to have you call him."

"Give me his number and I'll call him and block my number—don't give my number to him."

"I won't, I didn't." Bret paused. "He seems pretty wigged out if you ask me."

"How so?"

"I don't know, jumpy, twitchy. I don't know the guy, maybe that's how he always is. Some people who use get that way. I think his poison of choice is meth, that's nasty stuff."

"Did he seem high or anything?" I asked peering through the OR door's window. I raised my eyebrows inquiringly and my scrub nurse gave me a thumb's up. All seemed to be well.

"No, more like he was coming off something. I'll ask around and see what I can find out about him."

"Be careful. I have no idea what his involvement with Laura was or what's going on now. He may be harmless, or he may not. Be careful and stay in touch, okay?"

"I'll be careful."

Frost had brought Benny Tulio in and he denied knowing Laura, denied being her supplier, and refused to say anything else. He had no alibi, but neither Frost nor Talbot had any hard evidence to implicate him in Laura's murder. After holding him for the maximum time allowed without charging him, they released him. No one was happy about that.

I said nothing to Frost or Angel about the proposed phone call with Mike. It wasn't like I was meeting him in person, and there didn't seem to be any point in stirring up a hornets' nest unless I had to.

Talbot wanted to bring Mike in for another interview, but she had nothing she could use to compel him to come in. He'd been there once voluntarily, and there was no evidence that implicated him in Laura's murder. Over the course of the next few days, I called his number several times but got no answer.

Sixth time's a charm I thought when Mike Lewis answered his phone. "I want to talk to you, but it has to be someplace private, someplace my father won't hear about or someone won't overhear the conversation.

He doesn't want me to speak to anyone without the lawyer present," Mike said.

"I'm not going to meet you someplace private. Pick a public place where we can talk."

He tried to talk me out of a public place and then finally gave me an address of a restaurant and we agreed to meet the following morning. It had to be early in the morning because I was due at work for an eleven a.m. to seven p.m. shift

"Why do you want to meet with me?"

"I just want the cops off my back. I didn't have anything to do with Laura's murder. Bret said you work with one of the detectives handling her case, maybe after we talk you can convince them I'm not involved."

I noticed he said nothing about Laura's original abduction and rape. "All right, I'll see you in the morning."

Now the question was, did I tell Frost? These dilemmas always seemed to be the issue. If I told Frost, he'd insist on coming with me and Mike would take off. If I told Angel he'd try to stop me.

I had no idea what, if anything, Mike would tell me, and I didn't think it was risky talking to him. Of course, I never seemed to think that. What seemed riskier was telling Frost or Angel, and I decided not to unless Mike provided something useful. As usual, the need to know overruled common sense.

He'd picked a restaurant that I could never imagine his father patronizing or even knowing about. It was a tiny Greek place that took up part of the ground level storefront under an apartment house on the seedier end of Colfax Avenue's path through Capitol Hill.

A guy loitered near the entrance smoking, and the smoke clouded the doorway to the restaurant. I waved my hand in front of my face to dissipate the cigarette smoke. He looked at me and blew a stream of smoke upwards instead of at me. As I pushed through the door I saw him walk off. Spotting Mike at a table near the back of the restaurant, I joined him.

"Thanks for meeting me, maybe you can convince the cops I'm not involved other than to buy drugs from Laura."

An older woman with salt and pepper black hair and an apron tied over her waitress uniform approached. She brought glasses of water and pulled an order pad out of her apron pocket. I smiled and asked her to give us a few minutes, that I would signal her when we were ready to order. She didn't return the smile but walked away. I had no intention of eating, and I didn't want her to hang around.

"Talk to me about that meeting. I don't know if I can call the cops off, but I know talking to the police is unnerving. People often feel guilty or on edge even if they didn't do anything, so they stop talking."

"Yeah, they do, in the interest of keeping their asses out of jail."

I stared at him and saw him squirm. "Does your ass need to be in jail?"

"No! But I've been in lots of trouble, and I'd be the first one they'd suspect as responsible for whatever happened to her. They probably suspect me of her abduction, too. I'm not stupid. I'm a person of interest, which means I'm a suspect."

"Who paid for the attorney? My husband's an attorney, and he knows the guy who showed up to represent you. That guy isn't cheap. How'd you manage that?"

"My father arranged the lawyer. He called me and told me the cops were looking for me. He was pissed that the cops might come after him for saying the drawing wasn't me." He shifted uncomfortably in his chair. "I knew the cops were looking for me. My sister had told me, that's why I've been moving around."

"They told the police they'd cut you off and wouldn't help if you got in trouble, why the change of heart?"

"They tell everybody that, but they give me money when I need it." He shifted in the chair again. "I...I told them I hadn't done anything and was trying to stay out of trouble. My father said I needed to go in and explain my contact with her, and that he'd arrange for a lawyer. He said if I did that the cops would back off."

I nodded and wondered whether his parents were shielding themselves from legal trouble or if there was another reason behind their helping him. Most people claim innocence whether they are or not, and Mike's parents had probably heard that line from him a million times. From all accounts, Tom Lewis was a very self-absorbed guy. My guess was the lawyer was a means of keeping the cops from coming after him, not to help his son.

"You don't want your father to know we're meeting, but you asked to speak with me. I'm curious why you don't want him to know, or why you'd want to talk to me?"

"Because he'd cut me off for real if he knew. He told me not to speak to the cops without the lawyer present, but you're not a cop. I can't tell you anything other than what I told the cop who interviewed me…" He took a sip of the water in front of him. "I thought if I talked to you, you'd see that I told them all I know. I don't want to stop the gravy train."

"You mean the money they give you?" He shrugged and nodded. "You said you'd met with Laura to buy drugs, is that true?" He nodded. "How were you put in contact with her? It sounded like you hadn't bought from her before."

"I hadn't. Like I told the cops, the guy I usually bought from got arrested. A friend of mine turned me onto her."

"Did you recognize her?"

"Not at first, but the more I looked at her, she seemed familiar, and then it clicked."

"So, she didn't recognize you?"

"No. She'd only given me her first name. It took me a few minutes, but when I recognized her I told her who I was."

I nodded. "She wasn't the one who recognized you first?

"No, it was me."

"Why'd you lie about that?"

He fidgeted with his water glass. "I don't know," he said at last. "I just…I guess I thought it'd be better if I said she'd recognized me, like I wouldn't be responsible for setting her off if she remembered first. I don't know why I lied about that, habit maybe."

If he was in the habit of lying, that made me wonder how much of what he'd told Talbot was the truth. "Did you lie about the rest?"

"No," he said in agitation. "No, just about who remembered first."

"I was told that both of you looked upset during your conversation with her, as if you were having an argument, and that she took off after a few minutes. She was upset and unsettled in the days after meeting with you according to a person who was close to her. What did you talk about?"

"At first we talked about the buy, what she had, what she wanted for it. I made the buy, and told her who I was, that I was sorry for what had happened to her. Asked her how she was doing, and she got pissed and took off."

"Anything else?"

Anger flashed on his face. "No! What else would there be? I didn't hurt her, and I didn't kill her. I felt sorry for her."

"How well did you know her when she was a kid?"

"Hardly at all. She was my sister's friend. She came over to our house a lot, after school and on weekends. That's all I knew until the news broke about her."

"How did you hear about her abduction?"

"I saw it, a bit of the report, on the TV at a friend's house. His family didn't live in our subdivision, and I didn't mention it to him."

"And you said nothing to the police."

"No. I should have, I guess, but I didn't."

"Why? At the time, the police were trying to identify her and find her parents. Why wouldn't you call them?"

He wouldn't look at me, and he was struggling with something, some memory or maybe he was embarrassed by his behavior. "Look, I'd just had a DUI, the court had suspended my license, and school had barely started. I didn't want any more contact with the cops. The kid was fine as far as I knew—she was with the police—and I also knew that her parents would come forward eventually. It wasn't my problem."

I stared at him and shook my head. "There aren't any witnesses who can testify to what you talked about with her before she was found dead—"

He cut me off. "I didn't do anything wrong other than buy the drugs from her and make the mistake of telling her I remembered her. I should have kept my fucking mouth shut."

"Seems like your troubles started the fall of your senior year, around the time Laura was assaulted and abandoned. Is there a connection?"

"No!" he shouted as he shot to his feet.

"Then what caused the acting out?"

"I'm done talking to you. You're no better than the cops, always trying to set me up for a fall."

"She's dead, Mike. Her life was totally fucked up after her assault and abandonment. This isn't all about you."

"Fuck you," he snarled. He strode to the door and pushed out of the restaurant, walking quickly off and disappearing.

I turned, shrugged at the waitress who rolled her eyes, and I left.

Arriving at my parked, car I found my left front tire was flat and something was sticking out of it. Bending down I saw a screwdriver piercing a piece of paper and my tire. There were cigarette butts lying on the sidewalk. The guy by the restaurant doorway flashed through my mind. I hadn't recognized him, but it left me uneasy. I wrapped my coat hem around the screwdriver and pulled it out. The note read:

Back off or else!

Back off what? I wondered, *Mike Lewis?*

Mike hadn't vandalized the tire. He'd taken off in the opposite direction and had no idea what I drove. Then I remembered Bret's warning about Benny Tulio, and that he knew I had asked Bret to help with finding him and Mike Lewis. That was not good. Was the guy by the restaurant door Tulio? The idea that Tulio might have been following me and knew what I was driving scared me, but what was done was done. I'd just have to stay alert and hope that he felt the damaged tire had gotten his point across sufficiently.

I put the screwdriver on the passenger seat of my car and called Triple A.

THIRTY-THREE

MIKE LEWIS HAD STEPPED INTO FIRST PLACE as a suspect. Something about what he'd discussed with Laura had set this in motion. At least that's what it looked like to me. He didn't strike me as a killer, but something had occurred during his conversation with Laura that set the stage for her murder. I decided I had to talk to Frost so I grabbed some lunch for us and headed to the precinct.

"What the hell is this?" Frost said, holding up the salad I'd gotten him for lunch.

"It's a salad, people eat them for lunch. Try it, you might like it."

"Here, you eat it. I want a burger." He set the salad container on the desk and looked around the room. "Sanchez! You going out to get some lunch?" Sanchez nodded. "How about bringing me back a burger and fries?"

"Are you *trying* to kill yourself? There are easier ways to do it you know," I said in frustration.

He frowned at me and thinned his lips. "Fine, give me the fucking salad. Did you put any meat on the damn thing?"

"Chicken."

"Between you and Evie you're going to kill me; I won't need burgers," he muttered, then raising his voice he called out, "Sanchez? Forget it."

He grabbed the container, motioned me to the break room, and mumbled and fussed all the way there. I sometimes got the impression he wished he'd never met me, and I wondered whether my husband did, too.

As we finished our salads he asked, "What have you been up to?"

I sighed and put my fork down. He must have seen the worry in my face.

"Oh Christ, now what've you done?"

I frowned.

"Let's go into an interview room." He got up and walked with me to the room. After shutting the door behind me he flipped a switch to turn off the audio and video feed that activated whenever people entered.

"Sit." I sat. "What did you do?"

"I talked to Mike Lewis."

Frost's face lost all expression as he stared at me. Then his brows drew together, and his eyes went flat—that unnerving cop look of his. Maybe I'd gone too far this time.

"How did you get in touch with him and what did he say? Then I want to hear your excuse for not telling me, and it better be good."

I explained what Mike had told me, then said, "I didn't initiate the contact, he told Bret he wanted to talk to me. He said he hoped, if he did, I'd get you and Talbot off his back. It was an opportunity to talk to him without a lawyer being present. He knows something. He had some part in her abduction, and maybe her murder. I hoped he'd tell me." I twisted my hands together. "I'm sorry, Frost."

"Oh, fuck your 'I'm sorry,' that's supposed to make it better? You should have talked to me first. You're *supposed* to be staying out of this!" He ran a hand through his hair in frustration. "You realize that you may have jeopardized this investigation? If he did play a part in her abduction or her death, one word about him talking to you without his lawyer could derail everything."

"He asked to talk to me."

Frost shook his head and tugged on a handful of hair as if he might pull it out. "Everyone here and at the DA's office knows you're associated with me and Angel, you might as well be official, but you're not. At least if I'd tried to talk to him, he'd have no excuse for talking to me without his lawyer present. If he did, it'd be his mistake. I wouldn't be accused of trying to entrap him, and I'd be doing my job! *You're not a fucking cop. It's not your place to do things like this,*" he shouted at me, and I flinched. "How many times do I have to tell you that?"

I sat silently and waited for the ax to fall. Frost was quiet as he paced the small room. Coming back to me, he said, "This was a mistake. I should never have asked you to help me with the cold cases, and I should never have let my guard down and allowed you to listen in on the interrogations. You got nothing out of the kid that he didn't say when Talbot questioned him."

"I got some, like what happened when she disappeared. I think he's involved," I said lamely.

Frost threw his arms out. "Of course he's fucking involved! If he didn't kill her outright, I think he knows who did, and same goes for her abduction as a kid. But we can't *prove* it. I'm sorry, Annie, but I can't have you doing this. I'm not including you on anything further, or letting you work on the cold case files."

"Frost, please. He asked to talk to me. I thought I could help. Don't cut me off."

"I haven't got a choice. If Talbot hears about this, she'll have a total shit fit and tell the lieutenant who'll come after me."

I nodded. He shook his head. "You always do this. I don't know why I keep thinking you'll stop pulling shit like this. If we were doing the PI stuff, then fine, investigate on your own all you want, but not while I'm on the job, not on an official police investigation."

I could mess things up better than anyone I knew. Angel had said the same thing. And they were both right. I stood up, my arms wrapped around my middle where my stomach had started to hurt.

"You're right. I'm sorry, Frost."

He looked as pained as my stomach felt. We were friends, and I knew he didn't want to do this. I left the interview room, quickly gathered my coat and purse from his desk, and hurried out of the department to my car.

"Are you going to tell me what happened today?" Angel asked. He'd been home for about an hour and was fixing dinner.

"Nothing happened."

"Nothing. Then why have you been so quiet?"

"Look, I'm not on trial here. I had a bad day. Leave me alone!" I said storming off into our bedroom.

We were living on Angel's side of the two apartments, attempting to see if that arrangement would warrant staying or moving. It was cramped, and there was no way to have any private space if either of us needed it. You know what they say about familiarity breeding contempt? While it hadn't bred contempt, it was claustrophobic, and small irritants could quickly grow into large ones.

I didn't want to argue with him, and I most certainly didn't want any hassle about what had happened with Frost. I wasn't sure how I was going to explain no longer working with Frost on the cold cases. I had no idea how to explain talking to Mike Lewis that wouldn't result in another blowup between us. Angel ate by himself; I wasn't hungry. A few hours later, he joined me in bed and wrapped an arm around me.

"Annie, please tell me what happened."

"No, I don't want you to be mad at me too."

"It can't be that bad," he said, stroking my hair and murmuring endearments.

I couldn't take it. "Stop, please. I can't stand how nice you're being when I don't deserve it."

"Do you want me to yell at you and throw things?" I could hear the amusement in his voice.

"No," I said turning over out of his arms. "Just drop it."

"For God's sake, what's happened?"

I sat up and turned toward him. I saw the puzzled frown on his face and blundered on. "I screwed up. Frost's mad at me…you'll probably divorce me…and…" I couldn't manage to get the rest out.

"You've certainly given me enough reasons to divorce you over the last few years, but I'm still here, one more reason won't matter. What happened?"

I sighed and went for broke. "A suspect related to Laura's murder asked to meet with me—the kid whose parents hired the lawyer. I met with him and he told me about his meeting with Laura. I guess I've really screwed things up. Frost fired me, or whatever it's called when you're unofficially working for someone."

Things were ominously quiet for several minutes. I waited, wondering if this was the straw that broke the camel's back.

"What'd you hope to accomplish?" he asked, finally, in a very neutral voice.

The careful question and the neutral voice worried me more than if he'd been yelling at me, and I felt sick to my stomach. I could see his lawyer's face, that mask that was like Frost's cop face—blank, unreadable, and ominous. I had pushed Frost too far, and I had most likely pushed Angel too far.

"I thought…maybe he'd tell me something he didn't tell Frost and Talbot with the lawyer present."

I closed my eyes and huffed out a breath. "I guess I really messed up. If he's guilty, maybe his lawyer could say I prevented him from having counsel present when I talked to him."

"Did he agree to talk to you without his lawyer?"

"He asked to talk to me."

"Did he tell you anything that he didn't tell Frost or Talbot?"

"Not really."

Angel sighed and scratched at his chin absently. "Then legally, it probably won't matter. He didn't insist or ask that his lawyer be present. He asked to talk to you, and you're not a cop. That lets you off the hook at least as far as the legalities. With Frost, it could potentially cause a lot of problems for him. I'm not surprised he fired you."

"What about you?" I asked, dreading the answer.

"What am I supposed to say?" he asked, the exasperation in his voice clear. "I don't know why you get involved with these cases in the first place, and I can't seem to stop you. You shouldn't get involved at all, but you do it anyway, and I guess I'm just going to have to get used to it. Somehow. At least think before you do things like that."

"You don't have to worry anymore; I'm not working with Frost."

My voice hitched as I said that, as the reality hit home. I wouldn't be seeing Frost tomorrow, maybe not for quite a while depending on how angry he was.

"I fuck things up on an Olympic level sometimes," I said lying back down.

He didn't contradict me or pull me to him.

"Go to sleep, Annie. There's nothing to be gained by talking about this tonight."

He turned away from me and shut off the bedside lamp. He didn't gather me in his arms or give me a goodnight kiss, which reawakened all my fears about him leaving, and I had no one to blame except myself. It took me a long time to fall asleep.

THIRTY-FOUR

I **STOOD ON MY SIDE OF THE COMBINED APARTMENTS** and stared at the floor where Ian had died. I've heard people say that violent deaths leave a residue, an aura, something you can sense in the places where the death occurred. I guess they do. We'd had the hardwood flooring in that spot replaced. It was stained beyond repair with his blood, but his presence was still strong. I had tried to pretend that it didn't trigger me, but standing on the floor now, I relived the terror of seeing Ian holding a gun against Angel's temple and having no idea what to do. I figured it out, but Ian managed to inflict a lot of damage before I killed him.

Our conversation the previous night had stirred up things for Angel. He'd experienced one of the dreams he had about the confrontation. They always left him unsettled and jumpy the following day. It had broken my heart to feel him jerk in his sleep and begin struggling against what were now invisible restraints, to hear him beg Ian, "Don't hurt her, please, don't hurt her," and to know that I had caused his distress.

I had pulled him to me and held him, stroking his back and telling him Ian was dead, he couldn't hurt us any longer, until at last his body relaxed and his breathing slowed as he slipped back to sleep.

As chaotic and destructive as my involvement with Ian was, without that, I would never have met Frost, and most likely wouldn't be married to Angel. Those were two things that I was grateful for. Life was never all black or all white.

I wasn't sure if Frost was grateful for meeting me. We'd grown very close, but I hadn't made life easier for him. I chose to work in the OR because I wanted to see how the body worked and how it could be fixed. It was a fascinating puzzle; there, my curiosity was a good thing. Knowing Frost seemed to have triggered something in me, some insatiable curiosity that got me into trouble time and again. As the saying goes, curiosity killed the cat. I was beginning to think I was on life number eight and getting precariously close to life number nine.

If I hadn't gotten involved with Ian, Angel would still be doing what he loved—prosecuting cases. I sat on the couch and flopped back against it. There really was no point regretting any of it, nothing could be changed. Our only choice was to get on with our lives and be grateful he was gone. Maybe we did need to move. Staying was stupid and pointless.

I had never been fired before, officially or unofficially, and it had left me depressed. I knew that Frost had no choice—I hadn't given him one—but I had enjoyed working with him enormously, and now I couldn't.

I was startled by my phone ringing. "Hello?"

"Annie, what's going on between you and Alex?"

It was Evie. I had no idea what to tell her. "What?" I stalled.

"Oh, not you, too!" she said. "He won't tell me why he's been moping around the house since Friday, but I expect an answer from you. Now what happened?"

I blew out a breath and said, "He fired me."

"He *what?*" she asked, then paused and said in some confusion, "I knew you were helping him, but I didn't know he'd hired you."

"It was all informal review of cold case files. But as usual, I got involved in a recent active murder case and screwed up. He said he couldn't work with me anymore, even unofficially. It's all my fault. He had no choice, Evie."

There was silence for a few moments. "What did you do?"

I told her a quick version. "I've driven Angel, Frost, and Roberts nuts with my interfering. Angel didn't want me working with Frost in the first place because he knows how involved I get. Anyway, it's irrelevant now."

"Sweetheart, Alex has always enjoyed having you help him. Give him some time to cool down, and he'll come around."

"No, he won't. I've put him in an untenable position with my meddling. Don't bug him about it, please. Maybe if he retires he'll ask me to help him with the PI work, but right now it'd get him into trouble. I don't want that."

"I'll talk to him."

"Please don't. He did what he had to do, and it's my fault he had to."

I heard her sigh. "It'd be much easier if you were a cop, or he was retired and you guys were working as PIs."

I made a lame attempt to laugh. "True. As a PI, all I'd have to deal with is Angel. Besides, I don't think being a cop is really my style. The PI stuff? That I'd enjoy."

"Men can be a real pain, can't they?"

"They can, but, right now, I'm the biggest pain around."

"I like the house in the Highlands. Let's make an offer, the sooner the better," I said out of the blue at dinner that night.

"What?" Angel stopped reaching for a bread roll, his hand hovering in the air, baffled by the abrupt change in topic.

"I like the house, let's see if we can buy it."

"What brought this on?" He changed his mind about the roll and rested his forearm on the table.

"I've thought about it, and I think it would be a good idea to move." I ate a few bites of the lasagna I'd brought home from a nearby restaurant. Angel stared at me, knowing there was more to it than that. I put my fork down and frowned.

"Okay, fine. I went to my side of the apartment this morning and sat in the living room for a while. It feels like he's still there, he probably always will be in some way."

I pushed a bite of the lasagna around on my plate. "You've bent over backwards to accommodate my need to be involved with Frost's work, I think it's time I do the same for you. You said you wanted a permanent home. We'll have to move eventually, since you'll probably want kids at some point, and we don't have a basement to lock them in."

He snorted a laugh. "Sure this doesn't have more to do with Frost than eventual kids and the lack of a basement?"

"It has nothing to do with Frost."

"Sure?"

"Fine, let's stay here, let's see the bastard every time we walk in the back door or past my living room. Whatever," I said. It felt as if I couldn't win.

"Whoa, whoa, whoa, slow down," Angel said holding up his hands. "It's been better for me since we moved to this side of the apartment and we don't have to pass through your living room."

"I guess you don't remember dreaming about it last night. It hasn't settled down for either of us. It bothers me, too. I just didn't realize how much till I sat over there for a while. I think we should move."

"Annie, I may dream about it for quite a while. The shrink says I'm processing it, and that's good. You still dream about him, too. I don't know that moving would solve that. He shrugged. "It might make it less in our faces, though."

He reached across the table and took my hand. "We don't have to make any decisions right this second. We've only been sticking to this side for a week or so. Let's give it a bit more time."

"How much time?"

"A month?" he asked. "I think we both should be able to tell if it's made any real difference by then."

"No," I said. He gave me a surprised look and sat back in his chair. "We can't continue to pretend it's okay to stay here when it's not. We should move."

I did feel Ian's presence, though it was less noticeable now that we'd closed off my old side of the triplex. It would probably never go away living here. Better to get on with our lives so we could eventually put him behind us.

An hour or more later, I sat on my side of the bed and rubbed my forehead. I'd been depressed since my last conversation with Frost, and I had no idea what to do. Going to work at the hospital was a relief as it took my mind off the situation with Frost, but I kept hoping he would call and say he'd overreacted and needed my help. There'd been no call, and there likely wouldn't be. At least I had my job in the OR.

Angel entered the bedroom, sat down next to me, and wrapped an arm around my shoulders. He gave them a squeeze and kissed my temple. "Talk to me, Annie. Why all of a sudden do you want to move? You've been dragging your feet about this since I brought it up. What's changed?"

"I want to be done with this, with Ian, with Frost, with all of this," I said, sweeping my arm around indicating the apartment. "A new house would help both of us move on."

We sat quietly for a few moments. I leaned my head against his shoulder. "I *want* to move on. If we stay here, then it's beginning to feel like we're trapped with him."

"Would you feel that way if you were still working with Frost?"

"This isn't *about* Frost. I miss him, but moving is about what's best for us. It's not about him."

"Let's not make any hasty decisions. Let's give this separation of the units a chance and see if that solves the problem. If not, then I'll get in touch with Bob and go from there."

We sat silently for a few minutes. "You're upset and discouraged because of what happened between you and Frost. Even if he doesn't ask you to work with him, it's not the end of the world. You know he'd never cut you off completely. He'll want you back eventually."

I didn't know that. I was tired, and overwhelmed. "I want to move; I don't think things will change for us unless we do."

Angel shrugged. "Okay, I'll talk to Bob and see what we need to do."

"I need some sleep."

Angel gave my shoulders another squeeze. "Then let's go to bed."

"Do you take drugs?" I asked.

"*What?*"

"It's the only way I can explain your willingness to put up with me."

"It's the sex, *Corazón*. I'm willing to put up with a lot for that," he said with a grin.

I raised my eyebrows at him. "I'll have to remember that," I said as I pulled the covers back and crawled into bed.

THIRTY-FIVE

I **SAW PAUL ROBERTS'S CAR PARKED** in front of the triplex when I got home from a late shift the following day and I decided to ask him about the screwdriver.

When he opened the door of Gabriela's apartment, I held the baggie containing the screwdriver out to him "Can you see if you can pull any fingerprints off this? It was shoved into my car's tire."

"Yeah, any idea who did that?"

"I don't know for sure, but I suspect it was Benny Tulio, the guy who was probably Laura's supplier. Frost hauled him in for questioning about that, and I think he's pissed."

"Dare I ask why he's pissed at you and not Frost?"

"I had Bret Martin asking around about who her supplier was, and he gave me Tulio's name. Bret said people know he's asking around for me. I'm guessing Tulio didn't like it."

"Okay, give it to me and I'll see what I can get off it." He paused. "Sounds to me like he's been following you. That's not good. If you see him or anything more happens, let me know."

Paul didn't ask why I hadn't given the screwdriver to Frost, and I was grateful. I had no intention of telling Frost or Angel.

"I wondered if you'd meet me at Cody's," Frost asked over the phone a week later. I was shocked to hear his voice.

"Why?"

"Come and find out, or don't, if you're still mad at me," he said irritably.

A tiny flame of hope started to grow, and I forced it down as I walked into Cody's. He was probably trying to mend our personal relationship. He couldn't really do much about the job.

"How've you been, kid?" Frost looked uncomfortable.

"I'm fine. We're going to move," I said abruptly, afraid to let him proceed. I was as uncomfortable as Frost looked.

"Yeah, when?"

"I don't know. We're living on Angel's side of the units right now, but hopefully not for long."

"Whereabouts are you looking?"

I frowned, giving in at last to my curiosity. "What is this all about? You didn't arrange this get-together to talk about where we're moving."

"Christ, you never make things easy, do you?"

"Not if you and Angel are to be believed." I stared at him for a moment. "Did Evie or Angel put you up to this?"

"Can't I reconnect with you without you thinking there's some conspiracy involved?"

"No, or you would have done it sooner."

He shook his head and took a drink of his coffee. He'd ordered a turkey sandwich and a bowl of vegetable soup rather than his favorite burger and fries, which surprised me. At least a few miracles happened.

"Okay, fine. I wanted to apologize. I freaked out when you told me what you'd done. I let you go to cover my ass. Angel and I talked—"

"Goddammit! He should have stayed out of this." I threw my napkin down on the table and started to get up.

Frost held up his hand to stop me. "Stop. Sit down and listen."

"Why would he talk to you? He hasn't wanted me to work with

you since…forever…and now?" I threw my hands up in bafflement. "Why would he try to talk you into taking me back?"

"I think he sees how important this is to you. He may not want you involved with this work, but he loves you. Evie would rather I wasn't a cop, but she knows how important it is to me. It's what you do when you love someone. You're willing to move, even though I know you hate the idea."

I frowned. "I don't *hate* the idea." I watched Frost raise an eyebrow at me. "I just don't like the disruption to our lives."

"But you're willing to do it for Angel. Same diff with him." He took a couple spoonsful of soup followed by a bite of sandwich. "He had some good points, good lawyer points. Nothing the kid said to you contradicted what he told Talbot when his lawyer was present, other than he was the one who recognized Laura first and brought up what had happened to her as a kid," he said. "He contacted you—and he didn't insist on his lawyer, so he can't very well tell anyone he was coerced into talking to you."

"So what? I could have jeopardized the case. How does that change anything other than my husband came and begged you to take me back?"

Frost waved me off. "I'd been thinking about it anyway. I didn't tell anyone what I had you doing. Talbot doesn't know about you listening to the two informal interviews—Paul and I aren't going to tell her. I'd like you to continue to help me."

"Why? I'll probably do something equally stupid at some point."

That made him laugh. "Yeah, you're the wild card in the deck, that's for sure."

He took another bite of his sandwich and chewed thoughtfully for a moment. "I don't know. I saw the look on your face when you left. It broke my heart." He fiddled with his napkin and grinned. "My heart's kinda patched together anyway, I probably shouldn't let you break it any further."

When I didn't laugh, he huffed out a breath and said, "I wanted some time to think before I talked to you, I guess. And Evie gave me hell when she found out."

"God!" I swore in exasperation. "People can't leave well enough alone or do what you ask, can they?"

"You don't, why should they?"

"Look, I screwed up, I take responsibility for what I did, and I'll take the consequences. End of story."

"So, you don't want to work with me? Like ever?"

I closed my eyes and took in several deep breaths. "As much as I want to, I don't think I should, Frost. You know me, you know how I go rogue. I can't seem to help myself. It would put you in an awkward position if anyone knew what I did, maybe jeopardize your job. I don't want to do that to you. When you retire, I'd love to work with you if you decide to go the PI route."

"How about a deal then?"

"What kind of deal?"

"You tell me *before* you decide to 'go rogue' as you put it and keep me in the loop—even if you think it'll piss me off or that I would stop you. If I tell you not to do it, there'll be a good reason for it, but I gotta know before you do things."

I watched him and thought about it.

"You've been helpful in the past and this time around too," he added. "You make me nuts 'cause you go off on tangents without telling me. Your tangents aren't necessarily bad ones, but I gotta know before you go there, to keep us both outta trouble."

"What if you're not around or it's urgent?"

Frost gave me his *Are you serious?* look. "Kid, don't play that bullshit with me. You wanna help, you find me, and you tell me whatever you got planned—before you go off half-cocked. No excuses. If you can't find me, you don't do it. Either agree to that, and abide by it, or forget it."

"Okay, I'll try—"

"Nope, none of this try shit. As that little weirdo Yoda says, 'There is no try, there is only do.'" Frost shook his head. "He's weird, but he's got a point, so make a decision, either you agree or you don't."

I had to laugh at that. Frost quoting Yoda, that had to be a first in the history of the world. "Didn't know you were a *Star Wars* fan."

"From the first one, kid."

"Okay, I'll find you and I'll tell you, I promise." I held out my hand. "Should we shake on it?"

"I should probably have you sign something in blood." He shook my hand. "It'd sure be a hell of a lot easier to deal with you if you were a cop."

"So Evie tells me."

THIRTY-SIX

ANGEL HAD MADE THE TRIP to the state psych hospital in Pueblo to talk to Janet Casey's doctors. He said she looked somewhat better. As a younger woman, she'd been diagnosed with schizophrenia, but as often was the case with people similarly diagnosed, she had gone off her meds because of the side effects and her belief that she was fine. And she was, if she took her meds.

It had been a recurring problem. She had been showing signs of deteriorating mental health the previous year and her doctor had convinced her to go back on her meds. She'd been on them for a few months then stopped taking them. The voices, or command hallucinations as the psychiatrist called them, were a symptom of psychosis, and the rape had triggered the psychosis.

The psychiatrist said that in Janet's mind she was simply following the dictates of the voices who had told her to kill Ken Stevens and then God who'd told her that atonement was necessary by confessing. The meds she was on now were helping stabilize her and she seemed at peace with her decision to confess and with where she was, according to Angel. Perhaps confession was good for the soul after all.

Laura's cold case, however, was proving more difficult to resolve, as it had when her assault occurred. Thoughts about her murder were distracting me from the new cold case file Frost had given me—I hadn't even reviewed it. If he knew that, his blood pressure would spike, but I had agreed to his deal, and I planned to abide by it. I sat at our dining room table with Laura's original case file spread out in front of me. As in Crispy's case, it looked as though the detectives assigned had been thorough.

DNA had cleared Andrew Hutchinson, so that line of inquiry dried up. Testing Eleanor's DNA for familial comparison against the semen sample on Laura's dress had knocked her brother to the bottom of the suspect list, but his DNA was needed to definitively rule him out. Talbot had been unable to locate him; it was as if he'd dropped off the face of the earth. My guess was he had either died or disappeared into the huge population of homeless people who lived in cities across the US. It was unlikely he would ever be found unless he chose to contact his sister.

What struck me as odd, was the original investigators hadn't taken DNA swabs from men in the Hutchinson's neighborhood, but then, that was a lot of samples to process, and that cost time and money. None of the men interviewed had aroused any suspicions or they were alibied, so nothing was done. It was also a wealthy neighborhood, which often meant that residents weren't pushed. I also didn't see any mention of a search for like crimes in the file. I'd have to ask Frost why.

Mike Lewis as the killer didn't fit, for me at least. I doubted he would have mentioned the incident if he had been the one to rape Laura. He didn't fit as a pedophile either. If he liked little girls, chances were high that he'd have started by abusing his sister. It was clear Mike's sister cared about him. I couldn't see her standing up for him if he had abused her.

Something Mike had said to Laura set off a chain reaction, and it made me think she'd finally remembered who had abducted and raped her. If she had tried to blackmail the person, then whomever it was had put a stop to it permanently. It didn't take Sherlock Holmes to come up with that. The problem was figuring out who that person was.

"Frost, it's me. Gotta minute? I need to talk some things over with you."

"Okay. I'm driving, you're on speaker phone. Talk to me."

"No one could get Laura to talk or identify her abuser. Maybe she *couldn't* ID the person because she'd repressed that information, or perhaps she was afraid to ID him. You know how it is with kids who are abuse victims. They don't tell anyone what's going on because they fear the abuser will harm their family. That's especially true with young kids. They believe the abuser when he convinces them parents or pets will be killed if they tell what happened."

"Yeah, so?"

"It seems to me that as soon as she was old enough to reason that out, she'd have told someone. That leaves repression of the incident. Her friend Jayden Byers said she didn't think Laura knew who it was."

"You're not working on the new cold case, are you?" he asked resignedly.

"Um…no. I mean I planned to; then I got to thinking." I could almost see him shaking his head or pinching the bridge of his nose. "What if talking to Mike triggered her memory of who it was? She told Bret that she was coming into some money that would help them. That sounds like blackmail to me. Maybe talking to Mike helped her remember the person responsible for her assault and she approached them, and whoever it was killed her?"

"That may have been what happened, but we have no way to prove it, unless Mike knows something and will talk." I heard Frost drumming on the steering wheel. "She could just as easily have been mugged or have crossed her supplier or a buyer who overreacted in the moment, then finished her off. She borrowed five hundred bucks from Jayden Byers. That suggests to me she needed it to pay off someone she owed money to. The fact is, we have no idea why she was killed."

"True, but think about it," I said. "Who would Mike know who would have had the opportunity for contact with Laura? It had to be someone close to him to trigger her memory when she realized who Mike was."

"You're assuming her memory *was* triggered. Again, it could have been a random mugging turned lethal—she had no purse, money, or ID on her," Frost said. "It could just as easily have been a confrontation with her supplier."

I heard a horn blare, and Frost muttered, "Asshole," then he continued. "It's also possible that over a few days after talking to Mike she might have remembered what had happened. If she did, and he was the one responsible for her abduction, she could have confronted him the night she died, demanded money not to out him, and he killed her."

"If he was responsible, why would he even mention knowing her?" I asked.

"It could have been a fishing expedition to see what, or if, she remembered anything. You know, say you're sorry and see what happens."

"I don't think he'd risk it. If he was guilty, he's gotten away with it all these years, why risk getting ID'd now?"

"I'm just saying any of those scenarios are possible. But we have nothing to prove or disprove any of them."

"I think, if he was guilty, he'd have bought the drugs and left. He wouldn't have even had to mention his name—I doubt dealers or their clients exchange social niceties. I don't buy the drug deal or mugging gone bad either," I said. "The confrontation with her supplier is a reasonable possibility, but if the money was to pay him off, why kill her?"

"Who knows. By the way, Vice hauled Tulio in on an unrelated issue. Apparently, he's been causing all sorts of problems. Roberts talked to Kaye Jagerski and told her about Laura's connection, but he said they didn't get much more than we did."

Frost didn't say Paul had told him about the screwdriver, so I went back to Mike Lewis to divert him "Mike knows something about Laura's abduction and rape, I'm sure of it. Either he killed her or he knows who did."

"I agree that he knows something. The question is what? We've got no evidence, nothing that connects him, his sister, or his parents to Laura's murder, other than them attempting to keep us from finding him. Considering the trouble he's been in, that's not all that surprising."

"Yeah, I know," I said resignedly. "But I know there's a connection. We have to get Mike to talk—without the lawyer."

"That's unlikely, especially after your little chat with him. As a result," he continued, "he won't talk to us without counsel. My guess is he won't talk to you again, period. One of the many reasons you need to listen to me."

THIRTY-SEVEN

THAT EVENING, MY PHONE RANG. Thinking it was Angel calling to let me know he was either on his way home or to let me know it would be a very late night, I answered.

"May I speak to Annie Collins, please?" a male voice asked.

"Speaking, who is this?"

"Noah Granger, I'm the nursing supervisor in the ER at Denver Health. We have a patient here who asked that I call you. Do you know a Bret Martin?"

"Yes, what's happened to him?"

"He was assaulted. He won't give any details to us or to the officer who responded to the 911 call. I'm hoping you may be able to get more out of him, he claims you're his emergency contact."

I had been gathering my coat and purse as I held my phone to my ear. "I'll be there shortly, let him know I'm on my way."

I was escorted by security through the automatic doors to the ER nurses' station where I met Noah Granger. "How badly is he hurt?"

Granger walked around the desk and started to walk down the hall. "I'll take you to see him."

I grabbed his arm and halted him. "Answer me, is he badly hurt?"

"He's been beaten up, he has several broken ribs, a concussion, and a broken nose. He's taken some hard blows to his abdomen, so we're waiting for CT to come get him to make sure there are no internal injuries and no intracranial bleeding. The doctor doesn't think there is, but best to confirm. He's not doing badly all things considered." He stopped at a cubicle and parted its curtains. "Mr. Martin, your friend is here to see you." He nodded at me. "I'll be at the front desk if you need anything."

Bret's nose was splinted and the skin around both his eyes was bruised. He had a scrape on his jaw and had wrapped an arm protectively around his ribs. He had a line of stitches in the hair near his temple.

"Jesus, Bret, what happened?"

He shifted his position on the gurney and grimaced in pain. "Payback for asking around about Laura's supplier. He didn't like it, told me to stop asking or I wouldn't be able to ask. This was his idea of a first warning." The effort of telling me that exhausted him, and he let his eyes close.

"Why wouldn't you tell the cop who responded to the 911 what happened?"

He opened his eyes and glared at me. "Because I don't want to be killed and I don't want you to be either."

"Me?"

"Yeah, you. He knows that you're the one who wanted to know about him. People know I'm connected to you and Laura. People know I was the one asking around about the guy talking to Laura and word got around about the drawing. I asked people to tell him I wanted to talk to him. He said to tell you to stop causing him problems or he'd cause problems for you."

"Well, I can't do that, especially since he assaulted you. I'll let Frost know and he can pick him up—"

"No!" he said sharply. "You don't want to mess with this guy. Annie, please. If I don't say anything and you don't either, he'll go away."

"Bret he could have killed Laura and he hurt you."

"I'm pretty sure the five hundred Laura borrowed was to pay him back money she owed him. He got what he wanted; he had no reason to kill her."

Before I could continue the conversation, the nurse taking care of Bret walked into the cubicle and checked his vitals and did a neuro check. "Are they going to discharge him?" I asked.

"It's late; getting the tests done and read will take time. The doctor wants to see what the CTs show and monitor him for bleeding. By that time it'll be nearly morning, so we'll keep him here in the ER until then. Unless his condition changes, he'll be ready for discharge early tomorrow morning." She turned to him. "How's the head, did the Tylenol help?"

"A bit. I can't decide what hurts worse, my head or my ribs."

"No surprise there," she said with a smile. She left the cubicle and returned a few minutes later with a cold pack. "This should help your head. I'll be back later to check on you. If you need anything in the meantime, just use the call button."

"Thanks," he replied letting his eyes close.

"I'll come back in the morning and get you. Is there anyone I should let know about what happened?"

"No, not with Laura gone. You said if I needed anything to let you know, so I had them call you."

"I'm glad you did." I reached out and touched his free hand. "It's almost impossible in an ER, but try to get some rest. You're safe here and in good hands. We can talk more in the morning."

"Okay," he said, letting out a weary sigh. "Thanks." I turned and started to leave when he said, "I'm serious, Annie. Let this go and be careful, I don't want him to hurt you."

I left his cubicle and returned to the front desk. Spotting Noah Granger, I took him aside. "No visitors," I said. "No one except me is to be allowed contact with him. Okay?"

"Is there something we should be aware of?"

"I don't want whoever did this to come back. Make sure everyone knows, please."

"I will. Perhaps we should notify the officer who was here earlier."

I lied. "Bret won't say who did this, so that's probably pointless. Just make sure no one gets in to see him."

∽

"Where've you been?" Angel asked when I entered the front door. He was ensconced on the couch and had a frown on his face.

"I…" I hadn't thought about what to say, but decided it was best to be straight with him, he'd obviously been worried. "I got a call from the ER at Denver Health. Bret Martin, Laura's boyfriend, asked that they call me. He was assaulted and said I was his emergency contact."

The frown on his face deepened considerably. "Why call you?"

"Now that Laura's gone, apparently, I'm the only person he knows who'd help. Very few of his friends have cars…I guess."

"And you know him how?" I saw his lawyer's face drop into place.

"I talked to him about Laura, a while ago. He was able to get in touch with the person who'd seen her talking to Mike Lewis. That's how Frost finally ID'd him."

"Was his assault connected to that?"

I debated for a second about what to say then mentally shrugged. "Yes. I asked him to find out who her supplier was so Frost could find out whether he was the one who killed Laura and if the five hundred dollars she'd borrowed from a friend had been to pay the guy off. Evidently, he didn't like that."

The unreadable face dropped away. He slammed his hand down on the arm of the couch and jolted to his feet his face awash with anger. "Goddammit Annie! Why do you insist on keeping things from me? Jesus fucking Christ, you're right back in the thick of things aren't you?" He paced in front of me. "Things are better for me and I've tried to be flexible about this, but this guy could come after you if he knows you've been behind this kid's asking about him."

I chose not to mention what Bret had told me or about the screwdriver. There had been no further incidents directed at me. We were both silent for a few moments. I had no idea what to say, and Angel looked as if he was desperately trying not to say anything further.

"Look—" I started to say.

Angel shook his head and held his hand up to stop me. "No, I don't want to hear it. Just leave me alone."

He slept in the guest bedroom that night.

The following day, I called in sick for work so I could deal with Bret. Angel had left early and we hadn't talked. At least he hadn't disappeared on me. I hoped we could talk later.

Bret and I sat in my car in the parking lot across from the ER. The area around both his eyes was dark purple from the broken nose, and he guarded his ribs, each movement causing him pain.

"Did they give you a prescription for pain meds?" He nodded. He laid his head against the headrest and closed his eyes. "Bret, where did this guy attack you?"

"I was coming home from a friend's, and he took me by surprise, pulled me into the alley and started wailing on me. I feel like shit. Can you please just take me home?"

"Does he know where you live?"

"I don't think so."

"Okay, I'll take you home and then fill your prescription."

Getting him up the stairs to his apartment was a struggle, he was exhausted and every step jolted his ribs. After getting him settled I returned later with his pain med. I sat on the small coffee table next to

the couch where he'd insisted on resting and waited until he had taken his pain med.

"Keep your phone handy so I can check in on you later." I hesitated. "You're sure the guy doesn't know where you live?"

"Not positive, but I don't think so. I'm just gonna sleep. Christ I had no idea ERs were so fucking noisy." He saw the frown on my face. "Look, I'll be fine."

"I'll still check in, so answer your phone."

THIRTY-EIGHT

I F BRET WON'T PRESS CHARGES or confirm who assaulted him, then there's not much I can do," Frost said on the phone. "I can have Vice pull Tulio in again and have a chat with him, but I can't arrest him."

"I don't know if it's worth it. It could put Bret in danger if the guy thinks he talked to the police. Let it go, for now."

"Okay, let me know if the kid changes his mind about pressing charges."

I left the house to meet my friend and former coworker Chip Elliot at Saint Anthony's cafeteria for lunch. His shifts in the ICU there had been a bit crazy. This was the first opportunity we'd had to see each other in a while.

"For what it's worth, I think moving is a good idea," he told me. "Now that both of you are recovered and back to work, that place can't be good for either of you."

"I know. I wish I hadn't suggested separating the two spaces instead of agreeing to move when he first brought it up. I just want to move on, so we're looking. When's your tour here up?" I asked to change the subject.

"Two more weeks according to the original contract, but I'm going to stay on for another few months. I like the hospital and the ICU here, and my dads like that I'm home. Who knows? I may just quit the traveling nurse business."

"It'd be nice to have you around again. I've missed you."

Chip smiled and looked at his watch. "Damn, I have to go, sweetie. Let's talk tomorrow and plan a get-together, all of us." He stood up, walked to my side of the table, and gave me a kiss on the cheek. "Try to stay out of trouble, 'kay?"

I nodded as he made to pick up his tray. I waved him off. "I'll take care of this."

After dropping off our trays, I was on the way across the hospital entrance lobby, digging in my purse for my car keys, when I heard a voice say, "What are you doing here?"

I looked up to see Mike Lewis standing a few feet from me. "Visiting with a friend. Why are you here?"

He looked belligerent, then uncertain. "My mother's in the hospital."

"I'm sorry to hear that. What happened to her?"

He chewed on his lower lip. "She, uh, I guess she fell and hit her head on a table edge. My father came home to find her unconscious and called 911."

"Is she okay?"

He nervously rubbed the back of his hand under his nose. "I guess so. She seems okay. I wanted to…to make sure."

I nodded noncommittally. When I'd seen him last, he'd been twitchy, pale, and stressed and didn't look good at all. I'd wondered at the time if he was coming off something. Now he looked more clear-eyed than previously, which made me wonder if he was trying to quit drugs.

"I hope she recovers." I began to turn away when he stopped me with a hand on my arm. I stared at him until he removed it.

"Sorry," he said. "I was pretty upset the other day…but…" He glanced around furtively and frowned.

"Mike, what's going on?"

"Nothing! I recognized you and I wanted to apologize…I acted like a jerk."

I eyed him, sure there was something else he'd wanted to say. "Apology accepted." I reached into my purse, searching for something to write on. "Here," I said, scribbling my phone number on the back of a dry-cleaning receipt. "Call me if you need anything or want to talk."

He snatched the receipt out of my hand, shoved it in his jeans pocket, then said in a barely audible voice, "I don't think she—"

"Michael? What are you doing here?" Mike jerked around to see Tom Lewis striding toward us. Mike's eyes went wide; then his face went blank.

"I was going to check in on Mom and see how she was doing." He gestured at me. "This lady was just asking if I knew where the cafeteria was," he said, not realizing that his father knew I was connected to the police.

It was stupid thing for him to say, but I was stuck with it.

Lewis raised his eyebrows at me. "Really?" His eyes narrowed. "I know you—you're the woman in the car who accompanied the detective when he interviewed my wife and me at our home, aren't you? What are you up to, trying to entrap my son?"

"I was here to meet with a friend. I didn't know he was your son," I figured I'd best throw that in to calm Lewis down and keep Mike out of trouble. "I'm not sure why you think I was trying to entrap him." I chose not to address Mike's cafeteria comment.

The look on Lewis's face was skeptical. He stared at me long enough to make my skin crawl, then said, as he clamped a hand around Mike's upper arm, "Stay away from my son and my wife or I'll file a complaint."

He spun Mike around and escorted him to the elevators, leaving me standing open-mouthed as I pulled my phone out of my coat pocket.

"What?" Frost said when he picked up the call.

"I just had a rather odd conversation with Mike and Tom Lewis—"

"What the hell are you doing talking to them? I told you to clear things with me first."

"Stop! Listen to me for a minute." I headed for the parking garage and got into my car. Out of the corner of my eye I thought I saw the guy who'd been standing outside Mike Lewis's apartment, but when I turned there was no one there. Bret's assault and the run in with Tom Lewis had me on high alert.

"I didn't set up a meeting or seek them out. I was at Saint Anthony's having lunch with Chip. On my way out, I ran into Mike Lewis in the lobby. He stopped me and asked why I was there, then apologized for his behavior the other day.

"Apparently, his mother is in the hospital from a fall that resulted in a head injury. He acted like he wanted to talk to me but changed his mind. I gave him my phone number again in case he wanted to talk to me privately. He started to say something when his father showed up. Tom Lewis saw me sitting in Roberts's car the day Paul interviewed them. Unfortunately, he remembered me and accused me of trying to entrap Mike. Not sure what he thinks I'd entrap him into saying, but he marched the kid off pretty quickly. He obviously doesn't want him talking to me."

"You said the kid started to say something, what'd he say?"

"All he got out before his dad showed up was, 'I don't think she,' but he didn't have a chance to finish the sentence. I'm guessing the wife was admitted last night. Saint A's is where the ambulance service would bring an emergency from Evergreen. She's in for observation, which means it must have been a pretty serious blow to the head. I wonder whether Mike thinks it isn't an accident. I thought you should know, see what you can find out."

There was silence on the line. "Frost?"

"I'm still here, just thinking. I've got some sources to talk to. I'll get back to you later," he said and hung up.

I pulled the phone away from my ear and stared at it. The conversation had lit a fire under Frost.

⌒

"What'd you find out?" I asked Frost without preamble when he picked up my call the following day. I'd waited all morning for him to call, finally giving in and calling him on my lunch break.

"On the surface, not much. I contacted a cop I know in Jefferson County, and he looked into the 911 report. The call from Lewis came in at about three p.m. the day she was admitted. Seems on the up and up. He stated to the operator that he'd just gotten home and found his wife unconscious. According to the officer on scene, it looked as if she'd fallen and hit her head on a craft table of some sort in the basement.

"I talked to an ER nurse I know at Saint A's. She wouldn't give me any details other than that Charlotte had been brought in by ambulance with a head injury that required monitoring. She gave me the names of the EMTs who picked her up. They said that it looked as if she'd hit her head on the edge of a table on her way down to the floor. They wouldn't say anything more than that. I have no idea what caused the fall. The only one who can tell us how it happened is Charlotte Lewis.

"The cop I talked to said according to the officer on scene, Lewis seemed concerned, kept saying he shouldn't have left earlier, that she was complaining of not feeling well, he wished he'd come home sooner—the usual stuff people babble when someone's injured," Frost said.

"Not feeling well? How was she not feeling well?"

"Annie, neither the nurse nor the EMTs would give me any more info. At the moment, I have no reason to contact Lewis or his wife. The accident has nothing to do with their son or what happened to Laura. I wouldn't even know about this, other than your tip."

"Lewis hasn't forgotten me and filing a complaint wouldn't be good."

"Yeah, his threat complicates things a bit. Roberts never took you in on the interview, he had you sit in the car, and that's not a violation of protocol. If Lewis lodges a complaint about you, all Roberts has to say is you sat in the car while he talked to them. No one knows he let you listen to the recording. I'll give him a head's up just in case."

"Okay, but what about—"

"Hold your horses a minute. I'll try to come up with a reason to contact Tom or Charlotte Lewis that doesn't have anything to do with her accident to see what I can find out. I'm going to let it rest for a bit though. Seeing you pissed off Tom, best to let him cool off before I push anything."

"What d'you think?"

"I think it bears looking into. Her accident is a little close to our confrontations with them at headquarters for my liking—sorta similar to how close Laura's conversation with Mike was to her death. Makes me wonder if Charlotte knows something that either her son or her husband didn't want her to talk about. Or who knows? She could have passed out and hit her head, or tripped, or slipped."

"Frost? Before you go, I had a thought. I don't see any mention in the file regarding Laura's original assault about the detectives searching for like crimes to see if there were any then, or even now. I doubt if whoever assaulted her has stopped, maybe you could find a pattern or a suspect doing that. If you can, run the DNA from her clothing through the data base and see if anyone matches now. Maybe the guy got picked up for some other reason."

"That's not a bad idea. I'll take a look at the file we have here and see what was done and ask someone in the Sex Crimes unit to do a search for that and possible DNA matches."

"You'll keep me posted on Charlotte's accident and the search?"

"Yeah, just don't go doing anything on your own. Remember your promise."

"I remember," I said.

THIRTY-NINE

ANGEL AND I HAD TALKED but I felt as if we were right back on the thin ice. As I had promised, I told him about the encounter with Mike and Tom Lewis.

"You ran into him at Saint A's?" Angel asked.

"Yeah. Mike was as surprised to see me as I was to see him. I'd been there having lunch with Chip and was on my way to the car when he stopped me. Tom Lewis showed up, saw his son with me, and was not a happy camper."

"How'd he know who you were?"

I took a deep breath. "I rode with Roberts when he went to Evergreen to interview them the first time—but I sat in the car, I didn't go in with him. Lewis followed Paul out onto the front entrance of the house and saw me sitting in the car. He remembered me for some reason."

"Why did Paul take you with him?"

"He wanted to talk to me about Gabriela."

"If that fucker plans to dump her, I'll—"

"Angel, stop. He wants to ask her to marry him, but he's worried about how much younger she is than him. I didn't tell you because he hasn't asked her yet. Please don't say anything to her about it. He loves her; he isn't going to hurt her."

"Fine," Angel said with a scowl on his face. "Not sure I want her married to a cop," he grumbled.

"That's not up to you, big brother."

He shot me an annoyed look. Returning to the issue at hand, he said, "At least he made you sit in the car. Do you really think Tom Lewis hurt his wife?"

"Paul let me listen to the interview he taped." Angel started to object. I held up my hand to stop him, but for a moment, I thought he'd actually say "Objection!" as if I was being questioned in court.

"Based on what I heard, Lewis was helpful, but she pretty much let him do the talking. If she's intimidated by him, and she confronted him about something, I could easily see him hitting her. Falling and hitting her head may have been an accident unrelated to him or he could've hit her hard enough it caused the fall. Who knows?"

"Okay, but other than him *possibly* being controlling and *possibly* an abuser, what has this got to do with Laura's murder?"

"It may have nothing to do with it." I offered him a beer and sat down next to him on the couch. "When Frost and Talbot conducted the interview with Charlotte and her husband, he shut her down pretty fast. She's a bit of an idiot, though, so that may be why he didn't want her talking. Charlotte knows something, or maybe Mike does, and he doesn't want either of them talking."

I took a sip of beer. "I don't know if any of that's connected to Laura's murder, but based on his reaction when he saw his father, I think Mike didn't want his father to know he'd been at the hospital, and I want to know why. Charlotte's accident just seems a little too close to that interview. Maybe it wasn't an accident."

He raised his eyebrows at me. "Accidents do happen."

"I know that!" I snapped. "Her husband, though, is a real piece of work. They're all antsy about something. There's a lot of weirdness going on with that family, but it may have nothing to do with Laura.

I thought Frost should know, though, and do a little digging. Just in case it wasn't an accident."

"Thanks for letting Frost handle this," Angel said.

"That was the deal. I have to run everything by him first. I had to sign in blood before he'd take me back."

"When has that ever stopped you?" There it was again, that tone of frustration in his voice.

I was silent for a bit, then said, "Things have changed. I plan to cooperate." I took a sip of beer and returned the bottle to the coffee table. Resting my head on his shoulder I said, "I'll be careful. I want to work with Frost, but I don't want you to fire me."

"It's called divorce. You can't fire a spouse."

Ever the lawyer, I thought, but at least there was some humor in the comment.

"Maybe not, but everyone has their limits. I pushed Frost over his and I've pushed you too far." I was surprised to find myself choking up a bit, and I took a deep breath. "I don't want you to get fed up and leave me." I slipped my arm across his chest and snuggled in as he wrapped his arm around my shoulders.

We were quiet for a time. I wouldn't continue to withhold things from him, and would abide by Frost's conditions to work with him.

Angel interrupted my thoughts. "I'd never been in love before I met you," he said at last, giving me a small laugh that sounded more like frustration than amusement. "In like, in lust, maybe even infatuated a time or two, but never in love. It figures that when I did fall in love, I picked someone who doesn't just frustrate me but terrifies me. The thought that I could lose you, especially after what we went through…" He squeezed my shoulders, a little too hard, as if to anchor me to him. "I wish you weren't involved at all. It's not realistic or fair of me to expect you to give up something that you want to do. I'm not asking you to permanently. Just be extra careful for a while. I need some time to not have to worry about you."

He was quiet for a few moments. "It's nice to know you don't want to be fired."

"Or divorced," I said, not lifting my head off his shoulder.

"*Chica*, if I haven't divorced you by now, I think you're safe."

Think being the operative word, which wasn't all that comforting.

FORTY

WALKING TOWARD MY CAR in the parking garage after finishing my late-night shift, a man stepped out of the shadows and blocked me. I dropped my hand to my side and shifted the ignition key between my index and middle finger and gripped the fob in my fist to use the key as a weapon. Based on his appearance it was a good idea—he was the screwdriver guy.

"What do you want?" I asked keeping my hand at my side.

He stepped closer to me. "You keep causing me problems and you'll look a hell of a lot worse than that kid does."

"You're Benny Tulio?"

"See now, that wasn't the right response. The right response is you'll forget my name and stop asking questions. The fucking cops hauled me in, twice. I figure you're responsible for that. That wasn't smart."

"It wasn't smart for you to ruin my tire or beat that kid up. You're causing problems for yourself. They had no evidence, all you had to do was keep your mouth shut, and it'd be over."

"I hate smart-ass women." He took a menacing step towards me, and I backed up. Surprising me, he lunged forward grabbing my throat under my jaw and shoving me up against a nearby concrete pillar. "Back off. I didn't kill her. She owed me money, but she paid up. I had no reason to kill her, but I'm more than happy to get rid of you and Martin if you keep causing problems for me, got it?"

I nodded, but he continued to squeeze my throat, and didn't back off. Realizing this wasn't going to end well if allowed to go on, I raised my hand and drug my key down the side of his face as I brought my knee up and connected with his crotch. He howled and dropped to the ground. I ran for the door to the hospital, pulling my phone out of my purse.

"What?" Frost barked.

"Tulio found me at work—"

"Are you okay?"

"Shook up, but no injuries. He's got a slice down his face and his balls are going to be sore for a while. If you can find him, I'm happy to press charges."

"I'll take care of it. Have security make sure he isn't still there and have them walk you to your car. I'll be in touch in the morning."

When I arrived home, the shakes had stopped. I checked my reflection in the bathroom mirror. There were dark, red marks under my jaw that would no doubt turn into bruises before long. Undressing in the bathroom, I quietly crawled into bed, hoping I wouldn't wake Angel. I'd have a lot to explain in the morning.

Angel never woke up easily, and it took him a few moments to notice the bruises. He set his coffee mug down on the kitchen counter and walked over to me. Reaching out, he gently grasped my chin and turned my head from side to side.

"What happened?" he asked, and I could hear the worry in his voice.

"I'm fine—"

"I didn't ask how you were, I asked what happened. Who did this to you?"

"The guy who assaulted Bret Martin. Frost had him picked up a few days ago, then Vice did, and he decided that I needed convincing to back off."

He let go of my chin and closed his eyes for a moment. "Does Frost know?" I nodded. "When did you call him?"

"Right after it happened."

"But not me?"

"It was over, you were asleep, there was nothing you could have done. I intended to tell you this morning."

"Don't do this to me, Annie. If you want me to stop worrying, then you need to stop giving me things to worry about. At the very least, you should have told me when you got home." He ran a hand through his hair in frustration and paced away from me.

"Here's the deal," he said turning to me at last. "You text me when you're on your way home or if you get delayed. I'll do the same. If something like this happens you call *me first*, then Frost, because *I'm your goddammed husband!*" he shouted and disappeared into our bedroom.

I was changing in the women's locker room at the end of my shift a few days later when I heard a text message alert. Most likely Angel, I thought, wondering whether I'd left the hospital yet. I finished dressing and opened my texts.

<I need to meet w/u>

I frowned. I didn't recognize the phone number.

<Who is this?>
<Mike. Can u meet me tonight?>
<It's late, why tonight?>

<It's important, please>

After the run in-with Tulio, who had been arrested and jailed for the assault on Bret and me, I wasn't comfortable meeting him this late anywhere except the hospital I was at or the precinct where help was available, if needed.

<Where are you?>
<At the apartment where I'm staying, I'll send you the address. Can u meet me there?>
<No. What's this about?>
<Laura, what happened to Laura. I need to talk to u. Please>
<Why don't we meet at the police department, and you can talk to me and Detective Frost?>
<NO!!!>

That was a lot of exclamation points.

<Okay, if you'll come to the hospital where I work, I'll meet you in the cafeteria. Otherwise, it'll have to be at the precinct.>
<OK where?>

I told him and I went down to the lobby and into the cafeteria. *I should call Frost.* I pulled my phone out and hesitated. It was late, but I'd promised, so I called.

"Jesus, what time is it?" Frost grumbled.

"Frost, it's me. I just got a text from Mike Lewis. He wants to talk to me about Laura. He's got something that's bugging him enough to want to tell me. He's going to meet me here at the hospital—"

"I'll be there in ten."

"I suggested meeting at the precinct so you could be there, but he refused. If you show up, I think he'll bolt. It's the hospital, it's safe, I can talk to him and then let you know what he said."

There was silence on the line for a moment or two. "I'm coming over. I have to be there, Annie, in case anything goes down or he confesses."

"Okay, text me when you get here, but stay out of sight until I have a chance to convince him to talk to you."

I sat at a table in the corner and texted Angel.

<I'm going to be a little late. Frost and I are meeting Mike Lewis here at the hospital. I'll text when I'm on my way home.>

It was a few minutes until I got a response.

<Frost will be there?>
<Yes.>

Again, several minutes went by.

<Be safe, please.>
<I will. Love you.>
<Same.>

Same. That left a lot to be desired, but it was late and he'd most likely been asleep. Movement caught my eye, and I looked up to see Mike at the cafeteria doorway. I quickly opened my recording app and activated it, leaving the phone on the table. Mike came over and took a seat. I saw Frost walk in a minute later and quietly take a seat several tables over and behind Mike's back. Frost nodded at me.

"Thanks…thanks for meeting me," Mike said.

There was a scruff of beard on his face, and his hair was in disarray. His one eye was swollen and bruised, and he had a cut lip. "Mike what happened to you?"

He touched his face gently, closed his eyes, and shook his head as if trying to make something go away. "It's not important, I'll tell you later." He paused and again shook his head. "I can't carry this anymore. It's weighed on me…forever. I thought I was doing the right thing." He grimaced. "No, that's not the truth, and I promised myself to tell the truth. He said that's what was needed, to make amends."

"Amends? He? Who are you talking about Mike?"

He frowned as if in pain. "I've been attending an addiction recovery group, NA, you know, like AA except for drug addicts. I've been going there since I heard about Laura's murder. I feel responsible for that. If I'd told the truth years ago, it wouldn't have happened. If I hadn't talked to her, it wouldn't have happened. I went on a real meth binge after I heard, three days straight until I crashed. A friend took care of me and then took me to this group.

"Jack, the guy who sponsors me, said getting clean of the drugs was just the start, that addicts have to get clean in their heads, too. Be honest with ourselves at the very least, then make amends to the people we've harmed. I thought about that a lot, but I didn't know what to do. I asked to talk to you; I thought about just coming clean then, but I couldn't. When you said it wasn't all about me, it hit home."

I was afraid for him. I thought he was going to confess to killing Laura, and I stopped him. "Mike, you should talk to Detective Frost if—"

He cut me off. "No, no, just you."

I sighed. "No, Mike. You want to get clean, you want to make whatever happened right, you need to talk to Frost. I don't count."

He looked scared to death, and I was afraid he'd get up and disappear. Finally, almost imperceptibly, he said, "Okay. Do we have to go to the precinct?"

"No, Frost is here, you can tell us here." He started to cry, and I waved Frost over. "Mike has something he wants to tell you."

Frost clicked the recording app on his phone. "Let's hear it, son, get it off your chest. But before you do, I want to make this official." Frost recorded our names and then recited the Miranda warning. "Do you understand?" Mike nodded. "Do you want a lawyer?" Mike shook his head no. "I'd need to hear you say it out loud. I want all of us to know you're on board with this."

"I'm talking to you voluntarily, and I don't want a lawyer," Mike said. "I'll take the consequences, whatever they are." He reached for a paper napkin from the dispenser on the table and wiped his face and nose.

After taking a huge breath and letting it out, he began. "I should have said something a long time ago, but I figured it'd ruin what was left of my family. Mom and my father...I was a major disappointment to them. I guess I wasn't the son they wanted. That's what started the acting out and the drugs, a way to get attention, even if it was negative attention, but what happened made it worse. It ruined me...Laura, too, I guess."

"Mike, did you assault Laura? Did you kill her?" Frost asked.

He shook his head violently. "No...no...but I might as well have. I never told. God, it's been so hard, I never thought it would be. What happened had already happened, I couldn't change that." He paused and wiped at his face again. "Jack says not telling someone who could correct a wrong is a heavy load. He said I should stop carrying it and speak the truth, but he doesn't know what the truth is. I decided to do it, but it took me a while to figure out how."

"Do you know who assaulted and killed Laura?" Frost asked

"My...father assaulted her," he finally whispered and began to sob.

"How did you find out?"

I pulled several more napkins from the dispenser and handed them to him. He wiped at his face and blew his nose. Staring down at the table, he refused to look Frost or me in the eyes.

"I don't know if he killed her, but he assaulted her. I overheard him arguing with Mom the night Laura disappeared. Mom knew, and she covered for him. She took Laura into the mountains miles west of where we lived and left Laura alone there. He was furious with her for doing that. He said if she was going to do that, she should have killed Laura. Mom said that Laura wouldn't survive and when her body was found her death would be attributed to the kid getting lost and… exposure." Mike laid his head on his crossed arms and then raised it and continued talking.

"Mom was just as furious. She told my dad he'd been a fool to take a kid that close to their home, that that wasn't the agreement, that he'd taken an unnecessary risk just to appease his appetite. That's what she said. I don't know what she meant by that."

He twisted the paper napkin he was holding into shreds. "I was totally freaked out and left. Later, I wondered if I said I knew what they'd done and that I wouldn't say anything to anyone…I thought they would…that I wouldn't be such a disappointment to them. They'd see that I was protecting them, but it was stupid to think that.

"I waited until the end of the school year. I had to wait…I didn't have anywhere else to go. When I graduated, I told them I'd over-heard their conversation. I said I'd keep their secret in return for them supporting me, giving me money when I needed it.

"I stayed away from them after that. I don't trust my dad, or mom for that matter. A kid should be able to trust their parents, but I don't. He did this to me after he saw me with you at the hospital," Mike said indicating his face. "He told me if I said a word to anyone, I'd regret it." Mike finally raised his eyes and looked at me, a pained expression on his face.

"After I told them, I never met with them face-to-face, and I moved around a lot. It sounds crazy, but I thought they'd kill me if they could. They were my parents, but I didn't think that would matter if they thought I was going to say something to the police. All they had was my cell, and I would call them periodically for money, which they sent to a P.O. box I had. I always had a friend pick it up.

"I think, maybe, Laura remembered what had happened after we talked. I think she tried to blackmail my mother or my dad, and when they met with her, they—" His face was a mask of misery. Dropping his head in his hands, he sobbed. At last, he raised it and looked at me and Frost. "I'm so sorry."

"D'you know where the assault happened?"

"No."

"It won't bring Laura back, but it'll give her some justice," Frost said. "I'm going to take you to the precinct and talk to my partner and the DA to see where we go with this. Meantime, you'll need to make a formal statement."

I saw the flare of panic on his face, and I quickly said, "It's got to be official, Mike."

"Oh God, I should never have listened to Jack."

I walked around the table and grabbed him by the shoulders, giving him a shake. "Stop right now! You want absolution or to make amends for what you *didn't* do, what you *should* have done? Then man up. You stood by and let two people get away with ruining a little girl's life, then ending it, when she had a future ahead of her and a child on the way." His eyes widened in surprise.

"Did it ever occur to you that, in addition to Laura, your father may have sexually abused your sister or God knows how many other kids? Maybe that was the agreement your mother referred to. Allow him to 'appease his appetites' as long as he didn't abuse your sister."

It looked as if Mike hadn't thought about his sister being a possible victim, or any other child for that matter. Frost stood up and hooked his hand around Mike's upper arm. "C'mon, let's go." Mike tried to pull his arm away, and Frost stepped in close. "Cooperate or I'll cuff you right here."

◇

It was a long night. I didn't arrive home until nearly four in the morning. I woke Angel up when I slipped into bed and curled up around him. He turned over, took me in his arms, and we lay entwined for several minutes.

"People are incredibly fucked up," I said at last.

"Yeah, they are. What'd you find out?"

I told him. By the time I finished, I was in tears. "He could have put an end to this years ago. Who knows how many children Lewis molested and his wife covered up for him? Laura should never have tried to blackmail them; she should have come to the police. At least she'd be alive. Mike's gonna have to do a lot more than tell the truth to make amends for what he didn't do."

I hiccoughed a breath as I wiped at my face. "Frost took his statement and booked him. He'll be held in solitary until the Lewises are in custody. As soon as Frost gets an arrest warrant, he'll have them picked up. They'll pay for what they did, at least I hope they will, but Laura's gone. It won't bring her or her baby back."

"No, it won't," Angel said, as he kissed the top of my head. "If I've learned anything thus far in my career, nothing ever makes up for the crime committed. All you can hope for is that the person responsible pays for it. Go to sleep, *Corazón*. The world's troubles will still be there in the morning; you'll just be better able to deal with them."

FORTY-ONE

TALBOT SENT TWO SEPARATE PATROL CARS and officers to bring the Lewises in because she didn't want them to have a chance to come up with a story. Both of them refused to talk and immediately asked to contact a lawyer. Two high-priced lawyers, one for Charlotte Lewis and one for her husband, had eventually arrived. Frost had them in separate interrogation rooms, waiting for the lawyers to finish talking to them. I had come to the precinct in the hopes that I could listen to their interrogations.

Angel shocked the hell out of me that morning by offering to represent Mike. I wasn't sure how I felt about that. Mike was guilty of withholding valuable information that could have saved Laura's life. Angel reminded me that the kid had finally provided information that might help Frost and Talbot arrest and charge the Lewises. As my father would have said, Mike's confession was a day late and a dollar short, but at last he'd done the right thing.

Talbot asked that I give a statement about what had prompted Mike to call me. They had my recording of what he'd talked to me and Frost about, but she wanted to hear it from me. Frost had taken a while to explain how I fitted into the investigation. If a face could look like thunderclouds, Talbot's was doing a bang-up job. She didn't look happy with either of us.

"My guess is Tom Lewis isn't going to talk at all, but we might be able to get his wife to give him up," Talbot said. "Once they're formally arrested, we can get his DNA and run it against the evidence from the assault. I talked to the DA, and he's willing to deal if she'll talk."

"Let's see where we get," Frost said wearily. He'd never gone back home and looked exhausted.

"You," Talbot said pointing a finger at me. "You need to go home."

I looked at Frost pleadingly. "Could I listen in the observation room?"

Talbot frowned at Frost and then turned to me. "You're ass-deep in this and there's no reason for you to be. And you," she said to Frost. "You could get fired over this unless we can figure out a way to soft sell it to Lieutenant Walker."

"She's the one Mike contacted; it won't hurt to let her listen in the observation room."

"Fine, but you stay put and say nothing to anyone here, understand?"

Talbot was right, Tom Lewis never admitted anything or implicated his wife in anything, but Frost and Talbot had secured an arrest warrant. He was booked. DNA was collected, and Talbot was sure that it would match the DNA evidence from the assault. At least she hoped so. It was old, but the outfit the semen was on had been properly stored, the rape kit results were in evidence, and hopes were high it would incriminate him. Having obtained a search warrant, their home was being searched from top to bottom.

Charlotte Lewis was an easier target than her husband.

"I don't understand why I'm here…"

The lawyer leaned over and said, "Charlotte, let me handle this. What evidence do you have to hold my client?"

"We have a witness to the fact that she helped conceal the sexual assault of Laura Hutchinson by her husband and abandoned an injured child in the hope that she wouldn't survive. The only question is, did you kill her or did your husband?"

She rocked back in her chair, and before the lawyer could stop her, she said, "How dare you accuse either of us of anything that horrible. Who said that?"

"Charlotte! Enough." The lawyer put a restraining hand on her arm.

"We don't reveal witnesses' names, especially in a case like this. We have a first-hand account of conversations between Mrs. Lewis and her husband about the assault, the cover-up, and the murder." Talbot stared at Charlotte until she looked away.

"Your husband says you abandoned Laura to cover up his assault, and when she approached you about what happened and attempted to blackmail you and your husband, you met her in City Park and killed her." It was a lie, Lewis had said nothing, but there is no rule against the police lying to a suspect during an interview.

"That is a bald-faced lie!" Charlotte jerked her arm away from her lawyer when he tried to get her to stop talking. "No," she said to the lawyer. "I'll be damned if he puts this all on me. He's terrorized me long enough."

"Don't say anything more, Charlotte. Listen to me, please." But she didn't.

"He intended to let her go home after the assault. He'd been grooming her for months. He'd terrorized her with the threat to kill her parents and come back for her if she revealed what was going on. He was convinced she wouldn't say anything. I told him that was ridiculous and because she lived close to our house and would see him, the child would tell the authorities what had happened as soon as she was able. He was so smug; he said no previous child had ever said anything and neither would she."

She stopped and stared off into space, her eyes tracking back and forth. Finally, she began talking. "I had caught him coming out of Kathy's room one night a few months before she became friends with Laura. Fortunately, when I talked to her, she told me what he'd begun doing. He hadn't raped her, but he'd terrified her. I told him if he ever touched her again, I'd go to the police."

"Seems like that would have been the time to go to the police. Why didn't you?" Frost asked, speaking up for the first time.

"He'd agreed to leave her alone, and…I loved him. I was flattered by his attention when we first met. He pursued me. He seemed interested in me, not just my money. I know that sounds pathetic, but he was handsome and I…wanted him. I thought we had a good life, once."

She frowned and wiped at the tears on her cheeks. "Our relationship changed, gradually. After Michael was born, he lost interest in me. That's why there is such a big age gap between Michael and Kathy. I thought, initially, he was having affairs. He would come back to me for brief periods, but after Kathy was born, he never touched me again. I had no idea he was doing this kind of thing behind my back. Then when Kathy told me, I thought…God, forgive me…that Kathy might have encouraged him."

"She was seven years old. How would a child that age encourage him?" Talbot asked, revulsion clear on her face.

Charlotte blushed deeply. "I can't explain what goes through your mind at a time like that. He was her father and she loved him; she'd sit on his lap and tell him about her day, they played tickle games. I just thought—at first—that maybe that had given him the wrong idea. You deny and rationalize to avoid facing the truth.

"I should have realized that forcing him to leave Kathy alone wouldn't stop his behavior, that he'd just find another victim. But I never thought he'd be stupid enough to take a child from our neighborhood. I couldn't just let her go back home; I knew she'd tell. I thought by abandoning her, it would be a way to get rid of her without…I was so angry with him that I hoped, if she survived, I hoped she'd identify him, and he'd be arrested. But she never talked about it."

"So, you hoped she'd die of exposure or, if she survived, you hoped a traumatized seven-year-old would do your work for you? Jesus," Talbot said, shaking her head.

Finally, the tears began to flow without restraint, but listening to her talk, I felt nothing but contempt. How a woman—a mother—could let something like that occur and not call the police was beyond me.

"She never talked. I wanted to leave him, take my daughter and leave, but he said I knew too much and if I tried to leave him, he'd find and kill me and then Kathy would be his. I stayed to protect her, and I sent her to a boarding school to prevent him having access to her.

"I didn't know about Laura's attempt to blackmail him until after he came home that night. He'd said he had to go out to meet with someone and was very secretive about who he was meeting. When I heard about her body being found, I confronted him, and he said not to worry about it, she'd intended to blackmail both of us, and he'd taken care of it."

"Where did the original assault occur?"

"The house is a custom build. He had what he called a safe room built in the basement, but he used it as an office and kept it locked. I caught him coming out of it that night and saw her in the room. After the other detective showed up and then you accused us of shielding Mike, he and I got into a horrible argument, and he hit me. I fell against the craft table in the basement and hit my head and ended up in the hospital. I was terrified of him, and I didn't know what to do."

"Yeah, you did," Talbot said. "You just didn't do it. Charlotte Lewis, you're under arrest for aiding and abetting a sexual assault on a child, for endangering a child by abandoning Laura Hutchinson, not reporting the assault to the authorities, and covering up her murder. Stand up."

"Wait, wait, I didn't hurt her, I didn't kill her, why are you arresting me?"

"You colluded with your husband regarding the assault, abandoned a child that you hoped wouldn't survive, and you failed to report what you knew about Laura's assault and her murder. It's called conspiracy to commit and accessory to murder," Talbot said as she cuffed Charlotte. Then she led her to the interrogation room door and turned her over to the uniformed officer waiting outside.

"Take her to booking, I'll be down in a moment," she said.

In the days that followed, Frost told me that in the safe room they found Lewis's laptop, which was filled with encrypted child pornography, including photos of him with Laura and others. It made me sick, but at least she never knew about them. Techs were working on identifying the other children. They had also found the browser history, despite being deleted, that showed he belonged to several child porn and pedophile sites. The good news was the Sex Crime division was working on infiltrating them and arresting the participants. They had also found evidence of sexual assaults that could be connected to Lewis when he traveled for work.

Both Tom Lewis and his wife were arraigned, denied bail, and remanded into custody to await trial.

I met with Bret Martin at a local restaurant. He looked rough, still bruised, and his ribs still caused him pain. I'd promised to explain what had transpired. After I did, he closed his eyes and drew his lips in tightly, trying not to cry. I reached out, placing my hand on his.

"They'll pay for this, Bret. It doesn't bring her back, but they'll spend the rest of their lives in prison."

He nodded and finally looked at me. His eyes were glittering with tears and one rolled down his cheek. He quickly wiped it away. "Thank you for finding out who did this. I hope their son pays too. He could have saved her if he'd said something years ago."

"You're right. He could have. That's his guilt to carry. He's charged with the cover-up. Because he confessed and incriminated his parents, there'll be some leniency, but he's paid for his part in it since it happened, and he'll pay going forward."

I didn't tell him Angel had taken over Mike's defense. I didn't know if I was okay with that, but Angel said he and the DA were in negotiations for a plea deal, and Mike would serve time. He had finally done the right thing; it had just been far too late to save Laura.

We sat in silence until he said, "Knowing the why of it doesn't help, but at least they'll pay for what they did."

I nodded. I hoped the consequences for all three Lewises would be justice for Laura, although as Angel had said, justice never made up for the crime committed.

EPILOGUE

WE PARKED THE CAR in front of the house in the Highlands and sat in silence. Looking at it in February was probably a good idea. It could be a bleak time in Denver. Lawns looked dead and, other than the evergreens, trees in the neighborhood were bare. It had snowed. Despite the deceptive Colorado sunshine, it was cold. It was a time when everything except the ski slopes looked barren.

In contrast, the house looked snug and well cared for. The sidewalk next to the street and that leading up to the house was neatly shoveled and sprinkled with ice melt granules. A suet bird feeder hung from a hook on the front porch and birds visited regularly while we sat in the car. The tree in the front yard was bare, but the house looked inviting.

The realtor had called Angel to say the current contract on the house had fallen through and asked if we were still interested. Living on one side of our combined apartments had helped somewhat, but the urge to move was still strong, so we told him yes. We'd just come from signing the contract on the house. All that was left was to close on it and move.

So many things had changed. We were the only two still living in the triplex. Paul and Gabriela were engaged and she had moved in with Paul. Marisol had moved into an apartment of her own. We had the connecting doors between my original unit and Angel's removed, the wall repaired, and put the triplex up for sale. It was time to move on.

"This is it, I guess," I said at last.

"Sure you're okay with it?"

"Yeah, it's time. I like the house." We said nothing for several moments. "It's a good decision. Ian has no physical connection to this place, other than being the reason for the move. He was never here and won't be. I want to put him behind us, create a life that doesn't include him. I think we could do that here."

Angel reached out and pulled me across the car's central console and kissed me. "I think we could, too. And," he added with a grin, "it's got a basement."

That made me laugh. "It does; now all we need is a door we can padlock." It felt good to laugh with him. Maybe we really could move on and begin a new chapter in our lives in this house.

P LEASE CONSIDER LEAVING A REVIEW on Amazon and Goodreads. Reviews are extremely important for indie authors and are very much appreciated!

Read on for the first chapter in *The Woman He Used to Know*, which can be purchased in ebook, paperback, and audiobook formats on Amazon at https://www.amazon.com/dp/099924616X

THE WOMAN HE USED TO KNOW

PROLOGUE

HE LAY ON THE FLOOR in a pool of blood. She hesitated as she knelt next to him and watched his eyes open and close slowly, watched his breathing slow. She felt blood soak through her nightgown onto her knees and cover her hands as she braced herself to lean toward him.

"I'm sorry," she whispered as she grasped the knife handle that protruded from his abdomen, pulled it out, and dropped it on the floor next to him. "This isn't how I wanted things to end."

ONE

The house where dispatch had directed him was in Cherry Creek North, an area that lay to the northeast of the wealthy, old money, Denver Country Club part of town. It was the area where people with new money lived. Whoever lived here had a lot of money, old or new, Detective Nick Ryan thought as he approached the uniformed officer standing by the entry.

Nick looked as if he'd forgotten to comb his thick black hair, his lower face was covered in a deep black stubble—he'd been too tired to shave—and his suit jacket was wrinkled from being tossed on the chair in his bedroom and not hung up. At two in the morning, it was cooler than it had been earlier in the evening. A slight breeze ruffled his hair and played with his tie as he approached the house.

A patrol car, lights flashing, sat at the curb. A few curious neighbors had come out in their pajamas to see what was going on. They were quiet, watchful, and curious but restrained. No one snapped photos with smartphones. This was an area of town where pushing and shoving, or questions or abuse shouted at the cops were unlikely. That type of behavior, as the residents would tell you if asked, was for less fortunate neighborhoods.

"What've you got…Officer Kelly?" he asked reading the guy's name tag as he held out his badge and signed into the crime scene.

"We responded to a 911 call and found a dead husband and a distraught wife. My partner, Officer Jones, is with the wife. We secured the scene, called dispatch, they notified the ME's office, and I had them call homicide. I've got Officer Gillis out back to make sure no one comes in or leaves that way. It looks like the only person here is the wife. Jones has her in the study off to the left as you enter the house. Body's in the kitchen, straight back through the hall. Wife found him."

"What time'd the call come in?"

"Twelve forty-two. We got here at twelve fifty-five."

Nick nodded and moved through the doorway. He turned. "Don't let any of the looky-loos near. Call for some backup to help control things, if you need to, and get an officer on the sidewalk to head off any press. Get a couple of uniforms to start canvassing the neighbors who're standing around to see if anyone saw or heard anything or what they know about the couple. See what you can find out."

The officer nodded, and Nick closed the door behind him. He examined the front door carefully, no sign of forced entry. He pulled a pair of shoe covers out of his jacket pocket as he entered the foyer and slipped them on. *Nice house*, he thought, looking around at the graceful wood handrail that followed the carpeted stairs up to the second level. The cop had said nothing about any kids, just that the wife was the only one here. Seemed like a big house for two people, Nick thought.

The walls were paneled in expensive-looking wood, and there was a large flower display on the round, marble-topped table in the entryway. The scent of roses and lilies hung in the air, with a hint of something less pleasant underneath. He'd never cared for the scent of lilies, especially the white ones—they reminded him of funerals and Easter. Oddly appropriate seeing as there would be a funeral in the near future.

There was a bloody handprint on the inside door handle and a trail of bloody, barefoot prints on the slate entry floor that led up to the front door. He walked toward the hall, backtracking the footprints to what he'd been told was the kitchen and stopped abruptly near a side table on which rested a wedding photo and various other items. His heart rate jumped, and he swore softly.

"Ah, Christ." Talk about the universe screwing you over. Of all the detectives that could have been on duty, he'd gotten the call. Go figure.

He leaned in close to get a better view, not wanting to touch the frame or pick up the picture. He knew them well. No, that wasn't accurate—he'd known them. The photo showed Elizabeth on Oliver Harper's arm outside the church where their wedding, which he hadn't attended, had taken place.

He supposed it was Oliver who'd been killed and was surprised at the lack of regret or sadness on his part. If he'd been asked to guess, being murdered wasn't how he would've imagined Oliver getting his comeuppance. The fact that it had happened at all surprised him. He hadn't figured that Oliver would ever suffer any consequences for his behavior. As far as Nick could see, people like him were untouchable.

Karma is oftentimes an extremely tardy bitch, but a bitch nonetheless when she finally shows up.

"Looks like you pissed off one too many people, Oliver," Nick said.

He hadn't recognized the house, but since their marriage he'd had no idea where Oliver and Elizabeth lived. He remembered the last time he'd seen Elizabeth. The memory left him as angry as he'd been five years ago. He stepped back and closed his eyes taking in a deep breath and exhaling it slowly. He shook himself, pulled a pair of gloves from his pocket, slipped them on, and walked toward the kitchen.

Probably should get someone else to handle this, Nick thought. He and his partner Rob Keller had been the ones up next for a call, but Rob was at the hospital awaiting the birth of his first child, and Nick had come alone. One of the other detectives would take over if he called, and if he was going to call, now was the time. He wanted to see what had happened, though, and there were things he didn't want anyone else to know.

Read More at https://www.amazon.com/dp/099924616X

OTHER BOOKS

THE ANNIE COLLINS MYSTERY SERIES
The Mad Hatter's Son
No Pity in Death
The Burden of Hate

STANDALONE ROMANTIC SUSPENSE
Legacy of Secrets

THE DENVER MAJOR CRIMES SERIES
Finding Alex
The Woman He Used to Know

ACKNOWLEDGMENTS

I HAVE A LONG LIST OF PEOPLE TO THANK. This book was four long years in the making, and the following people helped birth it. Thanks to the fans who buy and read my books—I couldn't do this without you. Sorry to make you wait so long.

Thanks to my beta readers, Lois Miller, D'n, (AKA COmtnlady), and Donna Lefferdo, you always keep me focused. Thanks to my editor, Julie Cameron, Landon Literary, for her guidance, astute comments, and her humor. Thanks to KB Jensen, for her help with all the details that need doing to get a book published and for her 'title barfs.' Thanks to Victoria Wolf, Wolf Design and Marketing, for the great cover. And a huge thanks to Mandy Miller, J.D., Ph.D., for her gracious help answering my endless questions about defending a person with mental illness.

This book is a work of fiction, people, names, and places are in my imagination alone, and any mistakes are mine.

ABOUT THE AUTHOR

COLORADO NATIVE and former OR nurse, Helen Starbuck is an award-winning author of *The Annie Collins Mystery Series*, contemporary romantic suspense, and *The Denver Major Crimes Series*. No relation to the coffee bunch, she (sadly) doesn't get free coffee. When she's not writing, you can find her reading books about strong women and interesting men who find themselves in suspense-filled situations.

Follow her on Facebook (facebook.com/helensstarbuck), Instagram (instagram.com/helenstarbuck/), and her web site (helenstarbuck.com), where you can sign up for her newsletter to be the first to hear about new books, events, and cover reveals.

www.ingramcontent.com/pod-product-compliance
Lightning Source LLC
Chambersburg PA
CBHW021644110726
47902CB00007B/1822